I0542539

A Curse of Roses

ISBN: 978-1-7778460-1-5 (paperback)
ISBN: 978-1-7778460-0-8 (eBook)

Cover design by: Taireleidesigns

For more information visit mariabmoses.com

Trigger Warning

This novel contains scenes depicting sexual assault, and references to bullying. Reader discretion is advised

For my family.

Dad, mom, everything I am is because of you and for that, I will be *forever grateful*.

Pelumi, Ayoola, thanks for loving me as much as you do. *I love you*.

Maria B. Moses

A Curse of Roses

Maria B. Moses

Maria B. Moses

The Curse

We Purge your tainted blood from our world only to return once a generation. Never again shall it cross our own. With this seal, you are marked. Your children, your children's children shall bear it for all eternity as a punishment for your sin. For your betrayal. For your greed. Should this pact be broken, war shell reign. Should this line be lost, blood shall flow. A Curse of Roses is the scar borne upon your family for the sake of love.

Prologue

Burned

*T*o me it was a fairy tale.

The history and legends of Glorus tell of a child born of two bloods, and of two worlds. An abomination of love and despair. The embodiment of sin.

It all began in the southern kingdom of Halibel, when Princess La-Muse's parents tragically died during the *War of Bloods*.

Soon after, La-Muse became queen and Crown, but had grown weary from the conflict that had taken so much. Grieving, she found solace in Tarress, a world much like her own, and travelled there often.

It was soon discovered that she was in love with a man from Tarress. People warned her of the dangers, but by then it was too late. Queen La-Muse was pregnant.

There was uproar.

The Glories, high rulers of Glorus, demanded that Queen La-Muse stand trial for her sin, but she fled to Tarress, where the

Glories had no power. Enraged by this act of defiance, they ordered Dantre, La-Muse's younger brother, to bring her back to pay for her sins.

Dantre pleaded with the Glories not to kill his sister but instead allow the child to be born in Tarress. After all, it could do no harm in another world.

The Glories considered his proposal but insisted that a punishment befall the family. They decided that when the child turned eighteen it would live in Glorus for a year, surrounded by enemies, to attain penance for its existence. This cycle would continue generation after generation, and if a new heir to the curse was not produced, there would be war.

Dantre agreed, thankful for his sister's life. However, before he could breathe a sigh of relief, the Glories told him of the curse mark to be burned onto the flesh of each heir upon their eighteenth year.

Dantre told La-Muse of the curse. She pleaded for him to escape with her, but he declined for fear that a war between the realms would arise if he, too, tried to flee. They said their goodbyes and parted ways.

A mere year later, Halibel fell to ruins. The word of the Glories became law and the cycle of the abominations given the title *Renai,* began.

My name is Lillianett Adams, and I am the ninth *Renai*.

Chapter 1

Marked

So, this was it. My eighteenth birthday.

My heart was heavy as I stared up at the ceiling, hoping I'd miscounted the number of years I'd been alive. Tossing and turning, I tried to keep my eyes closed and skip the day, but I was wide awake and had been for hours.

I sat up and glanced at my drawn curtains, where sharp rays of the midday sun slipped through the slits. A grumble rose from my chest as I tossed my pillow at the window, cursing the sun for being so bright on such an awful day.

There was a knock at my door. Before I could answer, my mother threw it open. She stood in the doorway with a stern look on her face and fierce impatience in her dark eyes. A tangled bun of locs dangled on top of her head, seconds from coming undone. A smudge of flour on her face complemented the mess of ingredients on her red apron.

I pulled my knees into my chest. "Good mor—afternoon."

"Get out of bed. Now. I want you downstairs in ten minutes."

I frowned. "Can't we skip today?"

"Ten minutes," she repeated and grabbed her phone from the apron's pouch.

"But mom..."

"I'm timing you." She showed me the countdown and walked away.

I went still, mentally counting her footsteps like the seconds ticking by. When I heard her feet hit the creak in the staircase, I jumped out of bed and into the shower. I brushed my teeth furiously while looking for something to wear but tripped over a pile of dirty laundry I should've taken care of last week. After kicking the dirty pile into a safe corner, I rinsed my mouth and ran downstairs.

My mother was waiting with her phone in hand, showing me I was fifteen seconds over the limit.

"I'm proud of myself," I huffed, out of breath. "Ten minutes and fifteen seconds is a personal best."

She smiled and shook her head. "Happy birthday."

She hugged me. I hugged her back, taking in every detail. Her skin was bathed in the warm scent of dirt and lavender from working in the gardens. Her small, thin figure was fragile in my arms as she rubbed my back in small circles, like when I was a child.

I heard the snap of a polaroid camera and peeked up at my dad aiming a lens in our direction. I pulled away from my mom and hugged him, holding tightly to his lean, muscular body. I breathed in the cologne I'd bought him that smelled of sandalwood and fruity undertones. I glanced up at his sad green eyes that mirrored mine, full of anxiety. I could feel it in his heartbeat too. It was no surprise. He had the mark on his upper left arm.

"Happy birthday." He kissed my forehead and brought me into his chest for a tighter hug, as though he didn't want to let go. I know I didn't.

"Thanks," I whispered.

"Make a wish," my mom said, presenting a cupcake with caramel frosting and a single lit candle. It had to be the only cupcake to survive her horrendous baking. I stared at the flame and for a second made myself believe in the magic of a birthday wish.

As I blew out the candle the doorbell rang.

"Are you expecting someone?"

"No. I told all my friends I wanted to spend my birthday with family," I said, jogging to open the front door. As I opened it, I rolled my eyes at my guest. "Though I should have known you wouldn't listen to me."

"At least pretend you're happy to see me," Chris huffed, adjusting his backpack.

"But I'm not happy to see you," I said.

He grabbed me in a hug, twirling me around. I held onto him, giggling in his arms, almost as familiar as my father's.

"Don't lie," he said with a cheeky smile. His dark brown eyes glistened like two marbles. He was cleanly shaven, and had the same fade he'd requested since he was fifteen. His deep brown skin glowed against the midday sun, almost as bright as his smile.

"Yeah, yeah. It's always great to see you," I said, play-jabbing him in the ribs.

"I should have guessed," my mother said, pulling Chris into a hug. He towered over her like a bear, careful not to hug too tight.

"Hey. I hope you don't mind that I'm here," he said

"Of course I don't mind," she gushed. "Lilly, share your cupcake with him."

My mother walked away, and Chris stepped closer lowering his voice so that only I could hear him. "Cupcake? Singular?"

"Mom was baking this morning," I said. The woman cooked like a master chef but couldn't bake to save her life.

"That explains the flour," he said, rubbing his fingers together and releasing a crust of white dust. I stared at his dirty shirt and then down at mine, which had the same messy pattern. He snickered. "We're matching."

"Happy birthday to me," I grumbled, dusting myself off.

Chris followed close behind me as I made my way to the kitchen. "Why so grumpy?"

"I'm not." I grabbed a large kitchen knife from its holder and gave him an exaggerated toothy smile. "See?"

"Okay, you are way too dangerous to handle sharp objects," he said, taking the knife from me with caution. "And also, it's a *happy* birthday. Two words. Try to get them both right."

"I hate you," I hissed, grabbing the knife back from him.

He bopped me on the nose and chuckled. "Love you too."

I shook my head, suppressing a smile, and sliced the cupcake in half. I slid the knife underneath and passed him his piece. He took the cupcake with his fingertips and took a half-step away from me. "Like I said, too dangerous."

"I'm harmless." I dug my finger into the caramel frosting and shovelled it into my mouth. A little salty but not bad

"Is that what you tell all your victims?" he asked.

"Victims?" I asked, batting my eyelashes. "Whatever do you mean?"

"Don't do that. It's gross," he said. "You can't act innocent when you have priors."

"Hey, I warned them," I said, sliding my hand along a shelf with all the kickboxing trophies I'd won.

It was important that every *Renai* had some form of training as a foundation before their year in Glorus. I'd started earlier than the others. My mother insisted. It was a week-long argument in the house.

"And it's not like I go around beating people up for fun."

They deserved what was coming to them. Every one of them.

"That's true," he said with a shrug.

"Besides," I said, patting his shoulder, "we're a team. You've always had my back."

"And I'll always have your back."

I smiled at him and hoped that was true. I'd had nightmares of him turning his back on me because he found out the truth.

Shaking my head, I banished the thought. My parents were in the study, talking in hush tones, probably about Chris's sudden visit. "So, where's my gift?" I asked.

"Excuse me? You're demanding gifts from your oldest friend? Aren't I enough of a gift?"

"Don't joke. You're not funny."

"What if I didn't bring you anything?"

I lifted a brow and pointed at the strap on his shoulder. "So, you walk around with your backpack everywhere you go?"

"Maybe," he said.

I rolled my eyes. "Shut up and give it to me."

He took my hand, led me to the living room, and sat me down on the sofa. I devoured the rest of my cupcake, closed my eyes, and held my hands out in excitement. I felt something rectangular and cold in my hands. When I opened my eyes, I paused. It was a picture of us on the camping trip we took last fall. I remembered the sharp, cold rain against my brown skin, and the bug bites that remained for weeks. We got so drenched that water filled our rain-boots. My usually thick, curly, red hair was stringy, hanging over my shoulders and sticking to my head like wet toilet paper. My skin was flushed from the cold, especially around my freckled cheeks and nose. I was mid-laugh, making it an especially unflattering photo.

"Remember me," Chris said. I looked up at him with wide eyes, gripping the frame. "Who knows what you'll get up to while you're gone."

"It's only for a year," I said.

"A lot can happen in a year," he sighed. "So, keep that with you and try not to miss me too much."

I laughed but was seconds away from crying. I would miss him. I wished I could tell him that he was wrong, that my departure was only hours away, and my destination was another world where I would be a prisoner. Despite the well wishes and jealousy from him and all our friends, this upcoming year was a curse. The best thing that could happen was nothing. That's all I could hope for.

"Thank you," I whispered.

"I didn't think you'd like it that much," he said.

"I love it," I said and wrapped my arms around his neck. I took in his awful deodorant, that reeked of misguided adolescence, and laughed against his neck. A second longer was all I wanted. I wanted to hold on to this moment a little longer.

"You're acting weird," he said, pulling away from me.

"I'm normal," I said.

"Okay, see, that's never been true."

I smacked his arm. "We were having a moment!"

"And she's back." He pulled me in, then pulled away just as fast. "Let's get BeaverTails."

"What?"

"There's a food truck just a few minutes away," he said, standing and pulling me in with his best smile.

"No, I can't today," I said, pulling back.

He stopped pulling for a second, then said, "My treat."

I grabbed his hand and started running for the door. "Mom, I'll be back soon."

"Lilly!" I heard her shout before the door slammed shut.

We got on our bikes and rode off before reason could stop me.

Chris took me to the food trucks a few blocks away from my house. He ordered us BeaverTails drizzled with chocolate and crushed nuts. And we talked and talked and talked, but there was still more to say. There would always be more to say.

"The way to your heart is food," Chris said as he crushed his paper tray and tossed it into the closest trash can. "Never change."

I tore off a piece of my second pastry and let the warm sweetness play on my tongue. "I don't plan on it."

We'd been together for so long—he was my first friend. He'd saved me from my loneliness and anger. I didn't know how bitter I'd become by the time I was a teenager. I loved that I could talk to him without filters. It killed me that there was a whole part of me that he didn't know. He couldn't know. It was always at the back of my mind, scratching against my skull, pleading to break out. I was allowed to tell him, I wanted to, but the knowledge of different worlds, curses, and *Renai*, was best kept within the family.

"So, when you're back..." he started.

I nodded, swallowing the last piece. "I'll go to university and start the torturous process of becoming a vet." A late start to the rest of my life but I would be glad for any kind of start.

"You said someone in your family was a vet, right?"

"My great grandpa," I said. "He had a way with animals, like me."

Chris fiddled with the corner of the table. "You could become a zookeeper."

"You've made that offer before and the answer is still no," I said, flicking him on the ear.

"Ouch," he groaned around his laugh.

I smiled at him as he mumbled the odd reasons why being a zookeeper would be much cooler than a vet. It was the conversations about nothing that I would miss the most.

I looked down at my phone and groaned at myself for getting lost in the moment. I was out of time. It felt like time stood still when we were together and yet it flew by.

"What?" Chris asked.

"I should head home," I said and gave him a tight smile.

"Already?"

"I still haven't packed." I shrugged and stood up. I stretched my hands up to the sky as I wrestled with the tears in the corners of my eyes.

Chris hugged me from behind. "I'm going to miss you," he said.

His arms tightened and I wished they wouldn't let me go. I gripped his forearms, forcing my body to remember him, his awful scent, his voice, and his warmth. I had to take it all with me.

"I'm going to miss you too."

"Don't be a stranger," he said as he let go. I felt colder as he did but was determined not to let it show.

"Have I ever?" I asked.

"First time for everything," he said.

I shook my head. "Not everything." I hopped onto my bike and took one more look at him. "See you next year?"

"See you next year," he said with a wave.

I made a beeline for home, fighting back tears the whole way. It wasn't goodbye forever. All *Renai* had made it back before me and I would be no different. It was only a year.

As I pulled into the driveway, a sharp burning pain hit my spine, and I spasmed. I heard my scream before I realized it was me screaming and lost control of my bike. My body flew and tumbled down the pavement. Every searing jolt hit me like hot iron. My muscles shook, and I beat the ground with my fist, holding back my cries. My back was on fire, scorching my skin and burning a trail down my spine. I bit my lip until I tasted blood, waiting for the agony to subside. Dad had said it would only be ten seconds, but it felt like minutes.

When it was over, I gasped for air and pushed myself upright. I searched for something to ground my mind. The world was spinning too fast for me to grab a hold of anything. I was breathing too hard, hyperventilating.

"Lilly!"

My dad knelt to hold my head steady between his large hands. I hadn't noticed him rush to me. He pressed his forehead against mine and began to breathe audibly. He'd done the same for me when I had panic attacks as a kid or fits of anger as a teenager. I mimicked his breathing until I was calm and could think straight. My muscles buzzed and my heart lulled.

"Are you okay?" he asked.

I nodded, unable to find my voice. He helped me to my feet and led me inside. We stepped into the kitchen, and I took the glass of water he offered. I gulped it down in three sips and gasped.

"That…was intense," I panted, ready for my second and third cup.

"Are you okay?" he asked again, already fetching me my second round of water.

I frowned and resisted the urge to touch my tender spine. "I'm marked."

"Let me see," he said. I turned around and lifted my shirt from the back so he could get a good look. I heard his slow breathing and then I felt his cold fingers. I flinched at his touch. It stung like static in my veins. "I'm sorry."

"Don't be," I said. "How long will it hurt?"

"Give or take two days."

"No decent sleep for two days," I grumbled. "This keeps getting better and better."

My dad was about to say something but the sound of shattering glass from the den followed by my mom's scream stole his voice. He tensed up and was about to charge in, but I seized his arm and placed a finger over my mouth to silence him. I grabbed the knife I'd used to cut my cupcake and tip-toed towards the den—heartbeat loud in my ears.

Pausing at the entrance, I stole a glance inside. In the corner of my eye, I spotted a stranger facing my mother.

I ran out, shoved my mom behind me and swiftly raised the knife as a guard. I locked eyes with him and was quickly taken aback by the calmness that greeted me.

"I see you're quick," he said in a deep monotonous voice.

"Who—"

"Camerin," my dad said, stepping around me. "It's been a long time. You look well."

"Camerin?" my mom asked. "Oh, it is you. You shouldn't

13

appear out of nowhere like that. And you broke a vase coming in too."

I glanced at the broken glass vase behind him, next to the piano, now laying in a wet puddle of scattered flowers.

"It's been a very long time," my dad said.

"Eighteen years exactly," Camerin said with a stiff nod.

"Am I the only person who's never met him?" I asked.

"We met a long time ago," he said, taking a step forward.

"Eighteen years," I said and narrowed my eyes. "*Exactly* eighteen years?"

"He's your caretaker," my dad said. "He will train you and teach you everything you'll need to know to survive in Glorus. Hopefully you'll never have to use what he teaches you."

"Oh, so he's my babysitter," I said.

I met his gaze again and couldn't shake how steady they were, like large grey immovable boulders. He was tall and so stiff that I could practically see the stick poking out from behind him. His broad shoulders were tight under his long, deep green tunic that was belted at his waist. It was sleeveless, revealing a surprising abundance of lean muscle. He had his blond hair pulled back into a tight ponytail, and his beard was close-shaven to exhibit his sharp jawline. He appeared closer to my age than my father's and looked impeccable, not a hair out of place. I stared at him, trying to glean as much information from him as I could, but there was nothing much to gather. His face was the perfect poker-face.

I stepped forward suddenly, trying to get a reaction. For just an instant there was a glint in his eyes, as though he saw someone he knew and didn't expect to see again. A brief moment of wonder in his face, but it was gone, like the flicker of a flame.

"Are you ready?" he asked.

I opened my mouth to speak the truth, but I knew that wasn't an option, so I nodded.

My mom brought my duffle bag with only the essentials. My parents both held me in a hug, sandwiching me between their bodies. My insides squeezed. This wasn't goodbye. I knew it wasn't, but it felt like it was.

"I love you guys," I whispered.

"We love you more," my mom said.

"We love you most," my dad said. He kissed the top of my head, lingering a second longer than usual.

I pulled out of their arms and walked up to Camerin, trying to act like I was ready.

Camerin pulled out a small purple gem no bigger than a pearl and tossed it against the wall. The gem sank into the wall, sending ripples that darkened like rain clouds. The centre opened and shone with light.

My eyes widened. "Whoa."

"This way." He walked into the opening.

I followed, determined not to look back, trying to ignore the way my skin burned with anticipation. And fear.

Chapter 2

Sapphire

Cam's underground training hall had tall ceilings with three rows of lights and no scent. It was about a quarter of a football field long, with weapons and targets that hung on the white back walls. There were only two doors—one that led to a storage room, the other that led to his cottage above.

As I lay on my back, with bruises on almost every inch of skin, and a fresh, thin cut on my upper left arm, I couldn't help thinking how much I wanted to escape.

"Focus!" Cam shouted at me from the other side of the room.

I pushed myself off the ground and pressed my palm against the open wound with a hiss. Blood trickled down. It stung like a paper cut. I wiped the blood off on my black pants and got to my feet. Cam smacked the butt of his spear and gave me a stern look. There was no mercy in those eyes.

A grunt escaped my lips, as I straightened my spine. I ignored the unsteady way my legs swayed and kept my eyes on him. I filled my lungs with air to catch my breath and slow my heart rate. It didn't help.

Cam produced two daggers from their holsters and threw one of them. I tucked and rolled to my right and took off sprinting across the room, not taking my eyes off his throwing arm. He threw the second one and I stopped as the blade hit the wooden floors inches from my bare toes.

"He's going to kill me," I panted and ran straight for him. Despite how much it hurt to move I kept going, watching his hands for the next attack.

He lifted his spear, ready to strike. The first time he gave me that look I hesitated. Now, I saw it as an invitation.

As he thrust the spear forward, I slid my body across the floor with enough momentum to knock his feet out from under him. As his body fell, I grabbed the spear from his loosened grip and aimed it at his neck.

"Concede," I growled.

"Do you have the strength to make me?" he asked.

I clicked my tongue. My body was shaking from the pain. Blood slid down my arm and dripped from my fingertips. I sighed in defeat and dropped the spear.

Cam stood up and looked at me with the same impassive look I'd been getting since I arrived. "Again," he said.

"I'm tired," I replied.

"Again," he repeated.

I stared at him in silence for a minute, tender from head to toe in ways I didn't know were possible a few months ago. Shaking my head, I turned and walked towards the exit.

"Where are you going?" he asked.

I didn't stop. "You're not listening to me. I said, I'm tired."

I went straight for the shower after cleaning my wound and checking my skin over to make note of where I would need to apply the numbing salve later.

I'd been in Glorus for three months. It felt like longer. We lived in a small cottage at the edge of the northern kingdom of Tamikar, far from everything. Tall forest trees surrounded us. We were the only souls for miles. It was peaceful and boring. I felt restless most days, even after training.

The moment I stepped through the gateway into Glorus, I felt a surge of energy. I stepped into a forest like any other I'd find back home but there was something more alive in the air. For days, I felt electric, like there were fireflies in my veins.

I wiped the steam from my mirror and pressed my hand against the cool, damp glass. I turned to see my back and stared at the mark, like I did every day, as though I expected it to suddenly not be there. Its twisted vines stained my skin, spiralling towards the small of my back with thick threatening thorns and six tiny rose buds. The mark grew with every generation. Mine was the first with buds. At first glance, it was beautiful, almost mesmerising. But it was still a curse.

"Lillianett, I am leaving now. I will be back soon," Cam said, standing at my door.

"Okay, bye," I said.

"Please remember—"

"I know," I groaned. "Stay hidden. Run if you can. Fight if you must." I'd heard it every day for three months. I heard it in my sleep.

Cam threw me a steely gaze and departed without another word.

There wasn't much of a difference between his being here or elsewhere when he wasn't training me. He hardly spoke and almost never showed any sign of being alive other than breathing.

One look around my small bedroom fitted with the essential bed, dresser, and mirror, and I felt my lungs constrict. "I need air."

After applying the numbing salve that cooled by aching bruises, I fastened my high black boots over my pants and threw on my green shirt, which was two sizes too big. I pulled my hair back out of my face and was out the door without a glance in the mirror.

There were small, furry creatures that scampered about outside the cottage, making light rustling sounds that harmonised with the insects. The grass was rich and short, with pockets of bright flowers, and trails stretching out like spider webs all through the forest. The smell of trees and fresh grass wafted in the cool air, sending happy shivers down my spine.

I'd spent most of my first month in the forest, learning about the different plants and animals that existed. What I could eat. What could heal me. What would kill me.

The deeper I went into the forest, the more alive the world became. Rivers full of fish surrounded by rocks and flowers flowed. The trees grew tall and lush with colour, and their roots lined the forest floors like veins. I brushed my hand over a tree and took a lung-full of the natural woody scent. For a moment,

I wasn't weighed down by the boredom and loneliness of being in a world that thought I was a monster. For a moment, I could forget that my existence was a crime.

I was free.

I walked deeper into the forest, looking for a nice tall tree to climb. I paused when I heard a foreign sound. It was a grunt but not like any animal I'd heard before. I waited, searching for the sound and heard it again.

People.

My eyes scanned for movement, and when I heard it again, I crouched down low, moving towards it. This was my cue to listen to Cam's mantra and walk away but the noise was a siren song calling to my desperation. People were nearby.

I hid behind a thicket and peeked through a small opening. That's when I heard a gut-wrenching scream. My body tensed up, paralysed but my heart was racing.

I squinted hard to get a better look and made out three people. One of them was limp on the ground. The other two towered over him, holding some rope between them.

"I can't believe we got him," the man said, squatting in front of his victim.

"We need to get him out of here before his knights catch up," the woman insisted, impatiently.

"They'll never make it in time," he replied.

"Are you willing to take the chance?" she asked.

The man clicked his tongue, and they both crouched down, each taking a pair of limbs to tie.

Everything Cam taught me started ringing in my head like fire truck sirens. *Stay hidden. Stay hidden. Stay hidden. Run.* but the warnings were dulled by the person that lay lifeless on the ground. The thought of just leaving made my insides clench in guilt.

I reached for a nearby rock. "I know I'm going to regret this," I whispered and leapt out of the bushes.

Their heads snapped to my direction the moment I emerged. The woman was the first to react and stand. I threw the rock, and it hit her square in the chest. She sucked in air and stumbled back.

It didn't take long for her partner to move. He jumped and charged straight at me. I ran towards him and somersaulted across the grass as he swung his arms. As soon as he turned my way, I thrust the heel of my palm into his face, shattering his nose. He screamed, backing away with his hands inches from his injury.

I turned back in time to dodge the woman's left punch, which she followed with a right cross. I slipped to the left to evade her; saw my opening and I landed a right hook across her face. She sank down. I lifted my arms, ready for a second wave, but she was out cold.

"Are we done here?" I panted. The man nodded his head with tears in his eyes and a bright red nose. He hoisted his accomplice into his arms, and they disappeared into the bushes.

I sighed in relief. There was only so much the salve could do; I was already feeling the effects of moving so much.

A soft groan escaped the lips of the man still on the ground and I ran to him. More groans slipped from his lips as I tried to adjust him and threw off the ropes. He looked so much worse up close. He was so pale. His chest rose and collapsed heavily, as beads of sweat plastered his dark brown hair to his forehead. Scrapes dusted his cheeks, and fresh blood smudged the corner of his lip. His eyes fluttered revealing a glint of sapphire.

I pressed my hands against his body, examining him until I felt something wet. My heart almost stopped when I saw red on my right palm for the second time that day. I lifted his shirt and found a stab wound on his lower left side. I wasn't the squeamish type but even I felt uneasy at the amount of blood he was losing. I knew some people in Glorus healed quicker from physical wounds than others, but this kind of cut would kill anyone without treatment.

"This is bad," I murmured to myself. I lifted his shirt as high as I could. I touched his torso to feel for broken bones. He flinched. He had a bruise on the right side of his ribs, at least a fracture. The stab wound was the most urgent matter.

First things first. I had to stop the bleeding. I took a breath, trying to think of anything nearby that could help me. At the very least I had the knowledge Cam taught me about a few plants and herbs, but they were all for pain alleviation or food.

I smacked my forehead in realization. "Pocrat." It could stanch bleeding, and it grew in the river. Cam had to stock up for my second month, which was wise decision on his part considering how often I bled.

I pulled his shirt down again and ran to the river. He had to be okay until I could get enough.

As I reached the river, I plunged my arm into the cold water to grab the plants that swayed in the currents. I pulled out long seaweed-like reeds, easily the width and length of my forearm, with small, black bulb roots. They were slimy to the touch, and the bulbs had the texture of a sponge. When I gathered enough, I tore a part of my shirt into three pieces to use as rags and soaked them in the river.

I rushed back and found him struggling to sit up. I pushed down on his shoulder to keep him still. He looked up at me through strained eyes.

"Oh no. Stay with me," I whispered, tapping his cheek.

He opened his mouth and managed a few faint words. "Who...Alle...no... I need..."

"Don't talk," I whispered.

He closed his eyes and went completely still. My heart dropped. I searched for a pulse in several places with my two fingers. He was so cold and too still. I put both my hands on his face in a desperate attempt to feel anything. He then let out a pained groan, and I released the breath I hadn't realized I was holding.

I laid his head down, grabbed one of the wet rags and started cleaning the smeared blood on his torso so I could see the stab wound. It was smaller than I'd thought. I took a second rag, held the pocrat roots above it and squeezed to extract as much liquid as I could to wipe his injuries. He whimpered in pain.

"Hold still," I grunted, gripping his wrist. I knew exactly how much it stung.

I finished cleaning the cut and started plastering the pocrat reeds over the wound, layering them to be safe. He gasped and thrashed his shaky limbs. I was amazed by how much strength he had left. By all accounts he should've been unconscious or dead.

The layered pocrat reeds latched onto him and would continue to do so until they were dry and brittle. I wiped the sweat off my brow and used my last rag to clean his face. The bruises and scratches were already healing. He was even regaining some colour in his complexion. He was the kind to heal fast. *A Glorian*. He was even more dangerous now.

I took a moment to study his face. He had nice features: long lashes, full lips, and high cheekbones. I ran my fingers through his hair, pushed it back and smiled. "So soft," I whispered and then realized how creepy I was being.

He started to move and lifted his head. I panicked for a moment, trying to think of an excuse for why I was touching him without permission. He opened his eyes and blinked several times.

"You—"

But I couldn't let him finish. I covered his eyes and froze, trying to think of my next move. The panic made my head spin.

"Can you hear us?" A voice, not far off, called out.

My head darted to the side at the sound of even more people approaching. His assailants said something about knights looking for him. So, he would be in safe hands if I left him. Right?

"Who are—" he started.

"Shh," I hissed and covered his mouth. "I have to go."

I ducked into the bushes and ran towards the river as fast as I could. The only thing on my mind was escaping. I had no peripheral vision in my frenzied flight from potential danger. My legs carried me in a haze until I snagged my foot on a rock. I hopped awkwardly, stumbling to regain my balance, but tripped on a fallen branch and landed on my face. I grumbled in exhaustion and rolled onto my back, arms out in defeat. My body still ached with exhaustion from the morning's training, and it was hitting me again with a vengeance. I closed my eyes and exhaled all the tension in my muscles.

I flinched when a shadow fell on me.

When I opened my eyes, I chuckled. "Hi Blaze." I sat up. She nudged me with her wet nose, and I stroked her snout as she curled her large-as-a-horse body around me like an oversized fur coat. She was a beautiful creature—a kiliabi—a wolf-like beast with four tails and many horror stories surrounding her existence. We were kindred spirits in that sense.

Her red and black fur was dazzling. It created a vibrant pattern on her paws, the tips of her ears and four tails. She also had a little patch of red on her fluffy chest that closely resembled a flower.

Blaze lifted her head to meet my gaze with her large, golden-brown eyes. She stared at me for a little while, then laid her head back down. It was hard to be afraid when she was basically an overgrown dog. I nuzzled deeper into her soft fur.

"Well, aren't you docile."

She lifted her head and looked at me as though I insulted her. I could swear she had facial expressions. Maybe it was a side effect of my lack of human interaction.

"Well, look at you," I said with a laugh.

She growled at me, showing two sharp canines that I could imagine ripping a tree apart.

"Okay, okay sorry," I said.

She stared at me with a calmer expression and nudged me up as if I were the lazy one. She nudged my hands to lift them and sniffed. They still had a hint of red. She must have smelt the blood. "I know I have blood on my hands but it's not how it looks," I joked.

She made a low growling noise that vibrated through her gut.

"I saved someone," I said. She looked at me with tired eyes. "Is it that hard to believe?"

She looked away, shaking out her fur, which was enough of an answer.

"Fine. Believe what you want." I stuck my tongue out at her.

She stood up on all fours, bowed her head, and crouched forward. I climbed onto her back and grabbed her fur between my hands, staying low against her body.

"You're in the mood to run?" I asked and smiled at her answering growl. "Let's run."

She jumped across the river and dashed through the forest so effortlessly, she mocked the concept of air-resistance. She ran like a dream, flying at break-neck speeds and tearing through the wind without a care. She leapt off trees with so much force, they tilted.

I closed my eyes and focused on the feeling of shredding my way across the world with the most heart-racing sense of freedom. Deafening winds and blinding speed that tied knots in my stomach. I was untouchable to anything around me, even gravity. With Blaze, I could run forever, and no one could catch me. No one could stop me. I was almost free.

Cam was waiting with his arms folded across his chest when I got back. The sun had gone down, and a few stars dotted the darkening skies. My face fell the moment I saw him. He didn't look happy, but he never did.

"Where have you been?" he asked before I was even inside.

"Out," I answered with a shrug and walked past him. The door shut but he stayed silent. I felt his impatience build over me like a giant water-balloon ready to pop. "What?" I asked.

"You are covered in fur," he stated. "Why?"

I kicked myself. "Well, you see…" I started, trying to think of an excuse. I thought I'd gotten most of it off.

He lifted a brow but gave no other sign of wanting to hear my story. It looked like he already knew.

I bowed my head and grated my teeth. "It's my kiliabi's."

"Oh, I see," he said, nodding. "You are trying to get yourself killed."

"Hey!" I barked.

"Kiliabis are dangerous beasts, Lillianett, a likely threat. It could kill you. So, stay away from it," he said with so much calm I couldn't take him seriously.

"Blaze would never hurt me," I said, folding my arms.

"Blaze? You have named the beast?"

"She's not some beast! You're treating her like everyone in

this world would treat me. She's not a monster."

"Kiliabis kill," he stated.

"People kill. I'm still alive," I said, "She's all I have. She makes me feel less lonely and more free."

"Free," he repeated, "Forget that while you are here. Everyone outside these walls thinks of your blood as cursed. You are an abomination to them. There is no freedom in that."

"I know that," I hissed. My chest was on fire. All my frustration was building with no way out and had been for months. "But it's not fair. I'm not that different from them. If it weren't for the mark, no one would even know I'm the *Renai*. Why do I need to hide?"

"It's how things are done. *Renai* used to hide in plain sight, but something always went wrong. When people get close, they notice things. Isolation is the only option in the end."

"This forest was a great choice," I spat.

Not a soul to be seen. Mostly.

Cam's jaw ticked. "It is. No one comes here because of what lies in the depths of this forest. The area I've warned you of. I assume you've heeded my warnings?"

I nodded. I never travelled too deep into the forest, even Blaze didn't cross the large stream to whatever hid beyond. Cam never said what was there and I never asked.

"I shouldn't have to go through this," I grumbled. "And if I do, I should at least be allowed to keep a pet."

"You need to get rid of it," he said.

"That's what everyone outside these walls would say to you about me," I said.

He fixed me with one of his looks, deadpan and cold. It unnerved me every time. "You need to understand your place in this world."

"I understand my place in this world," I said. "Why do you think I'm so angry?" His stare tightened into a glare. I sighed in defeat. "Cam, I need her."

"Camerin," he corrected me. "It's a beast, not a pet."

"This is why I don't talk to you." I said. "We always end up fighting. I'm keeping her."

We glared at each other. Both refusing to back down. Cam closed his eyes, scrunched his brows, and pinched the bridge of his nose as he often did when we argued. I could almost see the physical signs of stress I caused him. I gave it one more month before he started losing his hair.

"How are your injuries from this morning?" he asked.

I pulled up my sleeve to show off my blemish-free skin. "I'm all better."

"Your body has adjusted," he said.

"I'm becoming more and more like them. The Glorians."

"You are of royal descent. It's only natural."

"A lot of good this royal blood is. All it does is make me a *Renai*." It was impossible to hide the bitterness in my tone.

"Yes, you will always be that, but you aren't only that."

"I am to them," I said. The frustration was beginning to bubble up from the base of my gut. It was middle school all over again. Alone. Scared. Desperate for something that would ease the slow building ache. "I'm tired of hiding in this tiny corner of the world."

"It's for your safety. I could never face your parents if anything were to happen to you."

I frowned. "All this time, and I never asked how you got stuck as my caretaker. Did you lose a bet?"

"Like in your family, it is passed down through the generations," he said. "I am a descendant of Queen La-Muse's most loyal knight, or so the story goes." He sounded detached as he spoke, as though he were talking about someone else and not himself.

I pressed my nails into my palms. "So, you're cursed too. I guess you do understand my frustration."

For the first time since we met, I felt a connection between us, but I wished it wasn't so twisted. I was his burden—his curse. Even in his eyes, I was an abomination.

He sighed. "Don't think of unnecessary things."

"I must sound so selfish complaining about my problems to you," I said.

We stared at each other in silence.

"Go wash the fur off and go to sleep. I'll be leaving early tomorrow. Try and get some training done on your own while I'm gone."

I pressed my lips into a tight line and turned to retreat to my room.

"Lillianett." I paused halfway up the stairs. "What happened to your clothes?"

"It was an accident," I said quickly and ran up to my room before he could start another round of questioning.

I took a bow and arrow from the training room the next day and went into the forest. My body had felt heavy since last night, and my heart was trying to plunge itself into my stomach.

"Can't this year go any faster?" I grumbled to myself.

I pulled the arrow back and aimed at a tree trunk a few paces away, took a deep breath, and released it with the arrow, which went straight past my target. Cursing, I threw the bow down and melted to the ground as if my muscles had given out. There was a mess of white noise in my mind. I threw my head back and squeezed my eyes shut counting back from ten to calm down. Frustration ran in me like scalding hot water. I was useless with a bow.

I never did find that tree to climb.

I opened my eyes and stared up at the sky, shrouded by tall colourful leaves that cast spotted sunlight over my skin. When I looked up, I could almost forget where I was—what I was. The forest was safe, but it was safe like a birdcage was safe.

How greedy I was. I had a whole forest, but I wanted more. The world called out to me, it made my muscles itch.

"I should get my arrow," I grumbled, standing up and dusting off my clothes.

I walked in the direction the arrow landed and found it with the head buried in the ground. I flung the dirt off the arrowhead and aimed it again but stopped when I heard the crunch of leaves. My body froze straining my senses to hear something else. It couldn't have been Blaze; she was large but virtually silent in the forest. Even if she weren't, she would've shown herself and there were no other large animals this side of the forest.

My heart rate spiked. Someone was watching me from the shadows, but I couldn't see anything. I felt eyes sweeping over my body, which made the hairs on the back of my neck stand on end. I heard the crunch of leaves again and released my arrow—it shot into the shadows.

I ran.

I didn't stop moving. Cam always told me to trust my instincts, and they were telling me to run. Branches and twigs snagged my clothes and hair, but I shook them off and clawed my way out of the forest.

When I reached the cottage, I dashed up to my room, where I stood gathering my thoughts and regaining my rationality. My shallow breathing was audible and so was the panic in my muscles. I opened my tattered curtains to see if anyone had followed me, but there was nothing there, barely even wind rustling the branches.

Maybe I was overthinking it and the adrenaline was making me paranoid. I lived in the middle of nowhere. The most terrifying thing out there was my pet.

I let out a sigh and almost kicked myself for overreacting. Cam trained me too well.

Once I'd completely calmed down, I skipped down the stairs and opened the door to the same sight I saw every day. Not even a twig was out of place.

In the corner of my eye, I saw him emerge from the forest thicket and stand ten feet away from me. At first, I didn't know who I was looking at. The shock of seeing another person besides Cam seemed to stun my senses.

"I found you," he said, his voice low and smooth.

A gasp escaped my lips before any words could. "You?" I couldn't disguise the horror in my voice.

He stood with effortless elegance, a smile barely touched his lips, and his blue eyes were focused on me. His long-sleeved white shirt was crisp, tucked into black pants that hung on his waist and swept into his long boots. There wasn't that much of a difference between what we wore, but I couldn't shake the feeling that he wore it much better than I did or that the quality was significantly better too.

"*You*?" he mimicked back with a confused frown.

"Oh, no. You have to leave." I marched forward to push him back. Who knew when Cam would return. There weren't enough excuses in the world to explain this.

"Excuse me?"

"Go. Leave. Get out," I said and started pushing him back the way he came.

"That's not the response I usually get," he said, dumbfounded. He turned to stop me from pushing him and gave me a once-over. "Hmm…"

"Please just—" Too late.

"I am home, Lil—" Cam became a statue and then his mouth fell. He was showing emotion. I was in more trouble than I could put into words.

I'm dead…

"You," he gasped.

I'm so dead...

"My prince." Cam bowed thrusting his upper body parallel to the ground.

I'm so...Prince?

Chapter 3

Dresses, jewels and kisses

By the way he lifted his chin just high enough to be elegant without being too snobbish, I could imagine him a prince. His smile was modest, polite, but with enough confidence to make it almost smug. His sapphire eyes regarded Cam and held a distant coldness.

Prince, huh?

"My Prince, I am honoured by your presence." Cam stood up straight. He spoke with a gracious and refined tone and kept glancing between us. "But why are you here?"

"For this girl." The prince took my hand, but I snatched it away.

"Her?" Cam's eyes darted to me and back to the prince.

"Yes. She saved my life yesterday." He was talking to Cam, but he was staring at me. I squirmed under his gaze.

"She did?"

The surprise in Cam's voice made my spine stiffen. In the last two minutes, I'd seen more emotions on his face than in the last three months, and that was unnerving.

"I came to thank her." The prince angled his body towards me and took my hand into an iron grip. "Thank you," he whispered.

"Sure," I mumbled.

He lifted my hand to his lips and kissed it. I kept my eyes glued to his face, unable to feel anything but unease. I wished he would disappear like a mirage. He smiled and his sapphire eyes sparkled. My nose twitched, fighting back the snarl in my throat. There was something off about his smile. Like it was especially crafted for moments like this.

"Please see our prince off," Cam said and was already in the house before I could attempt to protest.

"Does my saviour have a name?" he asked.

I frowned and took my hand back. "No. Goodbye."

He stepped forward, obscuring my path. He blinked like his own action confused him, but he quickly righted himself. "You must have a name."

I pressed my palm against his chest to maintain distance. "Look, does my name matter?"

He sighed. "I suppose not."

He took small steps towards me. I instinctively started backing away but soon bumped into a tree. He caught me between his arms, took my chin between his fingers and tipped my face up.

"What are you…?" I started to ask, but his other hand slid up my thigh. A disgusted shiver zipped up my spine, and my right palm hit his cheek, sending out the familiar ring of a slap. He stood paralyzed for a few seconds, blinking.

He turned his head and looked at me with wide, searching eyes that questioned my sanity. "Did you—"

"What's wrong with you?" I hissed and shoved him away. "Is that how you say, 'thank you?' You sick creep. I should break your arm for trying something like that on me.'"

There was genuine surprise on his face. His eyebrows almost touched his hairline. "This is…unexpected."

I shook my head, biting my tongue to keep from cussing him out. "Go away."

"You didn't want me to…" he started to ask, regaining his senses, "Despite knowing who I am, you have no desire for me?"

"I desire to punch you," I said.

"This is new," he said more to himself than me.

I felt an irritated twitch. "So, could you leave now?"

"Not yet. You never told me your name." He straightened up and was again the picture-perfect prince despite how brightly his cheek glowed.

"That was on purpose. I don't see how it's your business." I tightened my fist, ready to take a swing.

No. Slapping him was bad enough. He may have me hanged if I punch him.

The prince didn't look fazed but instead intrigued. He smiled up at the sky. "That's fine. I'll have every able man in my kingdom find out who you are," he threatened. Or at least it sounded like a threat. "None shall rest until I know your name."

"Wait." I lifted my hands so he wouldn't say another word. "I'll tell you my name. Under one condition."

"Condition?" The disappointment in his tone was audible, but he nodded.

"Don't do that."

His head tilted and a bemused smile graced his face. "You have my word."

I took a breath and decided to trust his word. It was just a name, what harm could it do? "My name is Lillianett."

He bowed with a flourish. "Prince Alixios de Velor, as I am sure you know." *I didn't know*. "It's a pleasure."

"For you, maybe," I mumbled.

"I look forward to getting to know you," he said, giving me a once-over like he'd just realized I was standing right in front of him.

It was like I was looking at a completely different person from the poised, almost cold prince I'd just met. This one had a glint in his eye, like a spark before a fire. Something in the last few seconds made him come alive.

"You've never been rejected before, have you?" I asked.

He looked me right in the eye. "It doesn't happen often. And never so passionately."

"Then here is a lesson in rejection. Goodbye." I shoved him away and started walking towards the cottage.

He chuckled. "I will take my leave then," he said, loud enough for me to hear him.

"Good riddance, creep," I said under my breath.

"Lillianett," he called out, but I didn't turn back to respond. "Let's meet again."

I closed the door behind me and found Cam sitting, waiting, giving nothing away. His grey eyes were two impregnable boulders. As usual, poker was his game.

"You are very rude," he said and shook his head.

"Do you want me to invite him back for tea and cookies?" I asked, gesturing at the door.

Cam stared at me. He was back to being emotionless, but I couldn't help but feel he was expecting an explanation.

"I'm sorry," I relented. "He was in trouble. I couldn't leave him. I know I messed up."

"I understand," he said, getting up from his seat.

I hesitated. "You're not mad?"

"I do not get mad Lillianett," he said. "You saved a life, a prince's life for that matter. I am sure it will be okay."

"Will it?" From our brief exchange after Cam left, I felt like I may have made it worse.

"I know I would not want to return if you were that rude to me," he said. "Well done."

I stared at him as he walked away. It was the first time he'd offered me any form of praise. I was grateful, but I couldn't shake the uneasiness creeping into the pit of my stomach.

Alix strolled through the palace corridors, his mind swirling with thoughts of his saviour. The sounds of his shoes tapping against the marble floors bounced off the walls, which were adorned with frames of past and present members of his family. The queen liked a quiet palace. The silence gave her the feeling of order and cleanliness. But it put Alix on edge and made his mind dull.

Servants and maids bowed to him as he passed. The maids blushed and giggled when he smiled at them in return. He sauntered past heavy drapes drawn open and windows that revealed the setting sun past the palace walls. The windows stretched from floor to ceiling, casting the palace in flattering light. He walked up a flight of stairs that swept up in a half-spiral and ended under a crystal chandelier that hung high out of reach.

He stopped abruptly when faced by a young man with a slender yet strong build and blond, ginger-tipped hair. "Alix, you're back. Want to go a few rounds?" he asked with a mischievous grin.

Alix cocked his head to the side. "Right here?"

"I'll have you beg for mercy," he declared.

"Stop it, Ryalie." Another young man came forward and hit Ryalie on the back of the head.

Alix smiled. "Be gentle with him, Jenos."

Jenos shook his head in exasperation. He was not as tall as Ryalie but had a broader build, along with long, curly, brown hair that he kept tied up, out of his face. He rarely let his hair down; said it was a nuisance and yet he refused to have it any shorter.

"Why'd you hit me?" Ryalie shouted, grabbing Jenos by the collar.

Jenos swatted his hand away. "What you were doing wasn't funny. The queen doesn't approve of sparring in the palace."

The queen didn't approve of many things.

"Sure, it was," Ryalie said, following him with an easy stride in his step. "Don't you think so, Alix?"

They began walking in the same direction. Everyone in their path parted without hesitation, bowing their heads as though to avoid their gaze.

"Do I think it's funny that you could even dream of besting me in a fight?" Alix asked with a thick layer of humour in his voice. "Hilarious."

"One day I'll put you in your place," Ryalie said with a wicked grin that promised to make good on his words.

"It's brave of you to say that to a prince," Jenos said.

Ryalie snorted. "It's just Alix."

"Are you saying I'm not a threat?"

"Judging by yesterday's events, you're more like a burden. Which reminds me," Ryalie started, resting both hands behind his head. "What happened to you?"

Alix turned to enter one of the rooms. A lit hearth warmed up the large, open space, and the sweeping ceiling-to-floor window revealed the brilliant landscape of the royal gardens, overflowing with vibrant colours.

"What do you mean?" Alix sat down on one of the cream couches, looking at Ryalie with amusement. "I was attacked, and you found me. My excellent knights."

"Don't act like you don't know. You were injured bad enough to need emergency treatment when we found you. Alle said you lost a lot of blood but got lucky," Ryalie said. "Also, you were alone when we arrived."

"That is strange, isn't it?" Alix said and rested his back on the chair. Ryalie grated his teeth, his patience waning. Alix suppressed a chuckle.

"It is peculiar that we found you in that state alone. Someone must have helped you." Jenos spoke with a calm tone, always steady, wiser than his age. "Also, you disappeared again today without a word to anyone."

"Not uncommon," he said with a shrug. His smile dropped. Sometimes he needed to get away from the palace and his title. "But to answer your previous inquiry. I was lucky. Very."

"You wouldn't have been in that situation if you'd listen to the queen," Jenos said. "You are busy as it is without taking unnecessary breaks."

"Who says they're unnecessary?" The prince stared down his knight. It was a disagreement they often had, one Alix knew Jenos understood but would not let sentimentality cloud his judgment. Alix's duty was to the throne. He was as tied to it as Jenos was tied to him.

"Do you remember who saved you?" Ryalie asked.

"I do. I thanked her today. That's where I was."

"You did?" Both Ryalie and Jenos asked.

"I got a glimpse of her during the ordeal. It wasn't that difficult to find her," he said. "Her eyes were...unique." A deep green, with a hint of brown, like the warm forests of the Moremi kingdom and just as dangerous.

"Please say no more," Ryalie pleaded. "Can we meet her?"

"I don't think you can," Alix said.

"Why?" Ryalie jumped up to squat on his seat.

"Something tells me she doesn't want to be met. She's strange—different," Alix said, rubbing his cheek. "But she's interesting."

"She's caught your interest from one meeting? She must have been very charming," Jenos said. His eyes were skeptical, trying to decipher if there was a future scandal he would need to deal with.

"Actually, she was quite the opposite."

Jenos raised his brows. "How so?"

"She was loud, rude, and violent." Alix still felt a slight tingle on his cheek. "She wasn't much of a *lady* towards me at all."

"That's a first. Most women endeavour to win your favour."

Alix shook his head. "Not her."

"How did you thank her for saving your life? Dresses? Jewels? A kiss?" Ryalie asked, making kissy-faces in the air.

Alix grabbed a pillow and threw it at the knight's face. "She wouldn't even accept my thanks. All she wanted was for me to leave."

"Do you know why?" Jenos asked.

"It may be because of the man she lives with. He was…familiar." It was at the tip of his tongue, scratching the back of his mind, but he couldn't quite place the man in his memory. The way he held himself told Alix that he was Syver trained, but not a knight; too young to be retired

"It's a strange situation you've stumbled into," Jenos said.

"Yes, strange," Alix said and smiled.

Jenos started. He must have seen something in Alix's eyes, a familiar warmth that he hadn't felt in a long time.

"You should still give her something to show your appreciation," Jenos said, forcing himself to relax his posture against the seat. Alix could see his mind working—the knight would need to find out who this girl was, or he wouldn't be able to relax. "It's only right."

"I will." Alix nodded. "Dresses, jewels and kisses."

There was a light, three-beat knock at the door, then a tall slender young woman walked in with a grace that fit her title.

"My prince," she swooned. She sat on Alix's lap, wrapping her arms around his neck with a giggle.

"Princess Aretia," Alix said. He smiled up at her but the warmth of it didn't quite reach his eyes. "When did you arrive?"

"I asked for you earlier, but they told me you'd stepped out." Her brown eyes warmed as she blushed. She tucked her thick auburn hair behind her ear, to reveal the beauty mark on her right cheek and her long slender neck.

"Ah, yes, I had a few matters to attend to," he said, kissing her hand as he'd done hundreds of times. "My apologies."

"I see," she said, then perked up, realizing they weren't alone in the room. "Jenos, Ryalie, always a pleasure."

"Princess," Jenos and Ryalie replied with a nod.

"Shall we retire to get reacquainted?" she whispered in Alix's ear.

"Let's," he purred and put his hand on her thigh. His mind backtracked to the way Lillianett had struck him for such a simple touch. He remembered the fierce disgust in her eyes, like a single strike wasn't enough to appease her anger.

"My Prince?" Aretia asked in a shrill, lady-like voice, gentle and with enough feminine charm behind it to rouse him.

But *her* voice was fierce and unyielding.

Aretia cupped the sides of his face. "My Prince, are you feeling unwell?"

"No, no. I'm sorry," he said and kissed her neck. "It's nothing. Let's go. I owe you a proper greeting." Alix stood with Aretia in his arms, and she shrieked with excitement.

Chapter 4

Friend

The next morning, the sound of rustling branches beat against my eardrums. It sounded like a storm had found its way into my bedroom. But when I opened my eyes, the sun was shining calmly through the holes of my curtains. I pushed my head up from the pillow and stared at the light, cursing the audacity of its brightness.

The wind died down, and there was a knock at the front door. I lifted my head off the pillow and paused to confirm I heard what I did. When I heard the knock again, I jumped out of bed and ran to my window. Cam never had guests. The chance to see someone felt like an opportunity that would never come again.

When I peeked through the curtains, I saw a large, winged creature. I stared at its bright yellow feathers, with its sharp beak wrapped in a bridle, and its black, puffed out chest. It looked like a sphinx, with its intimidating four-clawed limbs and large tail. Its eyes were big, black balls, blinking as it stared into space. Its head had a crown of feathers standing tall, like it was the king of the skies.

My limbs itched to touch its incredible wings. I wanted to fly through the air on its back and see the world from a place untouched by my circumstances.

I heard the door open, and my eyes darted down as I struggled to see who was at the door. No matter how I pressed myself up against the window, I couldn't see anything but the back of the guest's head.

He was there for ten seconds before he turned and walked back towards his giant bird. They flew off into the sky, leaving little trace of ever being in the area. All I saw was the back of the man's head, but it was still the most interesting event since I'd arrived in Glorus.

Well, the second most interesting event.

I narrowed my eyes and watched with envy as the bird flew away. I scratched my nails against the glass and sighed. It couldn't be me. I had to remember that.

"Lillianett," Cam called.

I paused for a second and mentally prepared myself for whatever training he had waiting for me.

When I arrived downstairs, Cam was sitting down and rubbing the back of his neck with his eyes closed. I worried that he was experiencing too many emotions in too short a period.

"What's with you?" I asked, pulling up a chair so I could sit in front of him. He looked up and I could see his age, worse, I could see his mental age.

He looked down. "I have to go," he said. "My mother is unwell, and her health has taken a turn. I need to tend to her."

"Your mother…" I trailed off. Somehow it had failed to cross my mind that he had a mother. I had to check myself. Even if he was robotic, he was still a person. "Of course. I understand. You have to go. But—and I don't mean to sound selfish when I ask this—what about me?"

"I'll get you a substitute caretaker," he said, getting onto his feet. His mind was clearly elsewhere.

"Substitute? That's a thing?" I asked.

"You will be in good hands," he said.

"If you say so." I couldn't help feeling uneasy again.

"I shouldn't be long. I will go now and get into contact with my substitute." He walked upstairs with heavy shoulders.

"When will you leave?" I asked.

"Tomorrow," he answered.

The room went silent. His words added weight to the air. I tried to imagine what this would mean for me. Would it be business as usual or was something going to change? And worse still, was Cam's mom going to be okay? Judging from how his eyes had hung, gazing into the empty space between us, it looked bad.

Cam descended the stairs with a hood over his head and a sack hanging on his shoulders. "I'll take my leave. I shouldn't be very long," he repeated. Maybe he was trying to reassure me. It wasn't working.

"Sure," I said and swallowed my lack of spit. He nodded and closed the door behind him.

I stared at the scratched wooden door, almost wishing he would walk back in. He wasn't one for jokes, but I foolishly hoped he was pranking me to teach me a lesson about his importance.

I shook myself out of my nervous daze and went into the kitchen. I grabbed all the fruit I could find and started scarfing them down. Sugar always calmed my nerves but at this moment I seriously missed chocolate.

After eating my worries away, I walked to the door desperate to clear my head with a run. As I closed the door behind me, the bushes rustled, and I froze in place. I grabbed the handle with caution, ready to hide in the cottage at the first sign of trouble.

The prince came into view.

This time I didn't hesitated and immediately opened the door behind me.

"Hello, Lillianett," he greeted.

"Goodbye, Prince," I said and closed the door. I gargled a sigh and stood contemplating my options.

I had none. His presence shrank my prison from the size of the forest to the size of Cam's cottage.

I jogged up to my room but paused when I reached my door. "What the hell?" I gasped.

The prince was leaning against my wall, looking at home in my space.

I stared at him, admittedly dumbfounded. "Did you climb through my window?"

He shrugged. "It didn't look like you were going to let me through the door."

"Most people take that as a sign that they're unwanted," I said.

"Do they?"

I glared at him. "Also, this is breaking and entering." He didn't respond. He just stared at me. We stared at each other like this for a while.

Finally, I sighed and asked, "What do you want?"

"You," he said, stepping towards me. "I want to thank you for saving me."

"You thanked me yesterday, and I said it was fine. Leave."

He smiled in confusion, like he understood my words but couldn't comprehend that I was saying. Instead of responding he strolled around the room analyzing every inch. I knew there was nothing that could give me away, but my eyes followed him for any signs of suspicion.

"I will give you whatever you want. Say it and it's yours," he said still walking and staring. "It is the least I could do for you."

I took a breath and held it. For a moment, I let his offer tempt me, then shook my head to dismiss the thought. "What I want, you can't give me," I whispered. I turned toward the door, but he blocked my path. His face mere inches from mine.

"What do you mean?" he asked, "What can't I give you?"

"It doesn't matter. You just can't," I said. He couldn't give me freedom and take away the curse placed on my family.

"I can try," he whispered.

No, you couldn't even try, I thought. The temptation didn't last as long this time. I shook my head. "It's nothing. It was an honour to save you. I don't need anything."

"You don't expect me to accept that, do you?" he said. He wasn't listening to what I was trying to say. "I will come back every day until there is something you want."

"I want you to leave," I snapped.

He took a step back like my words landed a physical blow. "Why? Why do you want me gone? Have I done something to offend you?"

Yes. "Maybe I'm dangerous," I said.

He shook his head and locked his jaw. All signs of warmth were long-gone. "You're not dangerous." His eyes searched my face like he was seeing me—truly seeing me.

To hear that…like a confession a part of me always wanted out in the world. There was a spark of gratitude in my heart, but it quickly died once I realized I was stuck.

"Why won't you leave?" I asked. "I happened to be walking by, and I saved you. It's not a big deal."

"You saved the future king of Tamikar. That is a big deal."

I suppressed a smile. "It was an honour, and that's enough for me. You can leave knowing I'm proud of myself."

"I won't leave. Not until I know," he said, sounding a little breathless as he inched closer.

I was seconds away from a migraine. "Until you know what?"

"Know you."

"You're annoying," I said.

"Persistent," he corrected.

"Stubborn."

"Diligent." He stepped closer.

"Creep," I breathed.

"Tell me what you want," he whispered, amusement dancing in his sapphire eyes.

"For you to leave!"

"Never," he laughed, locking me in his gaze.

"Like I said: annoying." I paused and smiled. *If he wanted to play this game…* "I want your kingdom."

He smiled like a wolf and pushed his hand through his hair. He reached out his arms like he was about to hold me. "In that case, shall we get married tomorrow?"

I lifted my hand to stop his outstretched advance. "Not what I meant."

"Too bad."

"I want treasures," I said.

"Enough to fill your pockets or this room?"

"A palace with my own servants?"

He smiled again. "Where would you like it built?"

I paused, trying to decipher his expression, but all I saw was the same calm politeness he had on yesterday. And that smile, trained to be bored yet charming.

"Are you serious?"

"Yes." He nodded, excitement suddenly bouncing in his eyes. Then he frowned, erasing all amusement. "But that's not what you desire, is it? No, you want something more valuable than anything material could ever mean."

"I want nothing, I'm fine," I said with a shrug.

"Oh?" He grinned. "Is that how it is?"

"Yup, it's like that." I snapped my fingers. "Bye." I waved my hand and was about to leave the room when he got in my way again. "Seriously, stop that."

"I won't leave. I'll keep coming back."

"Why?" I groaned.

"Because there is something about you, and I am determined to know what it is."

"I'll just have to run," I said. I tried to keep the anger out of my voice, but it was shaky, bordering a growl.

He stepped forward, and I stared into those eyes, so impossibly blue. I felt his warm breath tickle my skin. For a moment, he felt inescapable.

"And I will chase you to the ends of Glorus. You won't escape."

A shiver ran over my spine. There was no way he could know the extent to which those words scared me. If he knew the truth, he wouldn't be offering me riches. He would be asking me how I would like to die. No, he wouldn't even ask.

"Why won't you leave me alone?" I whispered and hated the fear in my voice.

"Like I said, there is something about you." The amusement was back in his eyes. He was like a child discovering something new and untested. It made my stomach churn. "It's easier to breathe around you," he murmured barely loud enough for me to hear.

I took a sharp breath. Before I exhaled, I ran. I sped down the stairs and erupted through the front door, rushing towards the forest. I didn't look back, but I heard him on my heels, and the steps were getting louder.

I took off sprinting into the densest parts I could find, ignoring the branches that ripped and tugged at my clothes, skin, and hair. My breathing became shallow, and the adrenaline started to blur my vision.

"Stop running from me," he shouted.

"Stop. Chasing. Me," I panted back. I hadn't been running for long, but I was running my hardest. I was faster, but I couldn't shake him no matter how I bobbed and weaved through the forest. Worse, he didn't sound tired.

I turned on my heel and hopped back struggling to control my momentum. This took him by surprise, and he ran straight at me, unable to stop. I grabbed his shirt and fell back with his weight, rocking onto my back while positioning my leg on his stomach. With our added momentum, I threw him over my head.

I scrambled to get up on my feet and lifted my fists. He rolled off the ground and stayed in a low crouch, staring at me with wild eyes. He took in my position, then stood up with an assured nod and expectant smile.

"Ryalie would love you," he said with a smile. "Well, come at me."

I swallowed and took a half-step back. He looked too confident. He could've been faking, but if he was, he had a Cam-tier poker face.

As a prince, he probably had knights to protect him all his life, but there was no way he wasn't well trained in case of emergencies.

I was so busy considering all the possibilities that I didn't notice he'd already made a move. I jumped back before he could grab me in his arms. I didn't have time to think. I'd have to knock him out and figure out the rest later.

I threw a right hook, but he slipped through and parried to his left. I followed with three more jabs. His movements were effortless, and he didn't take his eyes off me for an instant. I kept moving, trying to land a single shot, using the drive of my previous attempt to launch my next. I went in circles, over and over, trying to make a connection. Then he caught my right wrist and pinned my back against a tree.

"You're fast, with a decent amount of strength. But you're lacking experience," he said. I tried punching him with my other hand, but he caught it. "What are you? What's your Blood?"

"Let me go," I snarled.

He pulled me forward, twirled me, and crossed my arms so that my back was resting against his chest. His arms nestled my body. He rocked me back and forth, cocooned, as though he were trying to soothe my anger. For half a second, it felt nice, but I snapped out of it and threw my elbow back against his ribs. He grunted, releasing me, and I started running again.

I couldn't fight him, and running wasn't going to work either. It certainly didn't help that he knew where I lived.

I stopped and sighed, out of breath. Talking was my only option, but he wasn't listening. I pressed my fingers against the side of my head to try and massage the headache away.

My head snapped back. I listened, darting my eyes around. Silence. I couldn't hear him anymore. He didn't follow me. I lowered my centre of gravity and crept around. I wasn't buying it. He had to be somewhere. No way he stopped his pursuit because of one hit.

I heard the patter of footsteps scattered in the bushes. They moved in a distorted zigzag, throwing off my senses. My eyes jumped around, reacting to every shift. I shook my head and closed my eyes. I had to focus and filter out the excess noise. He could only come from one direction.

My eyes flew open. My head snapped to the left, but I was a second too late. He'd already leaped at me, arms stretched forward. It was a clean tackle from my blind spot. The impact of his body against mine as he wrapped his arms around me sent us tumbling across the ground. I instinctively held onto him as we rolled over rocks, cracking twigs, and dead leaves.

When we finally stopped, I peeled away from him and laid flat on my back. I blinked up at the sky that'd grown overcast with light grey clouds.

There was no escaping him.

He sat cross-legged beside me and dusted the dirt from my face. His brows creased as he frowned. "Are you okay? I didn't mean to hurt you."

I couldn't help laughing. *Now he felt sorry?*

"I'm not hurt," I grunted and pushed myself up.

He stared at me. When I stared back, he looked away, slightly flushed. "I'm sorry." He sounded like a kicked puppy.

Now I felt bad. "Well, I shouldn't have run."

"Why did you run?"

"You don't even realize what a creep you are, do you?" I laughed.

He pouted. "You don't realize I'm a prince, do you?"

"You don't make it easy to remember," I said. He pouted harder and I smiled at him. But I also felt sad. If he knew the truth, he wouldn't be so lighthearted. He would think I was a monster. Despite that, since I'd met him, I'd felt more alive than all my days being in Glorus. Blaze was great, but talking to someone who could respond felt so good.

"I know what I want from you," I said.

"Name it," he replied, ready for a challenge.

"Be my friend," I said, then laughed because it sounded even sillier out loud. "You're a prince and despite your current stalker tendencies, I assume you're busy. So, when you can, come by and visit me."

"You want me...to be your friend?" he asked with a voice so tender I could swear the words turned to crystal when they left his lips.

"Is that a no?"

"No, it's... I... I don't get that request very often," he said.

"Are the people around you not friendly?"

"Oh, most people who approach me are very friendly," he said with a smile, but his eyes glazed over with a sadness I couldn't explain. "But a request for nothing but friendship is rare. Why do you want me to be your friend?"

I shrugged. "Living here is boring."

"Yes, this place is pretty isolated. I don't understand why you'd stay," he said.

"Well, we became friends a few seconds ago. I'll need to get to know you a little longer before telling you everything about me."

He stood up and offered me a hand. I grabbed it, and he pulled me up against his body, so close that I could taste his scent. It was a pleasant, warm sweetness that put my senses in a flutter.

"Everything? Is that a promise?"

I gently pushed him back and shook my head "That depends on you," I said. I couldn't ignore the truth that telling him everything was impossible. But he didn't need to know that. "Also, keep this a secret from Cam."

"The man from yesterday? Who is he?"

I paused. "A family friend." Not a complete lie.

"And why am I a secret?" he asked.

"You ask too many questions," I said and started walking back.

"A secret friend," he said, walking in step with me. A small smile touched his lips. "How...novel."

I shook my head at his excitement. His eyes sparkled and something close to a real smile spread his lips wide. I couldn't deny that the idea was thrilling, but it was also terrifying. I was gambling with my life.

Chapter 5

Fairy princess?

A plain upright piano stood tucked away in the corner of the parlour, the least visited room in Cam's cottage. The years had chipped and cracked away at the corners, one of the white keys was stuck, and it was also in desperate need of tuning. Nevertheless, I made it a point to sit down and play once a week so that my fingers wouldn't lose their strength or dexterity.

I began with scales, moving my fingers over the keys, closing my eyes to immerse myself in the sound. My muscles danced over the black and white stripes, remembering the correct progressions, moving through arpeggios and staccatos.

I loved the sound of the piano. My grandfather and dad played together when I was a kid. I never forgot how at peace I felt falling asleep to what sounded like raindrops in the forest.

The door handle clicked, and my eyes flew open. My fingers stopped, and I waited for the footsteps to reach me. Cam dragged his body into the room and sat down on the nearest couch, rubbing his neck. I stared at him, unsure of what to say.

The silence was deafening, and the longer it went on, the louder my heartbeat sounded.

"Lillianett," he said, snapping out of his stress induced trance.

"Yes?"

He looked up at me, his usually grey eyes darkened by the shadows that plagued his face. How could someone age so much in a few hours?

"My cousin will take over my caretaker duties, starting tomorrow," he said but I saw his mind was elsewhere. He leaned back in his chair and released a sigh like breathing was the only thing keeping him functioning.

"Tomorrow," I repeated. "Does your cousin know about me? I mean my family."

His body sank further against the couch. "If anything were to have happened to me, she would have been your caretaker. She knows everything and she's qualified."

"Qualified?" I asked, resting my fingers on the keys and shadow playing so that my hands had something to do aside from remaining knotted in my lap.

"To train you," he said. He rubbed his brow and made himself sit up straight. The shadows played on his face making it look even grimmer. "I will leave when she arrives."

"So soon," I whispered, and my fingers froze, hovering aimlessly. "Will everything be okay?"

Cam said nothing. He looked at the space between me and the window. He stayed in perfect stillness, as though frozen in time.

"Cam?"

"Camerin," he corrected, then met my eye. Something he saw made his face soften an inch. "Everything will be fine."

The sun was dipping into the horizon as Alix strolled through the palace corridors, humming to himself while he twirled an arrow between his fingers. His mind replayed everything that had occurred. He couldn't help but smile every time he recalled her request.

"Friends," he whispered to himself. "How endearing."

She'd ran from him. It was absolutely ridiculous. And more ridiculous than that? He'd chased her. It took a split second for him to register her desperate dash and then he was chasing her. She'd lit a spark in him so overwhelming that years of proper training melted away in a heartbeat.

She'd ran and he chased her.

He could never tell Jenos, the lecture would be unbearable, the laughter from Ryalie would be just as bad.

He couldn't get her laugh out of his head.

"What's endearing?" Ryalie asked as he came up from behind and snatched the arrow away. He studied it, balancing the shaft on the tip of his fingers and staring at the point. "Why are you playing with this thing?"

"Give it back."

"Answers first." He skillfully dodged Alix's attempt to snatch the arrow back and instead pointed it like a sword.

"It was shot at me yesterday," Alix answered with a shrug. He'd happened to find it as he was leaving the forest and couldn't bring himself to leave it. Perhaps he would return it to Lillianett the next time they met.

Ryalie's eyes widened. For a second he let his guard down, allowing Alix to steal the arrow back and continue down the hall. Ryalie doubled back and spun around, racing to catch up.

"You were attacked yesterday? Actually, you disappeared again today."

"Yes, you and Jenos are terrible knights."

Ryalie snorted. "We could do a better job if you would stop sneaking out of the palace when no one's looking."

"As my knights, you should always be looking," Alix said.

Ryalie huffed but made no argument. "At least take me with you," he grumbled.

Alix smiled at his friend and couldn't help thinking how he and Lillianett would get along. He turned and walked into his private study, where Jenos stood waiting for him.

"How did you know I would be coming here?" he asked.

"You've been gone most of the day and still have a lot to do," Jenos answered, gesturing at the piles of paper.

"How dull. It disturbs me to think how long you've stood there waiting for me," Alix said. He crossed the large room, past the couches and drawn curtains. When he sat, he swivelled his seat around to face Jenos's frown.

"Violitt will meet with you tomorrow night, when you're done," Jenos said in an effort to lighten the mood caused by their staring match.

"Less dull," Alix said. "But that means I'll be working until tomorrow night."

"You reap what you sow," Ryalie taunted with a grin.

"Where did you go today?" Jenos asked, adding enough curiosity in his tone to not be demanding as he so often was.

"I went to see her," Alix said and showed off the arrow in his hand. Jenos furrowed his brows and examined the dirty tip.

Alix snorted. "She was less than thrilled."

"She was the one who attacked you?" Ryalie asked.

Jenos's brows jumped. "Attacked? Is she a threat?"

Alix shook his head. "No, no, it was a mistake. She didn't realize it was me. And besides, she's a terrible shot." He almost laughed at the memory of her frustration. The way she threw a short tantrum then melted to the ground in utter defeat. Yet she stood to try again.

Alix glanced at Jenos. He wasn't the best archer, but he was capable with a bow and arrow. She could benefit from his tutelage. He was a good teacher, definitely the most patient of the three of them.

"Alix?" Jenos's face was distorted with confusion and worry.

"It's nothing," Alix sighed. He twirled his chair back to look at his papers. "I assume all of these have to do with the EverSnow Night?"

"Yes," Jenos said. "There is much that needs your approval."

"I can't wait for this year's Night." Ryalie said, his face lighting up. He paused, the excitement dying out, then asked, "Will your sister or brother be attending?"

"No. My brother has declined, and Glory knows where in the world my sister is." Alix rustled through the papers.

Would Lillianett like to attend? He wondered. She did

mention how bored she was. He would rather have her attend than his siblings.

"Alix," Ryalie said, slamming his palm on the desk. "Are you okay? Do you need Alle? You've been distracted ever since your near-death experience."

The corner of Alix's lip twitched up. "Isn't that normal?"

"It would be if it were your first time, but it's not," Jenos said. "Something is different."

Alix smiled. "It is different. I made a friend."

Ryalie and Jenos looked at each other, neither one able to mask their confusion or concern. Alix smiled to himself, anticipating the next time he would see her.

The next morning, the sound of knuckles on hardwood woke me from a deep sleep. I buried my face beneath my pillow and groaned into my sheet, but then I sprang up as I realized I rarely heard that sound. This was Cam's second visitor in two days.

I tip-toed out of bed and snuck down the stairs. I heard the door close and tried to peek at who it was. It could be Cam's cousin, the prince, or someone else. I couldn't be sure. I strained my senses to hear what was being said but could only make out muffled sounds.

"You can come down," Cam said, loud enough for me to hear.

My body stiffened. I couldn't help feeling embarrassed thinking I was being sneaky.

I jogged down the stairs and faced a stranger. She was much shorter than Cam and me, with a shaven head and dark skin that matched her eyes. She had the stature of a child but held herself like a woman. I saw the age in her eyes. She was older than Cam.

"Lillianett, this is Estell. She will be your caretaker until I return."

I looked at Cam. He gave nothing away. Typical.

"It's nice to meet you," I said but I couldn't fully mask the uncertainty in my voice. There was something about her that made me feel on edge.

She glared at me, and I glared back out of habit. Her lips curled into a smile. "I hear I have a lot to teach you. Just so you know, Camerin is the nice one."

Oh yeah, this is going to be fun.

"I want her alive when I return, Estell," Cam said.

I gaped at Cam and his words and how serious he sounded when he said them. *Alive*? That was where the bar was?

"You get what I give you," she said and walked past me with a large bag tucked under her arm. She walked into a room and closed the door behind her.

"Take me with you," I pleaded as soon as she wasn't in earshot.

"Do not joke at a time like this," Cam said, narrowing his eyes.

"Who's joking?" I mumbled. "How long will you be gone?"

"I should not be long. I will be back soon enough," he said. "Listen to Estell."

I frowned. Would listening to her keep me more than just alive? "Okay," I said. It wasn't as though I had a choice.

He nodded. "I will be leaving now."

"Wait." The word was out of my mouth before the thought came to my mind. There was so much I wanted to say and ask, but what came out was, "What if something goes wrong?"

"Like what?"

"Something." I swallowed. "I don't know. What if I can't handle it?"

For the first time since I arrived, I felt a storm of anxiety choke the air from my lungs. Was it because he was leaving? Did I rely on him to this extent? Cam was all I knew. Although he wasn't warm, he was constant, and I didn't want him to leave me, even if only for a short time.

"You will be fine," he said, placing a comforting hand on my shoulder.

I looked up into his eyes, the certainty there. "What if you're wrong?" I whispered.

"I'm never wrong," he said. I found myself half-smiling. He was wrong about the prince not coming back.

I bit my lip to keep my secrets. He had enough to worry about without adding my troubles to the mix. He was right. It would all be fine.

"You're still here?" Estell asked, walking out from the back room. I turned to catch her shooing him away. "Leave already."

"Yes, yes, goodbye," he said.

When I looked back again, he was gone.

I poked my head out the door to try and see a departing figure, but there was nothing. "It's only cool when Batman does it," I grumbled and closed the door.

When I turned around, I almost walked into Estell, who grabbed my arm and started poking at my skin. I watched her examine me all over, trying to gleam what she could.

"Looks like you've adjusted. It usually takes a few months," she said. "Come down to the training room. I have a lot to teach you." I followed her down the flight of stairs and into the basement, where a board was set up near the entrance. "Sit down. Class is in session."

I did as she instructed, and she started writing. The first word she scribbled at the top of the board was *Glorians*.

"Do you know what this is?" she asked and underlined it twice.

"The people in this world with heightened abilities, kind of super-human," I answered. It felt like I was back in primary school. "My dad and Cam said that after my mark appeared, my body would change, and I would become one."

Estell cracked a sarcastic smile. "Cam was right. You don't know much. Your predecessor should know this. Why weren't you taught before you arrived?"

"My dad said because we live in isolation while in Glorus, it's safe to live in some ignorance before we arrive. That way every generation then gets to live a normal life before the start of their year."

She clicked her tongue. "Ridiculous."

I frowned. I liked it that way. I never had to dwell on what was or could be. My dad kept this part of my life at arm's length for as long as possible, while my mother prepared me in her own way. "What are Glorians, then?" I asked.

"You weren't entirely wrong," she said and started writing some more. She wrote the word *Arcania* and circled it. "This is life."

"*Arcania*?"

"Yes. You can find it in every person and everything, even in the air. People who can manipulate their own *Arcania* are Glorians. They train to master their skills, and how those skills manifest depends on their Blood," she explained. "There are five Bloods." She erased her previous words and jotted down five more: *warrior, hunter, seer, weaver,* and *healer.* "Depending on where one's talents lie, they can be one of five."

"So, how would I know which one I am?"

She snorted. "You?"

"I'm a Glorian too," I said. "Right?"

Estell chuckled. "You're like a newborn. Even if you were a fledgling, it would take a few days to see where your strengths lie, but luckily for you, you're born from royalty."

"That matters?" I asked.

"Each Blood has a regent," she said. "You are from the hunter lineage." She circled the word *hunter* and smiled at me. "You're a huntress, princess."

It was my turn to snort. "Princess?"

Estell shrugged. "Cursed or not, you're still royalty. Unrecognized and shunned, but royal blood flows in your veins all the same."

"What about Tamikar?" I asked. "What Blood do their royals fall under?"

"Good question," she said and circled the word *warrior.*

I couldn't help my surprise. That pretty boy stalker creep was a warrior? I couldn't imagine it. Then again, he did dodge my jabs and looked confident in his abilities. Even when he stood with smugness, there was an air of strength about him.

"Focus," Estell snapped. "Camerin did say you lacked focus."

"Sorry."

"A hunter's best traits are their heightened senses, speed, and swiftness. The ability to discern the world around them and tame creatures. The instinct for survival is what makes a hunter a hunter."

"Tame creatures? Like kiliabis?" I asked.

"Kiliabis are untameable. It's said the Crowns of old could tame them but that's a legend."

"Crowns?" I asked.

"That's what those of royal birth are referred to as."

I nodded. I was about to tell her about Blaze when I remembered how Cam reacted and decided against it.

Estell started writing again. When she stood back, the word *archery* appeared next to *hunter,* circled. "You should be able to use at least one weapon, as all Glorians can, and this is what it should be."

"I'm bad at archery," I said.

"I've heard. That's unacceptable. Camerin gave me a rough idea of your skill level. I understand that he was waiting for your body to mature, but now it has." She glared at me, and I squirmed. "Every morning, you'll be down here with me, learning how to be a huntress."

"Are you a huntress?" I asked.

"No, I'm a healer. Camerin is a hunter. But I'm a trainer at Syver Academy, so you are in good hands."

"Healer? Syver?" I asked.

"Syver is the island where Glorians are trained, and yes, I am a healer. I can use my *Arcania* to heal others." Estell pulled out a silver needle from her side pouch, half the length of my forearm and much thinner than a knitting needle. It had a blue, steely shine and a sharp tip. "Healers use needles to help concentrate their *Arcania*. They are kept on their person at all times." She pulled out five more and held them between her fisted fingers. "Any healer worth their title is an expert of their use. A true master can produce threads made of *Arcania* to stitch wounds."

I couldn't believe what I was hearing. It sounded like *Arcania* was magic. Was it magic? Did that mean I could use magic? Was I a fairy princess? I shook my head at the nonsense my mind was spinning. I wasn't even a princess let alone a fairy.

"I'll leave it at that for today. Get up," she said. "Time to train you."

"This is going to hurt," I groaned.

I could see it in her eyes. No mercy. But unlike Cam, there was also a ferocity, like *she* was the huntress, and I was prey.

She rubbed her hands together, taking a few steps backwards. "Don't worry. You're in good hands. No matter how much I hurt you, I can heal you."

"Yeah, but will you?"

Her responding grin sent shivers through me. "We'll see."

I couldn't help but think Cam set this up on purpose.

Reluctantly, I lifted my arms, bracing for whatever Estell would do, but she was too fast. I felt her fist against my cheek before I realized she'd moved. I stumbled back, sucking in air. The room was spinning. My jaw stung like I'd face planted against a hot iron.

"Too slow. Watch me," she said. "Again."

I shook my head and lifted my arms, and this time I was able to block her left hook.

She smiled. "Good."

Estell released a barrage of punches, each one faster than the last, coming from different angles. I couldn't defend against all of them. It was the blow to the centre of my chest that brought me to my knees.

"Oh my…" I sucked in air like it was my last, gripping my heart. She wasn't holding back. I felt the impact in my spine, and it spread like a river of blood.

Estell pulled me to my feet. "When you attack, always go at it like you're ready to kill."

"What?" I gasped, still finding my breath.

"Assume that your opponent will do the same." She gave me a steely look. "Don't forget what you are. Attack to kill if you want to live."

I nodded my head, but my neck was lead. I knew all that, but hearing it made it so real.

"Okay," I gasped, "Any other tips?"

She grabbed my hair and yanked. I screamed, and she kicked my legs out from under me. The next thing I knew, I was on the ground with her hand pressed against my head.

"Never let your guard down."

"Ouch," I moaned. The ache raced up my body like a heat rash. The blows to my back and chest were competing to see which hurt the most.

"Get up," Estell said. "Punch my hands."

I pulled myself up, and she lifted her hands on either side of her face. I punched both hands and she shook her head. "Add more weight behind it. Punch through. Punch faster. Go."

I adjusted my position and repeated the punches.

"Not bad but you're still too slow."

"You're going to kill me," I said between gasps.

"I'm a healer. You won't die," she said with a grin.

Somehow, that was worse.

"Okay, get ready. We're not going to stop until I say so. Keep light on your feet. Dodge as much as you can, and when you attack—"

"Attack to kill," I said.

I swallowed and lifted my hands. As soon as they were up, Estell rushed me with a blast of quick jabs. She was light on her feet and used her legs when I least expected it. I hit the ground, but she never stopped attacking. I rolled to safety and scrambled back up only to face another bombardment. I couldn't get a hit in. Even when I tried, she parried or dodged to my blind side and started all over again.

"Watch me!" Estell barked. Her sudden order gave me pause. She kicked my side, forcing me to take a knee. I pushed back, out of her reach, trying to catch my breath, gripping my ribs.

I understood now. I wasn't supposed to beat her—I had to

observe how she moved and learn everything I could. Like a hunter stalking its prey. Regardless of how it looked, I had to take the position of the huntress in this fight. I widened my stance and lowered my centre of gravity. I wasn't going to win, but I had to learn.

"Good," Estell purred.

Chapter 6

Perfect gentleman

P ain lined my lungs like razor blades. I lost track of how long we'd trained and how many times I'd hit the ground. The bitter taste of iron coated my mouth, and I was almost certain she'd knocked two of my teeth loose. My limbs were heavy and numb, weighed down by their fatigue.

My vision was starting to come back into focus.

Did I pass out?

"Look at that. You're alive." Estell walked past my body with a rectangular object in her arms. "Get up. One more lesson for the day."

My body screamed. I couldn't take much more. I would need a week to recover.

I rolled onto my stomach and forced my chop-stick arms to push my body up so I could at least sit. Estell hung a target on the wall, larger than the others.

"I said get up. Come on," she said and picked up a bow. "Take this."

I stared at her, hoping her nightmarish figure would disappear, but she remained staring back at me with no patience. I stood and took the short bow in my hand.

I couldn't grip. My muscles were sapped.

"Here." Estell handed me an arrow. "Aim."

I drew the bow back, but I couldn't keep my arms steady. The arrow vibrated between my fingers. "I can't. I don't have the strength." My arms collapsed.

"Try it again," she said.

I sighed and aimed again, and she poked one of her needles into my upper left arm. "Ow," I squealed.

"That didn't hurt," she said and stuck it in my other arm.

She was right, I realised. It didn't hurt. It was a small pinch, but it lasted less than a second.

"Again," she commanded.

I lifted and drew the bow. I couldn't believe how steady I was. My arms felt normal. The exhaustion in my muscles was non-existent. "How?"

"I've eased your fatigue," she explained. "Given the right circumstances, I can make you fight through the night, but I promised Camerin I wouldn't do that."

I had to remember to thank Cam when he returned.

I drew the bow back further and let go, missing the target as dismally as all the other times. I sighed in frustration. "I'm not focusing enough, right? Cam says so often enough."

"Everyone is different. Camerin talks too much. You learn better by doing, watching, taking risks," she said. "Focus isn't your problem here." Estell took the bow and drew back her arrow, hitting the centre mark with ease. "You just get bored.

"You make it look so easy," I said, and took the bow.

"You're a huntress. It should be second nature," she said. "See your target. Don't overthink the distance. You only need to know where to aim. Use your senses. Take in the variations in the wind, the way your bowstring tightens. Listen to when it tells you to let go. Camerin's taught you everything. Now use that knowledge."

I nodded and tried again. I took a deep breath and tightened my grip on the bow, felt the roughness of the curves, heard the tightness of the string. I adjusted my arm, eyes on my target. Nothing else was in the room. I released the arrow, and with a smooth whoosh it landed on the target. It wasn't a bullseye, but I got it in the target range. "Oh my gosh, I did it," I said.

"Hmm...passable. You've earned a goodnight's sleep"

"Finally," I cried. The sun was still high when we started.

Estell walked towards the exit. "Shout for me tomorrow morning if you can't move," she said.

I was dumbfounded. Was that a possibility? I looked around the room as though something would make me feel better. Then I spotted a splatter of blood—definitely mine—smeared on the ground and nodded. "Time for bed."

My bones creaked and my muscles wailed as I dragged myself up the stairs at a snail's pace. Every inch of me was throbbing. The only thing that kept me moving was the idea of lying in bed. The mattress was old and springy, but it would soon become my favourite place in the world.

I reached my room and collapsed against my pillow, releasing a stream of squeaks from the bed. I sighed in relief and dragged the blanket over my body, letting my weight sink low. I wasn't even comfortable, but I didn't have the strength to twitch a finger.

The bed creaked with extra weight, and I tightened my already shut eyes, praying Estell would let me sleep. If I stayed still, maybe she would leave.

A hand touched my shoulder, and I twitched. Her hands were bigger than I thought.

"Are you asleep?"

I jumped up and faced him. My body ached in protest, but the shock won out.

"Prince Alixios," I whisper-gasped and gripped the blanket. "You're taking this creep thing to a scary level."

He chuckled and smiled. "Still as rude as ever."

"What are you doing here?"

"Saying hello to a friend," he said and shrugged. He tipped his head to the side, a playful smile on his lips and in his eyes. "Hello, friend."

I glanced at my open window at the darkened skies. I shook my head. "Friends don't usually visit each other this late."

"You must not have very good friends then," he said. He narrowed his eyes at me and grabbed my arm, tracing his fingers over my blotchy bruises. "What happened?"

"Training," I said, taking my arm back.

"Are you training for a war?" he asked with a light laugh, inching forward.

I gripped the blanket and smiled, but I couldn't find the

humour in the truth. I was training to survive.

"I could train you," he said.

"You?" I almost laughed.

"Yes me, but you never told me…" He inched even closer, staring into my eyes. "What is your Blood? What are you?"

I stared back. "A huntress."

He cracked a wicked smile. "A little too old for training this intense. You act like a novice."

My fists gripped the blanket even tighter. "I lived a different life until now," I said.

"Childhood sickness?" he asked. There was a hint of sympathy in his voice.

"Something like that," I mumbled.

He took my hand and kissed it. "Don't look so sad, or are you tired?"

"Tired." I nodded. Maybe a little sad.

I scooted back into bed and wrapped the blanket over me like before. This time I felt a weight behind me shift. An arm hung over me while my back rested against a wide chest. I went still, contemplating whether or not the prince was actually spooning me, but the idea was crazy.

"Prince Alixios?"

"Yes?"

"What are you doing?"

"I'm helping you sleep. Doesn't this feel good?" he asked.

I couldn't deny that it felt nice. He was warm and smelled like a sweet mix of coffee and cut grass, like morning springtime, floral with a hint of warm bitterness. My body melted against his. The fatigue was hitting me even harder than before.

"You...we shouldn't..." I tried to protest while fighting back a yawn.

"I'm a perfect gentleman. I won't do anything to you in your sleep. You have my word," he said. "Sleep. Dream of me."

"I don't want to have nightmares." I smiled, sinking further away from consciousness.

Before Alix could open the door to his room, Ryalie poked his head out and glanced around the corridor like he was making sure it was clear. He grabbed Alix by the collar and pulled him in, closing the door behind him and sticking to it like a lock.

"Where have you been?" Jenos asked from the sunken lounge.

Alix strolled down the two steps towards the seat opposite Jenos. He sat, making himself comfortable, impressed with Jenos's endless patience. "Did I worry you?"

"You missed Violitt. She was waiting for you. She was sure you went missing," Jenos said. "For a moment, we thought so too. You weren't in the palace. You'd said nothing to us. Where were you?"

"Saying goodnight to a friend," Alix answered.

"That girl again," Jenos said. His brown eyes hardened as his nostrils softly flared. "What is it about her that has you so distracted?"

"That's a good question," he mumbled. His body already longed to pull her back into his chest. He wanted to feel her warmth against his own a little longer still.

Alix snapped himself away from the thought. "How did you handle Violitt?" he asked.

"We told her you were busy and that you would meet with her another time," Jenos said.

"You've never done anything like this before," Ryalie said, leaning on the couch Alix occupied instead of sitting. "Jenos is worried about you."

Alix lifted a brow. "Aren't you worried about me?"

"Nah, I'm sure you deserve whatever happens," Ryalie said and stuck his tongue out.

"Would you both be serious?" Jenos demanded, standing with needless urgency. "I demand you take us to this girl you keep seeing."

"And why should I?"

"We don't know who she is, and *you* don't know who she is. That's dangerous. We are your knights. It is our duty to protect you," Jenos said.

Alix smiled. Jenos never changed. His boundless, dutiful loyalty was something he inherited from his mother no doubt. It made it easy to get under his skin, but it also exhausted Alix. It reminded him too much of his responsibilities.

"I can't do what you ask."

Jenos paused. "Why not?"

"I don't want to." Alix shrugged and rested his back against the seat with a provoking smile on his face.

Jenos gaped at him. Alix hadn't responded like that in years. Not since the day he knew he would be the next king of

Tamikar.

"He's got you there, Jenos," Ryalie said.

"You're supposed to be on my side," Jenos said, rubbing the bridge of his nose.

"I never take sides," Ryalie declared, folding his arms in defiance. He couldn't care less about sides. He would follow whoever and whatever path reaped more rewards.

Jenos paused, stunned. He threw his hands up in defeat. "Do as you wish," he said and left the room.

Ryalie took the empty seat and stared at Alix, who couldn't help snickering at his unusually stern face, as though he were trying to mimic Jenos.

Ryalie leaned in and whispered, "Is everything okay?"

"Everything is great," Alix answered.

"Good enough for me!" Ryalie sprang up from his seat and started heading for the door, then paused just as he opened it. "I hope you're right."

"I'm never wrong," Alix said with all the poise he was trained to exhibit.

Ryalie sighed. "First time for everything."

Once he was alone, Alix frowned and lay on his side, remembering how Lillianett's body fit against his. She was warm, with the scent of the forest. He wished he had Jenos's senses, so he could break down the scent and decipher what made it so alluring.

He'd be lying if he said he wasn't uneasy.

Chapter 7

So close and yet so far

The sun woke me, piercing through my eyelids with a glaring burn. I groaned and covered my face, trying to hide in the darkness for as long as possible. When I found the strength to wake up, I would think of my revenge against the prince who must have left my curtains open.

"It's cute that you think you can hide."

I leapt out of the covers and dashed out of bed, standing at alert in the corner of my room like a spooked cat. I only calmed down when I realized it was Estell's voice.

"I know I was hard on you yesterday, but there's no need to be so afraid."

"I forgot you were here," I said.

Now that I was calm, the soreness in my muscles started to bubble to the surface. It hurt to stand—my knees were beginning to buckle. My skin looked like expressionist art: blotched with red and purple bruises.

"I look abused," I groaned, rubbing my arms.

"Catch," Estell said, tossing a small sack at me. I caught it. Inside were dark leaves blended with grass, balled together with a light green paste. "Take a warm bath with that and thank me later."

"What are they?" I asked.

"Unimportant," she said already half-way out the room. "Do as I say and meet me when you're done."

I drew a bath and poured the all-natural bath bombs into the water. They released a grassy scent with a hint of mint.

The longer I stayed in the bath, the more I didn't want to leave. Whatever she gave me melted my muscles down, undoing the knots and soreness. I sank into the waters and, for a moment, found inner peace. The steam in the room was intoxicating.

I sighed. "This is heaven."

"Get out."

I jumped, grabbing my shoulders when I saw Estell.

"I should've known this would happen," she said.

She unplugged my bath, and the water drained like my spirits. "Why?" I whined.

"Bathe for too long in that and you'll become paralysed."

"What?" I gasped.

"Again, you can thank me later," she said and left the room. I stared after her in horror. "Hurry up!"

Thank her for almost paralysing me?

I got out of the tub and met Estell downstairs like she ordered. She was waiting in the kitchen and pushed a bowl of mush towards me. It was an oaty mash of grains that had a weird, sour after-taste. I missed chocolate so much.

"You'll be doing some self-training today, until I get back," she said.

"Where are you going?" I asked, choking down the mush.

"Unimportant," she said. "I want you to run in the forest and open up your senses. Train them to feel everything: vibrations in the air, the dampness of the soil, the slight breath of every living thing around you. I need your senses stretched to their limits."

I swallowed a spoon of mush and fought the cringe that soon followed. "And you want me to run while doing all that?"

"Yes. I also need your stamina to improve. Open your senses before you run, and get used to the sensation," she said. "When you start, it'll be overwhelming."

"How will I know if I'm doing it right?" I asked.

She grinned. "You'll know."

"Will you know if I decide not to do it?" I asked.

"Yes, I will." Her tone was cold and direct, like her gaze. "If that's all, let's go."

I scrambled to my feet to follow her, glad not to have to suffer through eating more mush.

"How do you and Cam travel? On foot? I thought there isn't anything near here."

"There's a stable he manages outside the forest," she said.

"There is?"

"Don't even think of leaving this forest," she warned. "But yes, there is."

When we got outside, she walked me to the edge, where the

forest became thick and teeming with life. She slapped my back, and I stumbled forward, hissing at the sting that pricked my skin. I wasn't as sore after the bath, but I was still tender.

"So, I run and, uh…?"

"Open your senses," she said. "Fill your lungs with air. Power comes from the breath because breathing is life."

I took a deep breath, and then another and another, until I felt weightless.

"Listen to even the tiniest insects scurry across the forest floor. See everything, every animal, every colour, every shade. Taste the air, the dampness, the rich undertones. Smell them, separate them, know them each by their slight hums. Then feel all of it, the way they move in the air, the way your body lifts and collapses when you breathe. That is life."

I followed her words, slowly opening each of my senses, trying to take in as much information as I could. The fall and breaking of leaves, insects burrowing in the dirt and flying over bark. The dewy morning air tangling with dirt and the scent of warm sunlight. The bright, flaming colours overlapping with the deep black soil under the patches of grass that wilted against the stiff wind.

But my senses crossed.

I saw scents and tasted colours, soil on my tongue and vibrations in my eyes. It was too much at once. I stumbled back, blinking, trying to refocus as everything hit me like fireworks. Too much at once.

Estell grabbed and held me still.

"I can't…" I gasped.

"You must," she said. "Don't fight it. Run with it."

She pushed me forward and I ran. My body charged onward on its own. There was no thought, just action. My mind filled with everything my senses were picking up. The rushing shades of autumn colours and wet soil. The crunch of my body weight against the forest floor, each step faster than the last, pitter-patter like raindrops. The moisture in the air was in my lungs, pushing them harder. My body was high on electricity, dancing with energy through the forest. I didn't know it was possible to feel so alive.

I had to stop.

My breaths become shallower the farther I went. My vision became blurry, and my head was spinning. I couldn't tell where I was going. I felt like I was in a tailspin, and the only way down was to crash. There was too much information to process, and my mind couldn't keep up.

Just as it felt like I was going to overload, someone walked into my path. I closed my eyes and held my breath as our bodies collided. We toppled over each other into a mangled mess of limbs.

"Ouch," I whined.

"Are you okay?"

I looked down at Prince Alixios and wasn't sure how to feel about his presence. On the one hand, I was grateful he appeared just on time, but on the other I wished he would give me a day to myself. A day where I wasn't anxious that he would find out my secret.

"Prince…" I started but then felt a hand slip up my waist and shivered. I beat my fist against his chest and caught his sharp inhale. "Let go," I growled.

"Sorry. Old habits," he said and showed me his jazz hands.

"Bad habits," I hissed. I stood up, dusting off the leaves and dirt and plucking twigs from my hair.

"I've never had a complaint before," he said.

"So, people always just throw themselves at you?" I asked, fluffing my hair out for any stubborn pieces of foliage.

"Yes," he answered without a thought. It was almost annoying.

I shook my head. "Wow."

"You act like you've never heard of me," he said. "Like I'm not your prince."

"You're not my prince," I said sharply.

His face lit up in surprise. "What kingdom are you from?"

"Unimportant," I mumbled and walked away. He matched my pace and picked a leaf out of my hair. I glanced at him. "You have a lot of free time."

"I don't. I spent the better half of my day yesterday reading through documents and meeting officials," he said. "And I'm still not done."

"Then why are you here?" I asked.

"I'm on a break, hiding from my knights."

"Your knights? You have personal knights? Like baby-sitters?"

He chuckled, snapping a twig from a tree. "They're friends. We grew up and trained together."

"But they look after you, right? Where were they when you

were dying?" I asked, wishing they'd done their jobs.

"Not far behind. They found me just as you abandoned me."

"Saved you," I said, stopping in my tracks to correct him.

He didn't flinch and stared right back into my eyes. A smile flickered at the corner of his lips. "You still left me," he said.

We stared at each other until I turned away, lifting my chin. "You're alive. I don't know why you're complaining."

"I could've met you sooner," he said.

"You've met me now," I mumbled. "I'm nothing special."

"I disagree," he whispered.

He followed close behind me in silence. I felt him staring a hole into my back. He wanted to ask something, I could feel it, but he wasn't sure how, or maybe he wasn't sure what to ask. There was a tension between us, and the longer it went on, the harder it was to breathe.

I stopped and turned to face him. "Something about me bothers you, doesn't it?"

He stumbled to a stop, hesitating. "I would be lying if I said no."

Unease was plain as day on his face, and who could blame him? Everything about our relationship was strange even if one considered how it began. Why did I ask him to be my friend? There was no making friends. All I could have was enemies and loneliness.

"Go home. I'll do the same," I said.

"But—"

"Go home," I said again "And don't come back."

"Did I do something wrong?"

"No. You're a prince," I said, practically spitting in his face. "Get a grip and do your job before your babysitters accuse me of kidnapping their baby."

"Hey…" He reached for my arm, and I slapped his hand away. My actions shocked him just as much as when I slapped him in the face, but he recovered faster, staring at me with bewildered eyes. I glared back at him, as hard as I could make myself.

"Lillianett, why are you suddenly acting like this? I'm—"

"A prince," I said. "Start acting like it." I turned and walked away again, but he caught up and obstructed my path. "Get out of—"

"Is this goodbye?" he asked, cutting me off. "For good?"

"It has to be," I said and tried to walk around him, but he obstructed me again.

"Then one last thing before I go," he said. "I want to thank you for real."

"I don't want anything," I said.

"You'll like this, I promise," he said. "Please. Do this one thing for me."

I searched his face, but I couldn't find anything that would lead me to doubt him. He held his breath waiting for my answer.

"Okay," I said.

He grabbed my hand and pulled me deeper into the forest with eagerness on his heels. He held my wrist in his hand like he was afraid I would slip away. I watched to see if he would look back, but he trudged forward, silently, deeper than I'd ever gone. The more I looked, the more certain I became. He was pulling me to the edge of the forest.

"Hey—" I started.

"Almost there," he said and stopped. He turned back and stared at me with pursed lips. He was almost pouting.

"Your silence is scaring me," I said.

"I'm trying to waste as much time as I can," he said.

"You shouldn't."

"I know." He pulled my wrist, and we walked into a clearing, where the trees seemed to bend away from the open space. At the centre of the clearing was the creature I'd seen before, when Cam got the message about his mother.

It was even more beautiful up close.

As we got closer, it lifted its crowned head and stared at me. I stared back into its black eyes, feeling a mix of fear and intrigue. It was so foreign, but every part of me wanted to reach out and touch its yellow feathers, stroke its beak, feel its wings beat beneath me.

"You stare like you've never seen a pixa before," he said, tugging me forward.

"I have, but…never this close."

"You must have lived a sheltered childhood," he said.

"Something like that," I murmured and pressed my palm into its plush feathery body. I thought Blaze's fur was soft, but this softness was otherworldly. It was only my hand, but my whole body wanted to dive into its softness. "This is incredible."

"There's more," he said and grabbed my waist, hoisting me onto its saddled back. I looked around, disoriented for a second, but then he jumped on behind me and grabbed the reins. "Are you ready?" he asked, whispering low into my ear.

"Yes," I breathed, the adrenaline taking over, and grabbed the reins as well.

He whistled and tapped the pixa with his heel. I held my breath as it trotted forward and leapt into the air with one mighty beat of its wings. I felt the strength of every thrust beneath us, the next one more powerful than the last. It was like we were clawing our way into the sky.

Once we were above the trees, we glided into a tranquil calm, riding the air like a wave. I stared out at the landscape, unwilling to blink, afraid it would disappear if I allowed myself.

The world was vast, a sea of fiery trees spreading past the horizon, surrounded by rocky mountains with delicate white caps. Villages dotted the landscape, and rivers spread across the land like veins, twinkling from the sunlight. I saw three obscure towers in the distance past the many villages. There was so much more beyond the horizon that I wanted to see.

I wanted to reach out and see all the tiny details. It was so close, yet so far away. And it was beautiful. The vibrant colours played off each other. Every shade of red, orange, and yellow melted into the sparkling blue of the rivers. The snowy mountain tops mimicked the delicate white clouds, and everything was alive. I saw the pulse of the world in every breath I took.

"It's amazing," I breathed against the chilled air.

"Well, it is my kingdom after all," Alixios said.

I shook my head. "Don't ruin a good moment."

He chuckled. "Would you like to go farther?"

"Yes," I said. "But I shouldn't." *Can't.*

"A little more," he said. "I could show you Calla Lanae, the Niru Mountain paths, the edge of the world that lines the Hollow Forests. I could take you to the jewelled oceans, sail past the abandoned Lost Isle, and show you the lands richest with *Arcania*."

My lower lip dropped, tempting me to say yes—yes to everything he offered me. The world on a silver platter.

"Let me go home, Prince Alixios. You've done more than enough."

I felt his body tense up against mine, but he didn't say anything and guided us back down to the clearing. We landed, and he helped me to the ground without letting go of my hands.

I sensed the hesitation in the tender strength of his fingers. Despite it, I took my hands back and wrapped my arms around his neck to hug him.

"Thank you. Consider your debt repaid."

He held me and asked, "A glimpse of my kingdom is worth my life to you?"

I tightened my arms and let myself hold him close. "It's worth more than you know."

He wrapped his arms around my waist and buried himself against me. "Another day. I could give you so much more. So much more than a glimpse. Give me another day."

I pulled away and took a step back. "Another day could become forever."

"What's so wrong with that?" he asked in a whisper. "Forever sounds…nice."

I shook my head and curtsied to him. "It's been a pleasure, Prince Alixios de Valor. I wish you a long life, so take care of it."

"I wish you the same, Lillianett..." He paused. "What is your last name?"

I smiled. "Unimportant."

"One day, I will understand you," he said, shaking his head.

"No, you won't," I said, almost sad by it. "Goodbye."

He gave no indication that he was going to stop me, so I walked home in silence, forcing myself not to look back or reconsider. I wanted more of what he gave me today. I wanted to see much more.

He was right. A glimpse wasn't enough.

When Estell got home, I'd been in the training room for hours, practicing with the bow and arrow. I managed to hit the target four times, and it was never a bullseye. Maybe she was wrong, and I wasn't a huntress. I was a dismal shot.

"Fix your posture." Estell lifted my aiming arm and pricked it with one of her needles, melting away the fatigue. "How was the run?"

"Overwhelming," I grunted and released the arrow. I had to shake my head to get rid of the memory. It was like being on one of those carnival rides that spun too fast. Up felt like down and down felt like sideways.

She laughed. "Do it every day until it's not."

A protest bubbled up from my throat, but I kept it down. There was no way I was about to win an argument about my training against my trainer. For all I knew, she was going easy on me.

I lined up another shot with the bow, but Estell started groping me all over, and I froze under her touch.

She stepped away and nodded. "I can tell you've been here for a while."

I was trying to blow off some steam and hadn't stopped since I came back from the forest. There was no way for me to keep track of time. "I guess I have."

"Spar with me and go to bed. You're no good to me exhausted."

"Wouldn't it be better for me to go to bed straight away then?" I asked. My exhaustion multiplied tenfold at the idea of sparring with her.

"Don't act smart," she said.

I dropped the bow, and she lunged at me. She didn't give me time to think. I ducked down and rolled out of her reach, rushing to my feet. I had to watch her—how she moved, how she breathed, the flickers of her eyes, everything. She was prey, and to catch prey, I first had to observe.

She was as ruthless as before. I didn't have time to process her movements before I had to dodge or block them. Her fists came like an unforgiving storm. Her body was always moving, forcing me back. She was a small lady, but when she was on the attack, she towered over me.

I took a knee, clutching my chest, trying to get some air into my lungs. Spasms of pain shot through me when I tried standing up. My knees wobbled, then buckled. I fell on my backside. I had blocks of lead chained to my limbs, making me sink.

"Is that all you can give me?"

I tried answering but pain-filled wailings escaped my mouth.

She crouched down and stabbed a needle into my arm. I glared at her and bit my lip, so I wouldn't scream. She did that on purpose.

"A little pain is good for you," she said.

It took a while for me to get upstairs and drag myself into the shower. I couldn't even stand, so I sat in the tub while the water pelted me from above. I couldn't tell where my pain began or ended, or if there was any part of me that didn't hurt. My body felt like one big bruise.

But I couldn't deny that the emptiness I felt in my chest hurt most. I yearned to be in the sky again. The image was still burned into my mind, but the clearer I saw it, the more I wanted to see it again.

"This sucks," I grumbled.

"Lillianett," Estell shouted from downstairs.

I groaned. "Coming." I got out of the shower and half dried myself off while looking for some clothes to wear that weren't soaked in sweat.

"Lillianett!" Estell screamed again.

I wrapped a towel around myself and went to my door. "I'm coming. I'm still wet!" I slammed my door closed and grunted. Hearing her voice made me hurt even more. Patience was not her virtue.

As I was about to go back to the bathroom, I paused when I saw Prince Alixios in the corner of my eye. I clutched my towel and stifled a scream. He stood like a statue.

"You've taken your creep tendencies too far this time," I hissed.

He didn't say anything, but stared at me, wide-eyed, in stunned silence. He looked more startled than me. And I was the one in a towel.

"Prince…" I started and took a step forward, but he stumbled back as though my touch frightened him. "What's wrong with you?"

"Your back," he whispered.

"My back—" I grabbed my bare back and gasped in horror. He saw my mark. No wonder he looked like he'd seen a ghost. It was worse—he'd seen a monster.

"You're…you…" he mumbled out.

I'd wondered how people in Glorus would look at me and this wasn't what I'd expected. It was a brand-new look, twisted with a conflict of confusion, fear, and disgust. He looked betrayed. He stared at me, jaw slacked as words failed him. I felt cold, like my heart stopped beating to protect itself from breaking.

"Say something," I whispered.

"You saved my life," he said. "Even though you're…"

"Yes, I did," I said. "I'm not a monster."

"Lillianett, you're the *Renai*." He covered his mouth, like the word itself was a curse. He said it like he was trying to confirm it yet couldn't believe his own words.

"I am," I said and walked towards him. I grabbed his shoulder, dug my nails into the flesh of his collar, and forced him to look at me, like he'd made me do so many times. His eyes searched mine. "I told you to leave me alone."

I let go and walked back into my bathroom and locked the door behind me. I heard him exit from the window. When silence hit, I slid down to the ground. My head fell back against the door, and I closed my eyes in defeat.

"I'm sorry," I sobbed. Who was I sorry to? To the prince, for who I was? Cam, for not heeding his lessons? Estell for no doubt dragging her into this? My mom and dad...oh, my parents. More than disappointed, they'd be heartbroken. Was our goodbye all those months ago good enough? They knew I loved them, but would they know how sorry I was for everything?

"Lillianett!" Estell shouted again.

I pushed myself off the ground, the numbness like a rash. "I'm coming." I walked to my window about to close the curtain when I saw a glint in the trees. There was ruffling in the bushes, and it was too isolated to be the wind. I watched and waited to see if the prince would step out but instead, I saw a red paw claw the ground.

I got dressed and ran downstairs sprinting through the door. "I'm going out for a bit," I shouted.

"Wait. It's getting late, and I need to talk to you," Estell shouted back at me.

"I'll be careful."

I ran straight into Blaze and wrapped my arms around her large furry neck, digging my face into the earthy softness. She rubbed against me and let out a low purr

"I've missed you," I whispered. It was like she knew I needed her.

I climbed onto her back and felt at ease. She got low to the ground, muscles tensing beneath me. My heartbeat quickened, knowing what was going to happen next. I held my breath.

Blaze exploded with a broad jump, then broke into a wild sprint. The sound of her paws on the forest floor was like battle drums, and the growls that escaped her jaws were like war cries. The feeling of the wind pushing back on me and challenging my grip excited me and forced me to breathe deeper to survive. I tasted my own adrenaline, smelled it seep into the muscles that held on for dear life, chasing back the numbness. I could run forever. I could run away.

But I had nowhere to go.

Blaze stopped at the edge of the river that bordered the forest surrounding the mountains. I considered the forest my birdcage and personal playground, but I wasn't allowed in the mountains. Cam warned me that it was too dangerous, and it was forbidden, but whenever I reached the edge, I felt a different kind of danger. The mark on my back tingled like thorns scraping across my skin. Every hair on my body stood, and my heart raced at a nauseating pace.

Every muscle in my body wanted me to run. I was being watched. I felt dozens of eyes, scurrying through the shadows of the forest, watching me with a hungry curiosity. Even Blaze hesitated to cross the river, but she wasn't trembling like me— she was cautious—I was afraid.

"Let's go girl," I said unable to keep my voice level.

Blaze turned and started walking back. I turned around for one last look, my curiosity winning out over my fear, and for a second, I could have sworn I spotted a pair of yellow eyes.

Chapter 8

Monster

It had been ten nights since the prince discovered my secret. I kept expecting him to arrive with an army, or to attack and kill me in my sleep. But it was quiet, which made me even more paranoid. I was flinching at every sound and kept imagining all the reasons he could be taking so long. None of them were good. I was so anxious, I was getting random stomach cramps and couldn't eat more than a few bites at a time, much to Estell's frustration.

I still hadn't found the courage to tell her anything.

I couldn't remember the last time I slept well. I woke up at the crack of dawn every day, as exhausted as when I slept. Training was hell but it was the few hours in the day that I wasn't on the brink of a break down.

At night, I'd spend hours staring at my chipped and bulging ceiling.

"I need to sleep," I groaned. My body was drained, but my mind was restless.

There was a single knock at my door, and Estell came in with a bowl. She kneeled at my bedside and shoved the mush towards me. "Eat," she demanded.

I took the bowl and swallowed the food without tasting it. Every time I peeked up at her, she glared harder, like she wanted me to concentrate on eating.

"I'm not going to ask what's wrong," she said once I swallowed the last spoonful. "If you want to tell me, you'll tell me, but until you do, I still expect your absolute best in everything."

"Yes," I said.

"Go out for some fresh air tomorrow. Practice opening your senses."

"Do you want me to run?"

"No, just live in the moment," she said.

She had no idea how relevant her advice was. Living in the moment was all I could do, and it was all I ever did. It's what always got me in trouble, why my parents were so scared for me. And now the worst possible scenario had been realized.

Estell touched my cheek and smiled at me. "Don't forget to breathe. What did I tell you? Why do we breathe?"

"Power comes from breathing because breathing is life."

"Exactly." She nodded. "Now get some sleep."

"Don't you have a needle that can help me?" I asked.

"Not my specialty. I'm best at relieving pain and fatigue," she said. "Muscle your way through it."

I was speechless. All I could do was watch her leave, despite having so many questions. Like, how did one "muscle" their way to sleep? What happened to counting sheep?

Wait, is there a sheep equivalent in Glorus? I shook my head. It was a ridiculous question which revealed how tired I was. *I could count kiliabis.*

I reached for the table lamp and froze when I saw the prince climb through my window. My heart dropped and I couldn't react. My lungs seized up and adrenaline flooded my muscles. It was so sudden. I wasn't in the right state of mind.

He was alone and I didn't see any weapons on him. Was he going to kill me barehanded? I could scream. But then Estell would get caught up in all this, more than she already was.

"You're here," he said and sounded almost disappointed.

"That's my line. You took longer than I thought," I said, trying to keep the tremble out of my voice. If I was going to die, I would at least pretend to be brave about it. "So, what are you going to do now?"

He walked towards me. Every step he took sounded heavier than the last. The closer he got, the louder and harder my heartbeat became. He towered over me.

I waited.

He sat. "Now, I have questions for you."

"Excuse me?" I must have misheard him.

"I have questions," he repeated, then cleared his throat. He sounded almost nervous. "How long have you been here? In Glorus, I mean."

He took me by surprise. I shifted under my sheets. "Uh…a little over three months."

"What have you been doing? Did you attack anyone?"

"Of course not," I hissed. "I saved your life, remember?"

"You did," he said and shifted to come even closer. "Why? Did you know who I was? Did you think I would give you something? Was I part of a scheme?"

"You sound ridiculous," I said. My anxiety was replaced with annoyance. "I had no idea who you were, and if you recall, I tried chasing you away. I even ran from you."

"You slapped me," he said.

"Don't act like you didn't deserve it."

He pursed his lips and pulled back. He glanced around the dim room like it could tell him if I was lying. "What have you been doing all this time if you're so innocent?"

"Training," I said.

He narrowed his eyes in suspicion. "Why?"

"Why do you think?" He lifted his brows, and I rolled my eyes. "Can you honestly tell me that when you saw the mark on my back, attacking me wasn't your first thought?" He avoided my scrutinizing gaze. "I thought so."

"You're training for a war," he said.

"I'm training to survive."

We fell silent, staring at each other. He looked at me like he was trying to find something that confirmed his suspicions. I stared right back at him, determined for him to see it all.

"Do you…" he started, then paused. "Do you have a family?"

"Of course, I do. I wasn't born from thin air."

He frowned. "Your rudeness is still quite astonishing."

"Well, you're not my prince, so I don't see why I should placate you," I scoffed. "Besides, we're enemies now, right?"

His face twitched with discomfort. "I've had time to think. Knowing your true identity—so much about you makes sense."

"I bet you're disappointed. Disgusted too," I said. "You think I'm a monster."

"Well, what am I supposed to think?" he asked. "Your existence is a blight—a sin. You *are* a monster."

I scowled at him. My hand twitched, wanting to slap him, but the ache in my chest stopped me. I knew how they would see me. It was the main thing that stopped me from exploring past the forest boundaries. But knowing it and hearing it were two different pains. Knowing it was a hollow emptiness. Hearing it was a twisting knife.

"No, *you're* the monster," I said, gripping my sheets.

"What?" he gasped and sprang up from my bed.

"You heard me," I said, throwing the sheets and standing to face him. "You're the monster. The moment I was born, you labeled me a monster. I haven't done anything to anyone. You're the only person I've met, besides my trainers, and I even saved your life. At the cost of my safety! Of all the ungrateful, pigheaded, ignorant...ah!" I growled in frustration. "If you're not going to kill me, then leave." I shoved him towards my window. "Go, get out and never come back."

"Wait." He grabbed my wrists. "I'm sorry," he blurted.

I paused. "Excuse me?"

"I'm not repeating it," he grumbled and let go of my wrists.

"You're sorry?" I asked. "For what? You have a lot to be sorry for."

He walked towards my bed with a hand on his head and sat

down with an exasperated sigh. "Do you know why I took so long to come back?"

"I don't know. But you should apologize for that too. I haven't slept well in days."

He stared up at me, sullen. "You must've been frightened, not knowing your fate."

I sat next to him and nodded. "Not knowing when you'll die but knowing it's coming keeps a girl up at night."

"I couldn't accept what I saw," he said. "Sure, you were rude, rash, and strange, but a *Renai*? Once I accepted that, I couldn't accept that you saved my life, and I wondered what your reason was." He paused to look at me. "What was your reason?"

I shrugged a shoulder. "Do I need a reason to save a life?"

He chuckled. "And you're good. Being with you, even if for a moment, felt exciting. It made me question everything I knew about you even more."

I shrugged. "But you don't know much."

"And that's my biggest problem," he said with a sigh. "Discovering who you are, what you are, made me want to know you."

I hadn't noticed before but now that I had calmed down, I saw the dark circles under his eyes. I reached my hand up to touch his face and got a little closer. He wasn't sleeping either. I was glad not to be the only one.

"Lillianett," he whispered and put his palm on my cheek. I looked up into his eyes and froze. They were tender…and inching closer.

I jumped to my feet. "Too close."

"You started it," he said defensively.

"That is beside the point," I mumbled. "Anyway, what now?"

He frowned and stood up. "You saved my life, and that means something to me. In fact, it means something to this kingdom, and therefore, a large debt must be paid," he said. "I won't tell anyone I found you."

"You won't?" I asked cautiously, taking a step towards him.

He nodded.

I leapt forward, wrapping my arms around his neck. He lifted a giant weight off my chest, and I was so thrilled I didn't realize what I was doing until I'd done it.

I pulled back. "Sorry."

He stared at me with searching eyes, confusion playing at his features. Then he held me to his body, so close that I felt his heat seep into my skin. His scent, the warm bitterness with a hint of something floral, played on my senses, filling them.

I pulled away. "Wait, how can I trust you?"

"You would be dead by now if you couldn't, and I have no desire to hand you over to anyone. You're all mine, for now."

"It's creepy when you say it like that," I said holding back a laugh. It was unnerving enough to make his words believable. "But I'm grateful."

"And you're rude," he said.

I smiled. "Thank you for helping me."

"Of course, but I want something in return," he said.

"Isn't this already a fair trade?" I asked, losing my enthusiasm.

"I want to do something for you," he insisted.

"You've done more than enough." My voice was flat.

He smiled. "I want to introduce you to my knights."

I paused, my brows rising. "What happened to me being all yours?"

"Greed is unbecoming for a prince," he said with a laugh.

I stared at him. "No," I said.

"Think it over."

"No."

"Stubborn," he said, his eyes bright.

"Tenacious," I said back.

He shook his head with a genuine smile on his face. "This discussion isn't over."

"It is tonight," I said. "Goodnight, Prince Alixios."

"Call me Alix," he said and bowed to me, "Princess Lillianett."

"Ha! Call me Lilly."

"We need to do something about this," Jenos declared, storming through the palace halls towards Alix's room. He ignored every bowed head he crossed as he struggled to rein in his anger.

Ryalie was strolling by his side, his head in the clouds. He didn't reply or react, which made the muscle above Jenos's right eyebrow twitch.

"Ryalie, listen to me."

"I am listening," he said with a deep groan. "You're overreacting."

"Overreacting?" Jenos halted his heavy strides. "Alix has

spent the last few days in a daze, mumbling to himself, and has made little to no progress in completing his tasks."

"That stuff bores him. You should introduce him to a pretty girl. That always sets him right."

"I've tried. He rejects all of them."

"Oh. Maybe this is serious," Ryalie said.

Jenos shook his head and continued walking. He felt shame for not being by Alix's side more often, given how troubled he was as of late, but he was more annoyed by Alix's refusal to let them help him. That pride would be the death of them all. Alix had no problem leaning on them in the past, but now he kept them at arm's length. It had been happening for a while, but it had suddenly gotten so much worse.

"I'm sure it's nothing," Ryalie said.

Jenos glared at him, preparing to berate Ryalie, but then he saw a flicker of concern on his brow. "It's Alix. He's fine," Ryalie grumbled.

"I hope you're right," Jenos said. He pushed the twin doors to Alix's room open, expecting it to be empty, but was surprised to see Alix standing on his balcony, staring up into the night sky.

Jenos lost his composure, his anger dissipating in the cold breeze for a second but regained it when Ryalie shouted, "Alix! You're here."

Alix turned to face them, leaning on the railing with an ease they both hadn't seen in years. "It's been a while," he said, grinning.

"How are you feeling?" Jenos asked.

"Perfect," Alix said with a smile Jenos hadn't seen in days. It was as though Alix was a new man. Or the man he was before the fallout in his family.

"You look happy," Ryalie said with a naughty grin. He jabbed Alix with his elbow. "Who is she? I won't tell."

"And neither will I," Alix quipped

"It's that girl again, isn't it?" Jenos scowled. "Why won't you tell us anything?"

"Some secrets are not mine to tell," he said with a shrug.

"Secrets?" Jenos asked. "So, she is dangerous."

"I…don't know yet. I want to know." He sighed dreamily. "I need to know."

"Please, if there's any chance that she's dangerous, you need to stay away from her. You are the future king. If anything were to happen to you—"

"My sister could take the crown," he said.

Ryalie burst out in a fit of giggles. "Bad joke. No one has ever considered—"

"You've considered it," Jenos cut him short. "For how long? Since knowing her?"

Jenos knew it had once been a thought when the duties of an heir were thrust upon him. It shouldn't have been his burden to bear, but Alix took on the responsibility without protest. All to please the queen and keep a few promises.

Ryalie whistled. "She must be quite the woman."

"She's a threat to you," Jenos said, then glared at Ryalie. "Both of you, it seems."

Alix stared at Jenos and nudged his head to the side with a half-shrug. "I don't think she is. I may be the bigger threat."

"What do you mean by that?" Jenos asked.

Alix shook his head. "I'll find a way to explain it to you one day, if you're unlucky enough."

Jenos opened his mouth to start a new line of questioning, but Ryalie grabbed his arm and pulled him away. "Let go of me. We need to know who—"

"We need to let him sleep," Ryalie said. "He might finally get some tonight."

Jenos's facial muscles twitched, but he sighed in defeat and made a humble retreat. Before leaving the room, he glanced back at Alix's figure. He looked like he had shaken most of his uneasiness, but Jenos could feel his own multiplying.

Chapter 9

A Night of Magic

E stell never bothered to wake me up in person. She either knocked on my door loud enough to give me a heart attack or shouted for me from downstairs. I was shocked awake so often, I twitched when I heard so much as a faint tapping.

But today she nudged me awake. She was even poking my cheeks.

"Okay, I'm awake. Sto—" I stopped short when I saw who it was. "Oh," I groaned, wiping my face with both my hands, hoping it was only a nightmare. "Wake up," I groaned at myself.

"Good morning," Alix said, grinning with his eyes.

"How did you get in here?" I asked.

"The usual way," he said and pointed. "The window."

I lifted an eyelid long enough to see Alix bathed in light, smiling down at me with a taunting grin. "Why are you here, now?" I groaned with the full force of my grogginess.

"I'm here to see you," he said.

"Don't you have things to do?" I asked, pushing myself up.

He chuckled like my question was genuinely funny. "So many things. How'd you guess?"

"You're a prince. It would make sense that you would," I said.

"You're not wrong," he said. "I am busy, but sometimes I need a break."

"I need a break too—from you. And why do you keep using me for break time?"

He took my hands and pulled me to my feet so that I was face to face with him. He was a head taller than me, broad shoulders, sun-kissed skin...breathtaking good looks. I wasn't awake enough to deal with this.

"I enjoy being with you," he whispered. "And I think it's only fair that I keep an eye on you."

I blinked, deepening my frown. "Fine—" I paused as I realized something that had always bothered me in the back of my mind. I narrowed my eyes at him. "I locked my window. I've actually never opened that window."

"I opened it," he said.

My window couldn't open from the outside. I didn't know whether to be furious or dumbfounded. "Could you leave, please?"

"Lillianett!" Estell shouted.

The hairs on the back of my neck stood at attention. "This is not my day."

I jogged down the stairs and stopped when I saw Estell standing in front of the open door. My eyes scanned the room but there was no one else.

Estell greeted me with a once over. She was dressed in dark greens and had a black hood around her shoulders. "You look better. Do you remember your training for today?"

I nodded.

"Good. Oh, and I have a bit of good news for you. Camerin is coming back soon."

"He is?" I asked. I was surprised by the excitement in my voice.

"He's done all he can for his mother," she said.

I lowered my voice. "Will she be okay?"

Estell sighed. "No, but Camerin will be."

"You're a healer. Can't you do anything?"

"Not this time," she said.

I almost missed the slight tremor in her voice. Estell was Cam's cousin, which meant that his mother was also her family. She probably wanted to be with her instead of me. I was a burden on their family. It hit me again that my curse wasn't mine alone.

"I'm sorry," I said.

"Your apologies are unnecessary. Just survive your year and get home alive. That should be your only focus."

I felt guilty for not telling her that I'd almost failed to do that much. Last night could have been my last, but I got lucky. My mind shifted to Alix who was waiting for my return. Maybe 'lucky' wasn't the right word for it.

"Are you going somewhere?" I asked.

"A friend of mine invited me to a ball. I'm going to get fitted for a dress," she said.

"What?" I asked. "A ball? Like a royal party? Who are you?"

"Unimportant," she said with a dubious smile as she reached for the doorknob. "Do as you're told. Be prepared for when I get back. I want to get as much done with you as I can before Camerin returns."

She closed the door. A few seconds later, I heard footsteps descend the staircase. When I turned around, Alix scanned the room like I had when I descended. "Who was that?"

"My trainer," I answered.

"A new one?" he asked. "What happened to the man? Who are they? Do they know who you are? What you are?"

"Frankly, that's none of your business," I said. "Could you leave? I have stuff to do." I walked past him and up to my room, but he was right on my heels.

"Have I done something to offend you?" he asked.

I sighed. "You make me nervous." I started for the bathroom, but the prince stuck his hand against the wall, using his arm to stop me. He frowned and I avoided his gaze. "That's not to say I'm not grateful, but your presence makes me uneasy."

"Why?" he asked.

I stepped back. "Why do you think? Why do I keep having to explain this to you? You. Are. A. Prince. I'm enemy number one. This…us…it's a recipe for disaster."

"You're overreacting."

"You called me a monster yesterday."

"And I apologized."

"Talk is cheap," I said.

He frowned and dropped his arm. I had to admit that he did

look sorry. I rolled my eyes. "Once in a while is fine…I guess. But every day will cause problems in the long run."

"So, today?"

"Today's fine. You're already here, and I doubt you'll leave anyway," I said. "But leave for now, so I can at least shower in peace."

I hadn't been awake for more than ten minutes, and I was already fighting back a headache.

I'd wanted more excitement. The old saying was true: I should've been more careful about what I wished for.

Alix was waiting for me, sitting at the edge of my bed staring down at the photo Chris gave me. I paused, a small but sharp pain hitting my chest. I'd placed the frame down to avoid looking at it a month ago. It was too painful. Everything and anything that reminded me of home was safely packed away, out of sight. They just made the loneliness that much worse, almost unbearable.

I grabbed the frame from him and placed it face down on my bedside table. "Did we, or did we not talk about boundaries?"

"We did not," he said, leaning towards me with a smile.

I rolled my eyes. "Take a hint."

Alix chuckled and stood with a bounce. "What shall we do today?"

"I need to train today," I said and walked towards the door

"Boring," he said. "Let me fly you somewhere. I know you want to."

I did, but he didn't need to know that. "No, I want to train."

"Liar." He paused. "I could train you."

"You?" I scoffed.

"You doubt my skills?"

"I want to doubt your existence," I said.

We entered the forest and started walking in silence. My senses had gotten sharper since I started training with Estell. The more I trained, the more the forest started to feel like an extension of myself. My vision and reflexes were sharper. I could run for a full five minutes in a hyper alert state of mind and not get overwhelmed by it.

With Camerin, the changes in my senses were so small and gradual, but now I felt it even if I tightened my fists. A primal strength and power coursed through my veins.

"Are you done immersing yourself?" Alix asked, causing me to jump. I forgot he was right next to me for a second. I'd spread my senses too far. "I've been meaning to ask you something."

"Now you have boundaries? Ask."

"Is training all you do? Do you learn anything about this world apart from how to survive in it?" he asked.

"No. I need to survive. Which means I learn how to do that." I turned into a less dense part of the forest, brushing a tree Blaze had marked with her claws on one of our runs.

He frowned. "Do you know your enemy?"

"The Glorians?" He nodded. "There are five Bloods, but I don't know much apart from that."

"Shall I teach you?"

"Teach me what?" I asked.

"More about this world," he said. "You're here, you may as well learn."

"Why bother?" I asked, ripping a twig from a branch. I'm not staying long. Why bother learn something that I'd never get to experience?

"Because I don't want you to hate us," Alix said.

I stopped and stared at him, wondering if he understood the weight of his words. "Hate you?"

"There is more to this world than enemies. Like there is more to you than just being a *Renai*."

"Pretty good argument," I said with a nod. "Prove it. Teach me something."

"There are four kingdoms, each with its own royal family, traditions, and people," he said. "We are at peace and have been for many generations. We aren't unreasonable."

"Congrats to you all," I said with a layer of sarcasm.

"It would be so much easier if I could show you," he said. "Come to the EverSnow Night Ball."

"Ever…what?" I asked, "What is that?"

"A grand ball."

I lifted a brow. "And why should I go?'"

His face lit up. "Where do I begin? It's like a night of magic."

Alix grabbed my hands and brought me into his arms. The sudden action surprised me so much that I couldn't object. He guided me around the forest in a waltz, careful to avoid roots and rocks in our path. We moved to a song I couldn't hear but that he could feel. His warm right hand held mine, and the other lay on my hip as he swept me around. My feet followed his lead without warning.

"It's a night of light and music and dancing, and it's glorious," he said.

"Alix," I said, trying but failing to pull away.

He spun me around with a wide smile spread across his face, his sapphire eyes sparkled like gems, and then he dipped me down, taking my breath away

"It's the night of first snow," he whispered.

"First snow?" I was breathless. His words rang in my bones. I wanted to see it.

"Oh, yes, and I want to take you," he said, pulling me back up. "Go with me."

I laughed. "You're insane."

Alix laughed with me, then pulled me against his body and started waltzing me through the forest again, this time with more pep in his step.

There was an ease in his movements that he could have only achieved with years of practice, but I wasn't at his level and moved my foot too soon. We tripped over one another, and I landed on the ground. Alix managed to stop himself from falling on me. I opened my eyes and found him smiling down, eyes still sparkling.

"Alix?" I found my voice, but it was soft.

"Don't you want to see it for yourself?" he asked in a voice gentler than I'd ever heard.

"It's not that I don't want to. It's that I can't," I mumbled with a shrug and started to sit up. We sat facing each other barely six inches away.

"You're no fun," he said.

"I'm sorry that my will to live puts a damper on your spirits," I said, deadpan.

"I would keep you safe," he said.

I frowned and looked away. I almost believed him. I wanted to believe him.

"What was your opinion of the *Renai* before you met me?"

"The *Renai* is an impure abomination that will cause death and pain. It is an affront to all that is natural and good and should never be allowed to live peacefully in our world." he droned on with exaggerated boredom.

I nodded. "That's some pretty good brainwashing."

"I agree," he said. "Only half of that is true about you."

I laughed aloud, and it melted my unease away. "You never know. It may all be true."

"No." His tone became serious. I may have imagined it, but there was a lace of shame in it too. "You're just a person."

"And you're full of surprises."

I smiled and his lips spread into a slow grin, lighting up his face. He inched closer and tapped his forehead to mine. "I should get going. Jenos is probably having a fit right now," he said, letting out a heavy sigh.

"One of your knights?" I asked.

"And a friend," he said. "He's been worried about me lately."

"Sneaking out of the palace to dance with a monster," I said. "What's there to worry about?"

"Indeed," he said and pulled me off the ground. "It's all innocent fun."

I sensed the uneasiness from the tension in his fingers. Even if I hadn't seen the flicker in his eye, I felt it.

As soon as Alix stepped into his palace, a fist came flying past his ear from behind. He reacted, grabbing the wrist of his attacker, stepping back, and throwing them over his shoulder. When he saw his friend's grimace, he smiled. "You never learn, do you?"

Ryalie smiled up at him. "One day, I'll get you." He reached his hand up, and Alix pulled until they were standing on equal ground.

Jenos appeared and shook his head at Ryalie. "What is wrong with you?"

"It doesn't hurt to try, right?" Ryalie laughed with the wide smile of a victor.

Jenos strolled over and smacked his back, causing Ryalie to whimper and spasm.

"You were saying?" Jenos asked.

"You're so cruel," he cried.

Alix laughed. He placed an arm over each of their shoulders and made them walk with him. "It's good to be home."

He'd gotten five steps forward before Ryalie twisted out of his arms with fists up in playful defence. "You went to see her again, didn't you?" he asked. "Is she that important?"

"Important isn't the right word," Alix said. *Interesting? Dangerous? Alluring?* Like the forbidden desires his circumstances prohibited.

"Did you not find a worthy thank-you gift?" Jenos asked.

"The time I spend with her is my gift," he said. "Though whether she thinks so is uncertain. If not, I'm preparing something else."

"Perhaps you should be spending more time where you're appreciated," Jenos suggested.

"You bore me," Alix grumbled.

"You said before that she didn't want anything from you. It's strange for you to go out of your way to see one girl."

"Well, they've always come to me. This is a refreshing change of pace," he said. "And wasn't it you who insisted I thank her?"

"Yes," Jenos agreed. "But you seldom listen to me."

"I'm a changed man," Alix said.

Ryalie laughed. "And he's funny too."

Alix frowned. "Let's drop it for now. What is my schedule today?"

"You have a meeting with your father about the ball's budget. Catering plans with the queen, she also wants to know about the plans for your performance. You have more papers to look over and finalize. We need to screen the knights who will be on security and go through the guest list, also—"

"Enough," Alix said, cutting him off. "I don't think I can take much more. How many hours in a day do you think there are?"

"There would be more if you didn't sneak out," Jenos said.

Alix gave him a side-eyed glare while Ryalie held back his laughter.

Jenos opened the door to Alix's study, and they each took

their places. Alix took his seat behind his desk, Ryalie sat on the couch and Jenos stood on Alix's right side. "Please stay tomorrow, so we can get more done."

Alix sighed, pressing his fingers together. "I will if you give me a day off."

"I would like a day off too," Ryalie said.

"You don't do anything," Jenos said, glaring at him.

"I train the palace's new knights."

"From what I hear, they train themselves," Jenos barked back. He took a breath to calm himself. "Fine. You can have a day off."

"Nice," Ryalie said, placing his feet on the table.

"Not you, Ryalie. I need to see for myself how you're training the knights. They better be up to standard."

Ryalie's face went pale. "But—" he whined.

"No buts and no day off."

Alix laughed and patted his desk. "Cheer up."

"I hate this," Ryalie whined, dejected.

"And you only get a day off if you finish everything," Jenos stated, leveling a stare at Alix.

"Well, I'm highly motivated," Alix said with a smirk. "My princess is waiting for me."

"Princess?" they both asked.

Alix shook his head and pressed his finger to his lips. It was his and Lilly's little secret.

Estell returned and took me down to the basement. Without a

word, she lifted her fists and inched her stance wider. I didn't give her the chance and went straight for the first strike. She blocked my punch and smiled.

"Good," she nodded and jabbed me in the side.

I jumped back and she followed through. I dug my feet into the ground, determined to not let her push me further, and blocked her jab. Her fists came rushing at me, and I blocked them, looking for my window to attack. I waited too long. Her knuckles hit my face, cutting the skin on my lip. With the same arm, she elbowed my nose. The blowback made me stumble. I regained my balance in time to duck her next left hook and followed with a jab to her side. She grabbed my shoulders and kneed me in my chest.

I sucked in air and grabbed her waist, tackling her to the ground. I tumbled over her body and rolled up to my feet.

Estell was already running at me. I lifted my arms to guard, but she slid to the side and struck my blind spot, disorientating me. I went for a blind punch, which she caught. Her next jab hit my nose. My head began to spin, and the world twirled at my feet. She grabbed my shoulder and kicked one of my legs out from under me. My knee hit the ground, then her knuckles rammed my cheek. Blood spread in my mouth.

I fell onto my hands and knees, trying to breathe through my collapsing ribcage and strained heart. My vision blurred in and out of focus. I felt like my consciousness was pushed under dark waters. My muscles shook, burning everywhere.

"You've improved," she said. "You can fight back now."

I looked up at her through one eye, trying to discern whether she was actually praising me or teasing me. I could never tell with her. I crumbled to the ground, laying my arms and legs open like a starfish.

Estell squatted down and pressed needles into my arms, legs, and chest. My muscles decompressed and cooled, and I was brought back from the dark waters. I breathed a sigh of relief and curled back up into a sitting position.

"Time to practice your archery," she said.

I pressed my lips together, so my groan wouldn't escape. I took the bow from her and grabbed an arrow from one of the buckets. Inhaling, I drew the bow back, eye on the target, arms steady. The arrow flew and stuck to the ring closest to the bullseye.

"An overall improvement," Estell said with a nod. "I do fine work."

I couldn't deny that her training was effective. It was inhuman and cruel, but it was effective. I had improved exponentially in the time she trained me, and I was starting to hurt a lot less with every session.

"Twenty more shots like that and you can sleep," she said.

"Twenty?" I exclaimed.

"Did I stutter?" she asked. "And don't cheat. I'll know if you do. I always know."

I didn't know if she would know, but I wasn't willing to take the chance. Her normal training was hell. I didn't want to imagine what her punishments were like.

Chapter 10

It Hurts

W hen did you say Cam is coming back?" I asked, wiping the sweat off my brow and the blood from my lip.

"I had no idea you missed him so much," Estell said.

I wasn't sure if I missed him or if I wanted the daily beatings to come to an end. I know I missed not getting daily beatings.

"Well, he is a family friend, sort of."

Estell snorted, retrieving the arrows I'd shot earlier. "Our families are tied together and have been for generations, long before the curse was conceived. We come from a long line of knights and advisors, the most loyal of all to the Halibel kingdom," she said. "The Silva family."

"Camerin Silva and Estell Silva?"

She smiled. "Even now, still loyal."

"But why for so long?" I asked, rubbing my tender arms. "What do you get for staying loyal. That isn't to say I am not grateful for the life-threatening training."

"Some bonds run too deep for even time to whither."

Taking advantage of their loyalty seemed cruel to me, but my family couldn't have survived without them. It was a sick, parasitic relationship.

"Your family isn't ostracized for being loyal?" I asked.

"I don't know the story, but the Glories ensured our family retained its honourable standing," she said. "It was also such a long time ago no one really remembers."

"That's good."

Estell frowned, shaking her head with pity as she dropped the arrows in the bucket. Her look filled me with unease. Was I downplaying how bad it was for them?

"To answer your first question, Camerin should be back tomorrow."

"Tomorrow?" I perked up. "I hate to see you go."

"I'll visit often," she said and gave me an evil grin.

Was it evil? Or did she just scare me?

"I've been doing a good job. I'd like to keep doing it."

I nodded and stood up, stretching my arms above my head. Alix didn't come yesterday, so I got to laze around with Blaze after training. I was hoping for a two-day streak.

When I got to my room and found it empty, I almost squealed with joy.

After I showered and got dressed, I ran out into the forest with an ecstatic spring in my step, and then straight into something solid. Hands held my arms to keep me steady, and a familiar chuckle rang in my ear.

"Oh, no," I groaned.

"What has you in such a good mood?" Alix asked. I looked up at him with a frown, and he pouted, perplexed. "Or *had* you in a good mood."

"It doesn't matter. It's over now," I said.

"Are you sure?"

"Yes, I…"

Something felt wrong. My senses were confused, like a thought in the back of my mind played at the tip of my tongue. There was a presence, watching us, hiding.

"Did you lose something?" Alix asked. "You keep looking around like you don't know where you are."

I shook my head. I must have been more tired than I thought. "I'm fine," I said, trying to ignore the presence. "You're back today. I thought you would be gone longer."

"Why would I stay away?"

"Because I asked you to."

"Yes, but you didn't mean it," Alix said.

I laughed. No, I didn't mean it. In his own way, he was doing me a great kindness. I appreciated it more than I would ever admit to him or myself. If I pretended I wanted the loneliness, maybe it would suck less when it returned.

"So, are you here to convince me to not hate you and your people?" I asked. "Or are we going to dance some more?"

"I want you to tell me more about yourself," he said. "In your world, you're normal?"

Normal wasn't the right word but I nodded. "No one there knows anything about other worlds, so yes, I come across 'normal' even if I'm not. I'm only persecuted here for being a *Renai*." I was persecuted for other reasons back home.

"You must want to go home," he said.

I opened my mouth to explain how complicated it was, but then something dropped from above. I jumped back. It was a person, and then another. I took another step back, lowering my center, trying to gauge the situation.

"Jenos? Ryalie?" Alix exclaimed. Panic overshadowed his face, along with a drizzle of comical befuddlement.

The one with long, curly, brown hair bowed. "Alix."

"You followed me?"

"You gave us no choice," he said.

The blonde with orange tips put his arm over Alix's shoulders and smiled. "We're here to protect and serve, like good knights"

Alix pushed him away. "You disobeyed me. You tracked me?"

"Our duty is your protection, not your satisfaction," the curly-haired one said.

I wanted to creep away and let them fight it out amongst themselves, but I caught their attention when I took a step back. I froze under the gaze of the curly-haired one's eyes.

"What did you call yourself?" he asked.

"You first," I said and swallowed.

"Jenos, leave. I will explain everything." Alix grabbed his shoulder, but Jenos shrugged off his touch.

"I heard her," he said. "How are you going to explain this?"

"A *Renai*," the blonde said. The moment I locked eyes with him. I was trapped in his impossibly dark gaze. He stared wide-eyed, without blinking, like he could take in everything I was and swallow me whole.

"Stop it, Ryalie," Alix commanded.

"Why?" Ryalie asked, releasing me.

"We can talk when we get back to the palace," Jenos said and approached, reaching out a tanned hand towards me.

My muscles tensed, and my heartbeat started working overtime. He was like a predator about to lock me in his jaws. Every cell in my body told me to run.

"Wait, don't." Alix grabbed Jenos.

With that split-second distraction, I ran. I had to escape. It didn't matter where as long as I was not in their sights. Alix knowing was bad enough, but his knights would kill me given the chance. I wasn't about to give them that chance. If I could find Blaze, I could evade them, maybe even scare them

Too late. I heard their footsteps, and they were louder than I anticipated.

I had to stay calm. This was my birdcage. I knew it better, which meant I knew the best hiding places. I jumped onto the trunk of a fallen tree and used it as leverage to shimmy my way up to higher ground. My lungs were beginning to ache, and my limbs were turning to lead. Estell always healed me after training, but I never made a full recovery.

I looked up, searching for a way to get even higher. I jumped to grab a branch I could pull myself up on, but someone tackled me mid-air. I screamed, struggling to push them off. We hit the ground, rolling in brittle leaves that snapped and crunched under our weight. My body curled into a ball and tumbled until

I hit a tree.

I groaned, getting up while rubbing the lower part of my back that took the brunt of the impact. I locked eyes with Ryalie as he stood on his feet, fluffing the leaves out of his hair.

"Jenos may be the hunter, but nothing escapes my eyes," he said. "I'm bringing you back with me."

"I'm not going anywhere with you," I said out of breath.

His head whipped back as he laughed. "You don't have the right to refuse."

I lifted my firsts. I'd fight him if I had to.

Jenos and Alix caught up. I didn't think Alix would fight me with them but taking on two people at once would be hard enough on its own. With the distress Alix was showing, he wasn't going to be much help either.

"You'll fight us?" Ryalie asked with a wide, ecstatic smile.

"Yes."

He threw his head back again and laughed. The sound echoed through the forest like full-bellied thunder. I could tell by the playful look in his eye that he didn't take me seriously, which was perfect. He would underestimate me. My advantage.

Ryalie lunged forward with his arm stretched out like he was going to grab me. I met his waiting hand and interlocked my fingers with his, pulling him into my oncoming fist. My punch connected and he stumbled back, struggling to find his balance. I caught a glimpse of Jenos rushing from behind and kicked Ryalie into his path. Jenos pulled Ryalie out of his way and continued forward, unsteady. I smacked his face with my open palm, then grabbed his shirt and pulled his chest into my knee.

He sucked in air, stunned for a second long enough for me to throw his body down into the dirt. As I was about to take off into a run, I saw Ryalie in the corner of my eye.

"N—" I gasped. Ryalie was in my face. He released jab after jab in a relentless onslaught. I jumped back, but he was faster. I felt three quick hits connect: abdomen, chest, and shoulder. They felt like shallow love-taps, but then the pain struck like fire in my veins.

"Ah!" I screamed, staggering back into Jenos. He secured my wrists with one hand while his other arm crossed my neck.

"Don't kill her!" Alix shouted.

"How about you make sure they don't?" I shouted back.

I writhed against Jenos as Ryalie came back for the knockout punch. I gritted my teeth in frustration. I wasn't mad about them picking a fight with me. I'd gotten into plenty of fights, with all kinds of bullies and bigots throughout my life. At one point, I'd kept a tally on how many noses I'd broken.

But I couldn't remember the last time my blood was so hot with anger.

When Ryalie was close enough, I hopped off the ground, putting all my weight on Jenos and kicked Ryalie in the jaw with all the strength I could muster. His head whipped back, and his body hit the ground.

"Ryalie!" Jenos shouted. I thrust my head back into his face and wiggled my arm free enough to elbow him in the chest. He staggered back, and when he looked up, my knuckle cracked his cheek. He collapsed to the ground.

I stood above them, panting and furious. They looked up at

me in horror. I was fuming with rage. It was burning a hole in my chest, like all my anger, resentment, and frustration about the curse wanted to break out of me all at once.

"Stop," Alix said and wrapped his arms around me like chains. Maybe he was just holding me, but his touch was an unbearable weight.

I pushed him away and glared. Now he decided to step in? And he was telling *me* to stop?

"Lilly, please. I couldn't—" He reached for me, and I slapped his hand away. He looked betrayed, the feeling was mutual.

Instead of talking to the traitorous prince I focused on his blood hungry knights.

"You two. Look at me," I demanded. They stiffened and looked up. "I feel pain. Do understand that? *It hurts*. I'm not different from you." I paused to wipe the sweat from my face and clear my head of the various words I wanted to scream at them. "When you look at me like that…"

"Lilly—" Alix tried.

"Shut up," I growled. "They wanted to kill me. They don't even know me. You two." I pointed at them. "You hate me? You don't even know me. I've never even met either of you before, and within ten seconds you tried to kill me!" I wiped my tears with the back of my hand. "You *hate* me because I'm different from you." I looked at Alix, who struggled to keep my gaze. "And you all think *I'm* the monster?"

Alix flinched at my words. He couldn't meet my eye. Deep shame was etched in his frown. "You know I don't think that. Let's talk. I'm sure we can—"

"Stop. Leave me alone."

I ran into the forest and emptied my mind, letting my legs push me forward. I had to get far away from there, but I knew that no matter how far I ran I couldn't escape the way they made me feel. This wasn't the first, and it wouldn't be the last time. But the dull ache I had only intensified with every ignorant, hateful experience.

My leg snagged an exposed tree root and my world suddenly tilted. I ducked and rolled down a gentle slope bracing my body on reflex. Before I could figure out how to stop myself, I plunged into the ice-cold river. My body ceased up and I desperately held my breath. I pushed myself up, gasped air into my lungs and swam to land. I clawed my way out and sat beside the river's edge.

"No matter how bad a day is going, it can always get worse," I grumbled and wrung out my shirt. I shook my wet hair and pushed it out of my face.

Thanks to my sudden cold dip, I was a lot calmer.

I should go back and apologize. I sat up and flinched. I felt a slight sting in my chest from where Ryalie had hit me. *I should demand an apology before I apologize.*

I nodded, calm and ready to make them grovel, but then a shiver ran down my spine. Now that I was calm, I was more aware. The trees were different, larger, untouched by autumn colours, a green so dark it looked black.

Goosebumps raced up my arm, and I found all my senses on high alert. I hadn't realized at first, but I was in the part of the forest that surrounded the mountains. The forbidden part of the forest. The temperature dropped, and I became aware of the darkness the tall, thick trees created. It wasn't that different than the forest I usually roamed, but there was something in this forest that put me on edge. Something hidden in shadows. And in the air.

I was about to cross the river and retrace my steps, but as I turned someone knocked me out. The last thing I saw was a sharp yellow colour.

Alix wanted to run after her, but he didn't know what he would say once he caught up. Pathetic. He turned his gaze to his friends. He couldn't blame them. If he were in their shoes, he would have done the same. He almost did.

"We need to talk."

"Yes, we do!" Ryalie barked at him, "Why didn't you help?

"Why would I?" he retorted.

"She's the *Renai*. The half-breed abomination. The product of the unforgivable sin," Jenos said as though it were that simple. "And we are knights sworn—"

"I know." Alix lifted his hand. He didn't want to hear it. His feelings were conflicted enough.

"It hurts," Ryalie grumbled, clutching his jaw. "She was tougher than I thought."

"She's improved," Alix said in approval. Her movements were much sharper than when she'd last tried to fight him. To take on Jenos and Ryalie, even if they were caught off guard, deserved some recognition.

"She's dangerous," Jenos said, gripping a tree to keep himself steady. He met Alix with a warning glare that held more questions than anger.

"She trains to survive, not to hurt people," Alix explained. When she first explained it, he didn't believe her. He felt like such a fool. "You attacked her first."

"What is wrong with you? How could you stand there and watch? You're even defending her!" Ryalie growled.

"I stopped her at the end, didn't I? Where's the gratitude?"

"Alix." Jenos stared at him, demanding an answer.

His shoulders dropped in defeat. He couldn't talk his way out of this one with shrugs and half-smiles. "How could I attack a person who saved my life? She was selfless despite the risk."

His friends stayed silent.

"She runs at the chance of being seen because what happened now will happen every time." Alix looked up at the clear sky. He was beginning to understand. It was no wonder she refused to leave the forest. "But she still saved me. Knowing the risk, when everything within her told her to run, she saved me. She brought me back from the edge of death."

"Alix…" Ryalie shook his head in disbelief.

"I wanted to help her. I had to hold myself back. I know even I wouldn't be spared from punishment," he said. "But know that if it had gotten worse, you would have made an enemy of me."

"You can't be serious," Jenos said.

"She risked her life to save mine," Alix said. "And she's a good person, strong-willed."

"And ill-tempered," Jenos added.

"Wouldn't you be if two people you'd just met tried to kill you?" he asked. "Don't answer, because it's happened, and you were."

"What has she done to you?" Jenos asked, staring at Alix like the prince had truly lost all sense.

He shrugged. "She opened my eyes. Give her a chance."

"Why should we?" Ryalie asked.

Alix sighed in exasperation. "Have you not heard a word I've said?"

Ryalie pouted.

"Jenos, can you find her? I don't like the direction she ran off in," Alix said.

Jenos closed his eyes as he heightened his senses to trace her *Arcania*. "She went west," Jenos said, then flinched. "Too far west."

Before I opened my eyes, I felt a blunt pain in the back of my head pounding against my skull. Whoever hit me didn't hold back. My clothes clung to me, damp and heavy, making my skin heave in the humidity.

I pushed myself off the ground. The first thing I saw was a child crouched near me. I scrambled back and hit a stone wall with a force that knocked the air out of my lungs. I was in a cave, surrounded my tiny lights hanging from the ceiling. Rough brown stone surrounded me, as did the smell of the forest.

I wasn't too far from home.

Three kids giggled at my reaction. I blinked several times, trying to gauge if what I was seeing was real. They looked like normal children, but each of them had a different part of their skin crawling with grotesque, pulsing, bulging, black veins. But that wasn't the most striking thing about them. It was their eyes. The part that was supposed to be white was pitch-black and the irises were a bright yellow, like liquid sunlight. I stared in shocked awe.

I wanted to look deeper into those eyes to assure myself that I wasn't seeing things, but my body became paralyzed, unwilling to inch closer. It wasn't just their appearance that made me cautious. They exuded a deathly aura of wrongness.

I looked past them. Beyond the cave was light, the hum and steps of people, and probably a way home.

"You're awake."

A woman stepped into the cave; her arms folded across her chest. She had her guard up. Her appearance was a lot like the children, but the black veins covered more of her pale skin. I couldn't be sure where it began under her ratty clothes, but it had stretched past her collar bone and was spreading up her jawline. The dark circles under her eyes were prominent and almost matched her brittle, straight black hair. She had a sickly thin figure but somehow held herself with the dignity I'd observed in Alix.

She looked as confused by my presence as I was by hers.

She smiled down at the children. "Go play elsewhere." Her voice was low but feminine. "What were you doing in my forest?" she asked.

I didn't answer.

"You're not one of us," she said. "Well?"

"Where am I?" I asked.

"You don't know?" I knew, but acting like I didn't seemed like the wiser option. "Who are you?"

"Uh…" I couldn't tell her. I'd had my fill of near-death experiences for the day. "I got here by mistake. I'll leave now."

"Wait." She grabbed my wrist. My mark began to burn like it had the day it appeared. Fire ignited down my spine. I arched my back and choked back a scream.

She released me and took a step back. Her eyes were wide with fear, but it turned into confusion when she saw my face.

"What was that?" she asked. "That voice."

I shook my head, still reeling. *Voice?*

She took a step closer, and I stepped back.

"You're repulsed by me." The dejection in her voice gave me pause as I recognized the sadness in it. I could sympathise.

"No," I panted. But I didn't want her to touch me again. I never wanted to feel my skin burn like that again.

Her face twisted into a wide smile that made my stomach drop. There was a manic look in her eye that twisted my insides. "You're not afraid of me," she said and took a step forward, her eyes widening as she did. "I need to hear it again."

She reached her hand out, about to touch my neck, but I slapped her hand away and stepped out of range.

"No," I said. "I've had enough of pain for one day. And there are two jerks I have to thank for that."

"Who could you be talking about?"

I shut my eyes and fought back the migraine his voice gave me.

The woman stiffened and retreated out of the cave quickly. I followed her lead and my eyes widened at the large open space of carved rock. Caves, tunnels, and even more lights lined the walls making it impossibly bright. It must have taken years, decades, to create the stairs, slopes, and the small garden where dozens of people stood frozen, staring at Alix and his knights. They all looked like the children as well, with varying degrees of black veins.

Alix strolled in like he was expecting applause. His spine was bone straight, chin up and he moulded his features to show dignified boredom. He may as well have floated in on a cloud.

I frowned. "What do you want?"

"I thought you might enjoy being rescued," he said.

Everyone started whispering between themselves. Others were slowly peeling off into tunnels as quietly as they could.

"Queen Zalia," Alix said, ice in his tone. "Long time."

Of course he was on a first name basis with the queen of the forbidden forest. Why was I not surprised?

"Prince Alixios." She bowed. "I didn't expect to see you again."

"Well, I was around." He shrugged. "I thought, why not?"

"Why not?" Zalia repeated. She sounded calm but, I saw her trembling. Somehow her pale skin managed to lose even more colour.

"You have something that belongs to me," Alix said and nudged his chin at me.

I glared at him.

"But this is my forest," she said. "I'm the law."

"Yes, I'm aware, but…" Alix's frowned with distaste. "Make an exception."

"No, this is my—"

Before she could get the next word out, Alix walked up to her and was in her face. She stumbled back, shaken. "Did you not hear me?" he demanded, his voice dipping low into whatever icy reserves he had.

"Y-ye, yes," she stammered.

"Then step away." Alix offered me his hand, in a manner true to his title. I looked up at him, and I slapped it away. He frowned. "Don't be stubborn about this."

"You're a traitor."

"I would have helped if it got to that point," he said.

"Whatever," I said and sighed. There was no point in this back and forth. I was too tired, damp, and hurt to keep going. "I should be getting back anyway."

Alix chuckled. "You're a whole lot of trouble."

"No one told you to come looking for me," I grumbled.

We were about to leave, but Jenos and Ryalie stood in our way. I gritted my teeth. Would I have to fight them again?

They bowed.

I stepped back. Talk about a surprise attack.

Jenos was the first to speak. "We should not have done what we did. It was wrong. We are sorry," His voice was smooth and strictly polite. It created a wall.

"And if you still want to beat us up…" Ryalie straightened

and spread his arms wide. "You can."

I immediately took advantage of the opening and punched him across the face.

"Ow! I can't believe you actually hit me!"

"You know what, I don't feel that much better. Let me punch you again," I said, lifting my fist.

Alix and Jenos grabbed my arms.

"Hey," I whined.

"You need to get a hold of this temper of yours."

I opened my mouth to retort, but a sharp pain tore through me. I felt surge upon surge of sharp pangs race throughout my body. My knees buckled. I screamed, crouching into myself.

"Lilly?" Alix was on his knees.

I couldn't speak. My hand gripped my chest, hoping he would understand that I was in pain. I panted and the world spun out of control. I stared up at their blurred images, gasping for air and relief from all the pain, but as Ryalie began to reach for me, I could only see darkness.

It smelt like springtime. Alix was carrying me on his wide back. His steps were light. There was barely any light in the forest, and the hum of the night critters filled the chilled air. I took a deep breath, a dull ache greeting me in my chest as I did.

"Ow," I groaned when I found my voice.

"Oh, she's awake," Alix said, glancing back at me as best he could manage.

"What happened?" I asked. "Ah, why do I have heartburn?

"Ryalie, would you like to explain?" Alix asked.

I looked at Ryalie on my left. He scratched his head and gave me a toothy smile. My eyes widened at him. He had such a welcoming, kind smile, it warmed me up. His skin was fair and smooth, and his lips had a hint of pink. I stared at his hair. It couldn't be his natural colour. If I'd met him back home, he would be East Asian. Maybe things worked differently in Glorus.

"I'm sorry. You fainted because of me. I'm a seer, and I can see the flow of *Arcania*," he explained. "I stopped the flow in your body, and it built up in your chest."

"And you unstopped it?" I asked and he nodded. "How?"

Ryalie nodded. "I blocked it; I can unblock it."

"And if you hadn't?"

He looked down. "The *Arcania* would have built up, and your heart would've stopped…temporarily."

"I think I'll be staying away from you from now on."

"I promise not to do it ever again," he said.

"Talk is cheap," I said with a wry smile, resting my head on Alix's shoulder.

Ryalie's eyes widened, lost for words.

"I had no idea you were so forgiving," Alix said.

"What's the point in being mad? What's done is done and I'm alive. Being angry or hating him won't change what happened. Anyway, I don't have the energy to form a grudge right now."

"Is that so? You seemed pretty angry before," he said with a chuckle.

"Hmm…" Jenos mused. I lifted a brow at him. "I wouldn't

have thought you were the rational type with the way you stormed off."

"She's obviously not rational," Alix said, adjusting me on his back. "Going into the Exiles' Forest. What were you thinking? It's forbidden."

"Exiles' Forest?"

"They're war criminals who have committed such grave atrocities that they are confined to that forest," Jenos explained.

I furrowed my brows. "But there are kids there too."

"Born that way," Alix added. "The last war was more than two centuries ago."

"So those people…"

"Are descendants," Jenos said. "Their crimes were that severe. They're not so different from you if you think about it."

I frowned. "I guess you're right."

"You're almost home," Alix said, crouching down so that I could get off his back.

My feet hit the ground, and I managed not to buckle under my own weight. I flexed and stretched, still a little damp and shivering from my river diving accident. "Thank you," I said.

"It was fun meeting you," Ryalie said with a giant grin.

Jenos bowed, but when he straightened his eyes were hard. "Again, we apologize."

I smiled. He'd be hard to win over. "Sure, but never again, okay?"

"You don't smile at me like that," Alix teased.

"Give me reason to," I said.

"Enough flirting. Let's go," Ryalie said.

"Until next time, princess," Alix said with a playful bow.

I walked to the house and breathed a very heavy sigh as I walked through the door. "What a messy day."

Chapter 11

Famous Last Words

Alix was at his piano when Ryalie and Jenos found him. His fingers were spread across the keys, hovering in hesitation. The notes were a whisper out of reach.

"It's been a while, Alix," Ryalie said.

He didn't look up at the sound of his friend's voice. "You saw me an hour ago."

"He means it's been a while since you were at your piano. Composing a new piece for the EverSnow Night Ball?" Jenos asked.

"Well, you and the queen have been pestering me about it." Alix attempted to jot down some notes but produced nothing legible.

"We wanted to ask you something," Jenos said after a few seconds of silence.

Alix looked up from his paper. They both held his gaze, frowning. Jenos was often serious, but when Ryalie mimicked his behaviour, it was worrisome.

Alix straightened his spine. "Is this about Lilly?"

Jenos nodded. "It is."

"I won't stop seeing her, and I won't let you take her."

"I know. There is no point in even trying," Jenos said. He of all people knew how stubborn Alix could be, it was why Ryalie stood beside him instead of a knight like Kais, from a family much like his own. "You've made up your mind."

"Perceptive as always," Alix said, sliding his attention back to his notes.

"But I ask you don't meet her alone," Jenos said.

Alix paused. "What?"

"We want to be there whenever you meet her, which means no more sneaking off alone," Ryalie said. He slid onto the bench, softly bumping Alix. "I get bored too."

"What are you planning?" Alix asked, ignoring Ryalie.

"No plans. We want to keep you safe," Jenos said.

Alix rolled his eyes. "She's not dangerous."

"Ryalie's jaw would disagree."

"She got lucky. I went easy on her," Ryalie protested and jabbed the air. "Next time, she won't get a hit on me."

Alix smiled. Given time, he had faith they could all get along. Despite Jenos's apprehension, Alix knew he wasn't completely against Lilly.

"I agree to your terms."

There was a single, hard knock on the ballroom door which drew their attention. A man walked into the and went straight up to Alix and his knights. He bowed and announced, "Prince Alixios, the king seeks an audience with you."

"How rare," Alix said, getting up from his seat.

Alix joined the messenger, walking close behind him. Jenos and Ryalie walked close behind Alix in silent vigilance and departed before they turned the corner that led down a long hallway and ended at a large wooden door worn with age. Alix lingered for a second, trying to recall why no one had bothered to change it or hide the flaws.

The messenger bowed and took his leave. Alix opened the door to the king's study without hesitation.

"Father," he said in way of greeting.

King Alpan put down his documents and looked up at Alix with eyes that reminded him of his older brother, dark brown with a shock of light near the iris like burning wood in a hearth.

"Why don't you ever knock?" his father asked in a tired voice.

"My apologies. You sent for me?"

"Alix," he started, "why do you keep leaving the palace each day? I thought we were past this already. Have you forgotten your position?"

Alix shrugged, his shoulders heavy. "A prince should know his kingdom."

His father shook his head. "You have been neglecting your duties and have fallen behind. Tomorrow you will catch up on all your work, and later, we will meet with Princess Aretia for dinner."

Alix nodded. He couldn't refuse an order from the king.

"What do you think of Aretia?" his father asked, changing his tone from commanding to mildly curious.

Alix had known her all his life. He had grown up with her and even spent a great deal of his childhood in her palace. Of all the Crowns, she was the one he was closest to. "She's beautiful in every possible way," he said.

"Indeed." His father nodded.

"She is a tad obsessed with me though," Alix said.

"She likes you," his father said with a hearty chuckle.

"I know." There was a flicker of sadness in his eyes.

The king eyed Alix for a second then refocused on his documents.

Alix swept his gaze over the room. It was smaller than his own study with books and papers crammed into every space imaginable. A portrait of his mother hung on the wall above his father's head flanked by two long windows. The floor had a carpet as old as the door, and there were no other chairs in the room aside from the one his father sat upon. No one sits in the presence of the king.

"If that is all." Alix bowed and made to leave but paused. He turned back to his father and asked, "Father, why do women test us?"

"To see if we are worthy of them," he answered, not bothering to look up.

"Shouldn't we be testing if they are worthy of us?" Alix asked, frustrated by the thought of Lilly testing to see if *he* were worthy. Maddening girl.

"We start the chase, son. We have already shown them they are worthy. Now we must prove ourselves."

Alix frowned as thoughts of a particular woman crowded his mind. He couldn't understand why he was so captivated. "Some women are a mystery."

His father suddenly burst into boisterous laughter. "Indeed," he said. "Women are the greatest mystery in all of time. In fact, they are a mystery to one another as well. But you should investigate the mystery."

"Why do you say that?"

"Because," The king looked up at his son, his brown eyes bright with amusement. "It's always a mystery worth investigating."

I sat with Estell in silence, stirring my unappealing breakfast as though making it mushier would make it more appetising. It had the opposite effect. I was better off scavenging for my breakfast.

Estell was drinking herb water and reading some papers, which were causing her forehead to furrow.

"You'll need to self-train today," she said.

I paused and perked up. "What? Again?"

"Camerin is coming back and I'm going to meet him. It's a long trip and will take most of the day." She glanced up at me from her papers. I couldn't hide my excitement. A day she didn't punch me in the face was a good day. "Self-train doesn't mean laze around."

"What kind of self-training?" I asked.

"I'm feeling benevolent. You may choose." She stood up and packed her papers into a sack, then threw it over her shoulders. "Well, I'm off."

"Bye," I said and waited for the door to shut. When I heard

the click, I pushed my breakfast away and stretched my arms up in relief.

Now if Alix doesn't show up, I can relax.

A breeze welcomed me as I strolled through the forest. Brittle leaves fell like rain and crackled under my feet like soft fireworks. The weather was getting cooler each day, and the trees were becoming more barren.

I made my way deeper into the forest.

"Blaze," I breathed.

I'd never been so happy to see her. She was as beautiful as ever. Her fur looked almost alive, like fire against charcoal. She raised her head when I called out to her and looked at me with knowing eyes. I stroked her soft fur, and she cuddled into my chest.

"You won't believe what happened to me."

I jumped onto her back. She sprinted through the forest, but we didn't get far.

We'd been moving for less than five minutes before she stopped by a fallen tree. Suddenly she crouched down and released a deep-bellied growl. I'd never seen her react that way before. My eyes searched for the cause and spotted two figures inching closer.

"Lilly?" Ryalie's voice was a surprise. His eyes were wide, and his muscles were tense, like he was ready to run.

"Ryalie?" I dropped down from Blaze's back. I patted her and whispered in her ear, "It's okay. Relax."

"Are you crazy?" Ryalie asked when I was close enough for him to grab. "Kiliabis are dangerous!"

"Does she look dangerous?" I gestured to Blaze but realized she still had murder in her bright eyes. "Oh."

"Is she a pet to you?" he asked, not even trying to hide his hysteria.

"Yeah, kind of, her name is Blaze." I smiled. "Why?"

"You tamed a kiliabi?" Jenos asked, still eyeing Blaze. Every muscle in his body looked primed to make a run for it at a drop of a hat.

"Tame? Uh, I guess you can say that."

"I know you're the princess of hunters, but that is impressive."

I scoffed. "Thanks." He looked at me with such sudden admiration, I felt awkward. He was a hunter too, maybe that's why he felt it was such an amazing feat.

I looked over their shoulder. "No prince today?" I asked.

"No. He has other obligations. Orders from the king," Ryalie explained scurrying around Blaze like a fly. She looked ready to lift a paw and swat him.

"So, why are you here?" I asked.

"He requested we bring you with us," Jenos said.

"Yeah, he says you get lonely," Ryalie teased.

I frowned. "He said what?"

"Oh, and he sends his love." Ryalie made kissy-faces towards me, but I covered his mouth with my palm. Blaze inched forward and released a soft growl. Ryalie's face paled and he went still beneath my hand.

"You can keep it," I said and pushed him back. "What'd you say about bringing me with you?"

"We've been asked to guard a high-ranking seer," Ryalie said, moving to a safe distance. "Nothing too dangerous."

I didn't say a word. Did yesterday not happen? Why were they so chummy all of a sudden? Even asking me to hang out. Or what I assumed a knight's version of 'hang out' was.

"A high-ranking seer? Like you?"

"No." Ryalie shook his head. "I far outrank her."

"She sees auras. Because she works with the royal family her skills would fetch a high price on the black market," Jenos explained.

Wait, were they talking about human trafficking? "Who's after her?"

"Mercenaries," Jenos said.

"Mercenaries?" I repeated. "You want me to tag along while you protect a seer from mercenaries?"

"Exactly, so let's go." Ryalie grabbed my arm and started pulling me into his pace.

"Wait, wait, wait, wait," I said, digging my heels into the dirt. "I didn't say yes."

"Why would you say no?" he asked with a pure innocence unfit for his age.

"You guys know I can't be seen by *anyone,* right? We shouldn't even be having this conversation," I said. "Why do you want me to come anyway? Don't you hate me?"

"Alix and Jenos said we need to get along," Ryalie said.

I glanced at Jenos, who shrugged. He stole glances at Blaze, looking at her like a child would look at a candy bar in a store.

"I don't know. A lot could go wrong," I said.

"Nothing will go wrong," Ryalie said.

I frowned. "Famous last words."

"You have our word as knights," Jenos said.

"Yeah, and we promised Alix we'd keep you safe," Ryalie said.

I let myself consider it for a second. It was tempting. Despite three people knowing about me, I was still alive. What harm could a little adventure do? Then again, this could be a trap, and they could be setting me up to kill me behind Alix's back.

I shook my head. "I'm supposed to stay hidden in this forest."

"It's a large forest," Jenos countered. "Our destination is far but within the forest."

I groaned. But he then looked at me with a gentle smile that made my heart squeeze. It caught me off guard. He struck me as the type that smiled only out of necessity. "Please, Lilly. We want to get to know you. Understand you."

"You want to make sure I'm not a threat," I said.

Jenos's smile flinched but he held it together. I could respect his tenacity.

"Fine, I'll join you."

Ryalie jumped forward putting his hands on my shoulders. He gave me a bright smile. "Good to hear. You should go back and change into something more presentable."

I looked down at my worn clothes, rips and holes made it clear I wore it often and with little regard. There was nowhere to go and no one to impress so I never gave what I wore a once over.

"Fine," I said with a shrug.

"Great," Ryalie said with a clap. "Jenos, you go back with her to make sure she doesn't run."

"Where would I run to?" I asked, getting onto Blaze's back.

"We don't quite know what you're capable of." Ryalie gave me a side eye.

Blaze strolled to their side and bowed so that Jenos could get on. He hesitated to touch her, but when he did, his eyes shot wide open as he felt how soft she was. I chuckled under my breath.

"Hurry up."

He got on behind me in silence, but I felt how stiff he was. He wasn't sure where to put his hands.

"Meet you where we almost caught you?" Ryalie asked, with an inappropriate amount of nonchalance.

I glared at hm.

"It's memorable," he said and took off running.

I looked back at Jenos and tried to comfort him with a smile. "Hold on tight."

Blaze leapt into the forest, and Jenos grabbed me with urgency. I laughed and bent lower, digging my fingers into her fur. She could go faster. She wanted to. If I didn't know better, I'd think she didn't want to scare him.

We trekked through the forest towards the agreed meeting spot. Jenos walked a step ahead of me and kept his eyes forward. His posture was immaculate: his hair was tied back neatly into a bun, and he was a wall of muscle and stoic tension.

"Tell me more about what we're doing."

He glanced back at me, and paused for a second, considering his words. "I should begin with who exactly we are going to be guarding. She's an apprentice seer with the specialised ability to see auras. It's not a common trait, and that makes her valuable."

"How is the ability to see auras useful?"

"Auras don't lie," Jenos said. "They can tell you a lot about people."

"Can they tell you when someone is lying?" I asked.

He nodded.

"So, where is she going that she needs protection?"

"Seers like her have problems with their eyes. They start to lose their ability to see auras, and their normal vision becomes sensitive. Therefore, they need to...cleanse them, so to speak."

"How do they do that?"

"We are going to guide her to a kilypsi, a pure body of water rich in *Arcania*. It's one of the three great creations of the Glories."

My spine stiffened. The Glories were the creators of my family curse. I wasn't taught much about Glorus, but I knew to fear them. Hearing their name made my mark burn.

"Kilypsi," I repeated, shaking off my nerves. "Why not bring the water to her?"

"It's most effective in its given area," he said.

"Why are you guarding her?" I asked.

Jenos sighed with an exhaustion that made it very clear he was tired of my voice. "Ryalie explained that already."

"No, why are *you* guarding her? I thought you were Alix's knights. Does he rent you out?"

Jenos frowned. "It's what her closest friend would have wanted."

We were getting closer to our destination.

"What does that have to do with anything?"

"That friend was my late sister."

We were fulfilling the wishes of the dead?

He said it so matter-of-factly that I couldn't absorb the information. I repeated the words in my head to try and gauge the emotional weight of them, but Jenos's stony face could have given Cam a run for his money.

"It's me, isn't it?" I asked, deciding to focus on the less obvious issue. "You're not comfortable with me being a part of all this."

"I've accepted it," he said.

"You're a good liar, but you're not that good," I said. "You don't like that I'm friends with Alix either."

"His obsession with you is troubling," he said.

"On that, we can agree," I said, then frowned. "I'm not a monster, you know."

"That is yet to be seen."

Jenos turned to face me with a steely gaze. I looked him straight in his brown eyes, clear and steady. There was a wide sharpness to them, like he could capture the world.

"What're you two doing?" Ryalie asked, walking towards us.

Someone trailed behind him like a lost sheep. She had a small, fragile frame and slouched like the air was weighing her down.

Her short black hair stuck out like needles, and her skin was so white that it almost glowed. A black blindfold lay over her eyes, yet she moved and stood like she had perfect eyesight.

"Shechire, this is…a friend. Please refrain from any rude questions," Jenos said.

"Who is she?" Her voice matched her frame.

"She's not important," Jenos answered.

I scoffed. "Wow, thanks. Some friend."

"Hey," Ryalie whispered to me. "Do you want to see her eyes?"

"Her what?"

Before I could stop him, Ryalie loosened the blindfold. I stifled a gasp. Her eyes looked like they were fading. They had a smoky grey glow to them, like the remnants of a dowsed fire. When our eyes met, she narrowed her gaze into a sharp glare and kissed her teeth.

"Ryalie!" Jenos barked. He grabbed the blindfold and tied it back over her eyes. Jenos glared at him with disproportionate intensity.

"Sorry," Ryalie said and slipped behind me. "I wanted her to see it."

"You're wasting time," Jenos huffed. "Let's go." He offered his hand to Shechire, but she ignored it and started walking ahead without us. Jenos followed close behind her like an unwanted Glorian angel.

I glanced at Ryalie, who was still hiding behind me. He smiled, lifting his hands for forgiveness. I rolled my eyes and followed them.

We walked in tense silence with the moaning wind and pitter-patter of scurrying animals. The wind was chillier than usual, and the leaves fell like snow from their branches. Some trees had already moulted down to their twigs, and their leaves blanketed the forest floor like a dry rug. Despite the sun being out, there wasn't much warmth and the deeper into the forest we went, the more I could see it. We were going deeper than I had ever been. It was too far from home for Cam to tolerate.

"Hey, Ryalie," I whispered getting his attention. "How long until winter?"

"Not long," he whispered back.

I was curious about what winter was like in Glorus. Did it snow everywhere? Did they have traditions? Alix mentioned something about a ball. He sounded excited about it. I had to admit a part of me was jealous.

"We should take a break," Jenos said when we reached a clearing. Small boulders lined the edges like a natural border. Green moss covered everything, and vines hung from trees like clothes on a line. Tall trees and buzzing bushes encircled us like a fence.

"How long until we get there?" I asked, plopping down on a boulder.

"Not too long," Jenos said, looking around. His eyes darted from side to side. "We're being followed."

"Yup," Ryalie said, stretching his limbs. "No worries. They won't do anything. They're observing for now. How many?

"Two. They have a hunter amongst them" Jenos said.

Ryalie grinned. "I feel underestimated."

I felt something in the forest too, but I assumed it was animals. Jenos's senses were sharper than mine. I sighed in dejection and peeked up at Shechire, who had curled herself into a ball at the edge of the clearing, as still as a statue.

I moved to sit down next to her, but she didn't even flinch.

"What's your story?" I asked.

"That's none of your business," she hissed.

"True, but they," I said, pointing at Ryalie and Jenos, "made it my business."

"Well, they shouldn't have."

"I agree," I said with a nod but frowned. "I heard your close friend died."

Jenos talked about it like it was nothing, but there had to be more than that. He acted like she was a stranger, but Shechire was important to him. That much was obvious. There had to be a story there.

"She died for me," she said.

"For you?" I asked. "How's that?"

"Why don't you ask Ryalie.?" Even with the blindfold I could tell she was starring daggers at me. Every muscle in her face was taut as her hands curled into fists.

"I'm asking you," I said.

"Well, stop," she barked, hard and loud. "She was an idiot who threw her life away. Talking about her brings back bad memories."

"You don't mean that. I'm sure you're just hurting."

She scoffed. "It was years ago. It doesn't matter. She doesn't matter anymore."

My whole body stood still as I took in her words. I let her venom melt down into my bones.

"What did you say?"

"What, are you hard of hearing?" she asked with a bitter sharpness at the tip of her tongue. "I don't care that she died. Why should I?"

A humourless laugh escaped my lips. I felt my blood run hot and cold at the same time.

I stood up. "I'm leaving."

"What?" Jenos asked, startled.

"Don't even think about stopping me. I'm not risking my life for her. From what I can tell, she doesn't have a heart, and that makes her as good as dead to me."

"You'd leave and risk her getting kidnapped? Why?" Jenos asked.

"Don't act like I'm leaving her defenceless. She has the two of you—personal knights to the prince. She's more than fine."

"Wait." Ryalie spread his arms out to obscure my exit.

"What are you doing?"

"I don't know what happened, but don't go."

"Why shouldn't I?"

"Because Alix likes you and I want to like you too," Ryalie said. His eyes kept darting over my shoulder, his face was a mess of desperation. It was odd.

If I was honest, I wanted them to like me too. It would lower my chances of death a great deal for one.

Jenos walked up to me. "Please stay and see this through."

I pouted. It felt almost cruel to refuse. "Fine," I said.

Ryalie grabbed me in his arms and spun me around in a bear hug. His skin felt hot against mine, and his scent, like vanilla and pine trees, warmed me up further. "Thank you."

"You're welcome," I said. "Now put me down."

I glanced over at Shechire in time to see Jenos crouch down in front of her. I couldn't hear what they said, but she gritted her teeth and tightened herself further into a ball like she was seconds away from tears.

Chapter 12

Smile

Y ou don't like her, do you?" Ryalie asked me.

We were crossing a low bridge over a river to reach the other side of the forest. There'd been silence since we resumed our journey.

"Oh, no, I can see us being the best of friends," I said. Try as I might, I couldn't erase the cynicism in my voice. To be fair, I didn't try very hard.

He smiled. "So can I."

I lifted my brow. "You don't have sarcasm in this world?"

Ryalie laughed, his eyes sparkling in the strange way that they did. "We do, but I'm serious."

"You see me and the harbinger of death being friends. Should I be insulted?"

"She wasn't always like that."

"What happened?" I asked.

"If you believed your best friend died because of you, wouldn't you change?" he asked, "At least a little?"

I sighed. "I would change a lot." I couldn't imagine Chris dead—my mind rejected the very notion of the idea. Ryalie was right. Shechire lived a type of hell I couldn't begin to understand.

Swallowing my pride, I picked up my pace and caught up with her. "I'm sorry for what I said," I started.

Before I could finish, she cut me off. "You should be."

I shook off the bite of her response, steeling my resolve to keep speaking. "I should've known how hard it was for you. I reacted without thinking."

"I already told you. I don't care. She died and that's her problem. Good riddance. It's what she probably wanted."

Something inside me snapped. I pounced, but before I could grab her, Jenos snatched my shoulders and pulled me back. I fought against his grasp on instinct, but he held my arms in an iron grip.

"You're supposed to be proving to me that you're not dangerous," he hissed.

"Let me go," I barked.

"If I do, you'll hurt her," he said.

I let all my anger boil to the surface and let it all out in a huff. Calm washed over me, releasing the tension in my muscles. Jenos let go.

"We're supposed to be protecting her," Jenos said, giving me a cold glare, piercing and brutal.

That's when I saw it, his anger. His wasn't an explosive rage, it was like ice. Ice that burned. All that rage couldn't have been for me alone.

"It must be hard on you," I whispered.

Jenos blinked, the icy rage shattering for a moment. "Stay focused on the task." He walked away, holding Shechire as though to shield her from me.

"It's hard on the both of them," Ryalie said, appearing next to me. "What were you thinking, attacking her like that?"

"I wasn't thinking," I admitted. I rubbed my arms, and we started walking again.

Ryalie watched Jenos and Shechire with dull eyes, like he was seeing through them. I nudged him.

"Tell me what happened."

"What makes you think I know?"

"Shechire said you did."

"What makes you so sure she's right?"

"You're both good liars, but not that good," I said. "You've been pretty decent at hiding your tension, but I can tell being around her makes you uneasy too."

Ryalie laughed, but there was no humour. "Barely a day in and you know everything about us?" He paused and chewed on his lower lip. "My family are the mercenaries who killed Jenos's sister."

My brows shot up. "The plot thickens," I said. "You come from a family of mercenaries. Your whole family are mercenaries? Even your parents?"

"My whole family." He nodded. He spoke like it was so simple, but it couldn't be. "I was born into one of the most notorious mercenary families in Tamikar."

"They must be proud," I said. "How does a mercenary like

you become a knight to the future king?"

"It was a chance meeting," Ryalie said. "We were a bunch of kids running around town, just outside the palace, causing mischief. It was fun, and I didn't want the fun to end."

"What happened?" I asked.

We walked in silence for a minute, the crunch of our footsteps the only sound. I waited.

"Jenos comes from a dignified family that has produced many loyal knights. Shechire is also part of a prominent family, one that was targeted."

"By your family," I said.

Ryalie nodded. "By my family. Jenos's sister, Jiya, happened to be there on the day. She put up a good fight until others came, but she was young. She didn't make it. I was too young to be included on the job, so I don't know who requested it, but I remember the day they left. It was the last day I saw them."

My eyes widened. "Your family is gone? Dead?"

"My brother is still out there somewhere, but everyone else is dead or locked up." I couldn't sense any grief or hurt in his voice.

I shook my head. "I can't even imagine the mixed feelings you must have for each other."

"It was years ago," he said.

"That doesn't matter," I said. "Not with something like this.

Ryalie stared at me, his black eyes searching with acute bewilderment. He then wrapped his arm over my shoulder and pulled me closer. He held me so close we were stumbling to move forward. It was faint, but I could feel him trembling as he chuckled under his breath.

"We're okay," he said.

I folded my arm around his waist and tapped his chest. "It's okay if you're not."

He peered down at me, his black eyes assessing. "I see why Alix likes you."

"Why?" I asked.

"You're like an animal that runs headlong into a brick wall to get through instead of walking around it."

"Are you saying I'm dumb?"

"I'm saying you're not afraid of pain as long as you get through," he said.

"I'm not sure that's a compliment," I said.

He cuddled me closer into his side and kissed the top of my head before ruffling my hair.

"Hey," I whined, swatting him away like the pest he was being.

Ryalie grinned at me, and my slight annoyance melted away. Then he ran forward and jumped onto Jenos's back, much to his frustration. Ryalie ran from Jenos with abandon, and laughter trailed his every step. He moved with such weightlessness and fleeting joy that it made his dark eyes sparkle. Yet, I couldn't help feeling like he was more weighed down than he appeared.

"I'm going ahead!" Ryalie shouted and sprinted deeper into the forest.

I lagged behind Jenos and Shechire, staring at their backs, looking for an opening to talk to them but the atmosphere was so tense. Maybe I messed up and Jenos would tell Alix I couldn't be trusted. There had to be a way to fix it.

The sound of Ryalie's sprinting died down suddenly. We all stopped as everything went silent. There was something in the air, an inaudible buzzing that ran through me like electricity.

Ryalie came flying out towards us and hit the ground rolling. He pushed himself to his feet as he came to a stop, shaking his head like he was ridding himself of a bad dream.

"What happened?" Jenos asked.

"I'll give you two guesses."

Every muscle in my body tightened. My senses searched for a culprit, but my adrenaline was throwing me off. Then I saw a shift in the shadows, and two men walked out into the light.

Their size difference was comical. The bald one with a beard towered over the small, fresh-faced man with long hair. They were barehanded, but I knew by the way they stared us down that they didn't need weapons.

"Friends of yours?" I asked.

"Hide Shechire, now," Jenos ordered.

The mercenaries began to roll up their sleeves, revealing muscular arms decorated in scars. The pressure I felt as I faced them was foreign, like a heavy wave pulling me to my knees. The air around Jenos and Ryalie shifted so that they now looked like the calm before the storm. They had unshakable focus. Only the enemy existed.

"Me first," Ryalie said. He ran forward with Jenos on his heels.

I grabbed Shechire and tried to make a run for it, but she gripped my hand and wouldn't budge.

"Hey," I hissed. When I looked at her, she was shaking.

I pushed her behind a nearby tree.

She grabbed me, and a panicked gasp escaped her lungs. Her blindfold had slipped off revealing ghastly eyes wide with fear and on the brink of tears. Her body trembled so hard that her fingers couldn't grip my sleeve. Small, panicked breaths came from her like haunted whispers. It was the same for her as it was for Jenos and Ryalie, only the enemy existed.

Holding onto me was the only thing keeping her standing.

I placed my hands on her shoulders and made her look into my eyes. I gripped her small, trembling figure. "It'll be okay. We'll protect you," I said.

She lost her grip and swallowed hard. Her body was as stiff as the trees around us, and she stared at me like my words were a slap to the face. I released her and was about to join Ryalie and Jenos when she grabbed my arm, digging her nails into my flesh. I clenched my jaw to hold back a scream.

"Hey…" I started.

"Don't go," she whispered. "Please don't go. Stay with me. We can hide together."

She wasn't looking at me. She wasn't talking to me. I knew she was older than I was, but at that moment, she was a scared child again, reliving the trauma that had stolen her friend.

"No," I said.

She looked up at me with tears streaking down her cheeks. "Please!" she begged, tugging at my clothes. "Don't go."

I pulled her hand off and took it in mine. "I have to protect you. I said I would."

She melted to her knees, succumbing to her violent sobs. As much as I wanted to comfort her, keeping her alive was all that mattered.

I ran out from behind the tree, and the smaller guy ran towards me. I couldn't react in time, and he tackled me to the ground. He pulled me up, jabbed my ribs and landed a straight hook across my face. He followed with a kick which I managed to block but still caused me to stumble back onto my knees. Every place he landed a blow throbbed.

Estell kicked harder, but that didn't mean his didn't hurt.

He grabbed me again and threw me against a tree, knocking the wind out of my lungs.

"Yup, knew I was going to regret this," I grunted.

I stood up and tried to stand straight, but my balance was off. The long-haired man approached me with a nasty half-smile. I almost smiled back at him, thinking how I would repay him back for my bruises.

"You could sell for a high price too," he said, leering at me.

I fought back my disgusted shivers.

He laughed and walked up to me with audacious confidence. He threw a right hook, and I evaded by cocking my head to the side. I grabbed his extended arm and jabbed his shoulder. It buckled, and I backhanded him across the face. Before he could recover, I swung my foot into his shin, and his knee hit the ground. I kneed him in the chest, and he gasped, his body crouching forward, crumbling until his face was in the dirt.

I was about to knock him out when someone crashed into me, knocking me off my feet.

"How's it going here?" Ryalie asked, out of breath.

"I want to go home," I croaked, struggling to talk with him laying on top of me.

"Don't say that." He pulled me to my feet, and I dusted the grass off my clothes.

As I turned around to finish the job, the long-haired man grabbed the sides of my head with his fingertips, and I couldn't move. A shadow began to creep over my mind, encroaching on my consciousness, pushing me under. My eyes fluttered.

I was so tired.

I grabbed his wrist, but there was no strength in my hands and my fingers slid off.

Ryalie threw a fast punch from the side, pulled me from the mercenary's grasp and shook me by the shoulders. My head snapped back and forth, forcing my mind to the surface. I gripped his arms to make him stop.

"Are you okay?" Ryalie asked.

"No, you shook me like a pom-pom," I growled.

"You can't let your guard down. He's a weaver."

"Weaver?" I knew that word, but my mind wasn't there yet.

Ryalie grabbed the man and put him in a headlock. He struggled, clawing and pounding at Ryalie's arms. There was no escape. His movement began to lag, then his eyes rolled back, and he passed out, sliding to the ground.

"You make it look so easy," I said.

Ryalie smiled. "Because it is."

"Shut up," I grumbled.

"Jenos!" Ryalie shouted in realization and started running. I followed him without thought.

The big guy had Jenos pushed into a corner, defending against a hail of attacks. Ryalie jumped onto the guy's back, grabbed his jaw, and pulled back with all his weight, steering him away. I grabbed Jenos in time to steady his stumble. He looked like I did after sparring with Estell.

"Are you okay?" I asked.

Jenos spat out blood and nodded.

"You're getting worse at lying as the day progresses," I said. He gave me a withering look. I bit my lip and looked away. "Never mind."

The big guy grabbed Ryalie and threw him over his head. Ryalie tucked and rolled across the ground. He ended up on his feet, arms up, ready for a fight.

I admired his tenacity.

"Give me an opening." Ryalie clicked his fingers into a fist.

"Let's go," Jenos ordered me.

"Go?" I asked.

"Follow your instincts," he said and dashed forward.

The big guy swung a strong straight punch, but Jenos twisted to the side dodging the brunt of the attack by a whisper. He grabbed the extended arm and crushed it between his knee and elbow with all his strength. The mercenary let out a cry that shook the trees and retreated. I ran up to him and jumped up and off his chest, pushing him back against a tree and knocking the wind from his lungs. This left him unguarded, giving Ryalie the opening he requested. Ryalie followed up with two swift jabs to the chest that caused the big guy to shudder and fall to his knees.

He clutched his chest and released a sharp gasp before collapsing face-down.

The whole forest went still.

"Is he...dead?" I asked, a little stunned.

Ryalie gasped melodramatically, though I could tell he was truly out of breath. "He's unconscious. What is wrong with you?"

"Thank you for your help," Jenos said before I could release a hail of retorts at Ryalie.

"No problem. It was..." I paused to look for the right words. "Interesting. Can we never do that again?"

"No promises," Ryalie said.

Once we collected ourselves and restrained the mercenaries, we found our way to Shechire, who was still on her knees, staring into space. She came to as she saw Jenos, but her eyes widened in horror as he offered her his hand.

Shechire exploded into a scream. She slapped his hand away and retreated as far as she could before stumbling over her feet.

"Stop smiling at me!" she screamed. "You have the same smile. She died smiling. Did you know that? That horrible smile like she was happy. What was she so happy about?"

"Isn't that obvious?" I asked.

"She was happy to die? Then let me die too!"

The echoes of her screams made the forest silent again. Jenos and Ryalie were speechless. They looked down at their feet with wide eyes and tightly gripped fists. Their chests rose and fell, and it wasn't entirely because of the battle they'd just waged.

"This is getting too painful to watch," I said with a sigh. I pulled Shechire up to her feet. Before she could look away, I grabbed her face and forced her attention.

"Lilly!" Jenos shouted. "You can't—"

"Oh, yes, I can," I said. "It seems neither of you will."

I locked eyes with Shechire until I was sure she saw me. Her milky stare was the stuff of nightmares. They belonged to someone who knew the meaning of fear and the agony of loss.

"Do you want to know why she died with a smile on her face?" I asked. The question grabbed her attention, held her body impossibly still. "It was for you. She knew you would live."

Shechire bared her teeth at me, but her eyes no longer contained any anger.

"How do you think she would feel if she heard the way you speak? What was the point of doing any of what she did if you're just going to complain?"

"But—"

"No." I flexed the fingers at her temple. "I know it hurts, and it probably won't stop hurting. But don't make the pain everything. Don't let it be more than the life that was saved." I pressed my forehead against hers. "Your life is precious. It is always something worth protecting. Remember that."

She trembled. "Who are you?"

I smiled. "That's unimportant."

Chapter 13

Winning

After a brief rest, we continued onward until we were out of the thickets and faced with a mountainside. I stared at the dark, ragged rocks, keenly aware of the ache in my muscles. There was no way I could climb a mountain after a fight like that.

"Shechire, if you would," Jenos said and cleared the way for her.

Shechire walked forward and pressed her palm against the mountain. A towering double-doored entrance began to open pouring sunlight into the cave beyond.

My mouth fell open. "Wow."

"Wait until you see the inside," Ryalie whispered.

Inside, the cave was a vast landscape of rough grey stone. Stalagmites and stalactites gave the illusion of towering columns, and the air inside was warm and damp. Running water hummed like a soundtrack of serenity from all directions. I could almost feel water droplets forming against my skin, but it was soothing instead of stifling.

Crystals grew out of the walls, ceiling, and floor. Some of the crystals were large and stood alone; others were clustered together, like a family. They glowed a bright white, illuminating the cave and making the stone shimmer. It was magical.

"Beautiful, isn't it?" Ryalie said. The glow of the crystals gave his complexion a dewy tinge that had me blinking in amazement.

"Keep moving," Jenos ordered.

I pouted. "Can't he let me stop and smell the… crystals?"

"What?" Ryalie asked.

"It didn't translate as well as I'd hoped."

We travelled deeper into the cave, careful not to fall into any sudden trenches or trip over the small, protruding rocks. The deeper we went, the bigger and denser the crystals lining the area became and the more fauna we saw. Simple patches of flowers grew where the light of the crystals were concentrated, like the light created life itself.

"Hey, what are these crystals?" I whispered to Ryalie.

"They're *amerine*. They form in areas that are dense in *Arcania*," he explained. "The Glories can refine *amerine* to create *ameris,* or it can form under the right conditions. Depending on their colour, they have different attributes. They were especially useful during the war."

"For weapons?" I asked. Ryalie nodded. I stared at the crystal, and a thought occurred to me. "Have you ever seen a purple one?"

Ryalie furrowed his brow. "No. Have you?"

"I'm not sure...maybe. I think it..."

"We're here," Jenos announced.

In front of us stretched a large pool of water. Stacked rocks formed small waterfalls, all illuminated by a cluster of crystals—*amerine*—above it, like a giant glowing chandelier. The area erupted with tiny, budded flowers that looked like fire lights reflected in the water. There was a constant flow that caused the water to ripple, yet there was a perfect calmness around us.

"Wow," I breathed. I wanted to walk in and somehow absorb the feeling that radiated towards me. The air here was alive and electric. There was a buzz as my heart rate steadily rose like a rushing stream of adrenaline was pumped into my veins.

Shechire knelt at the edge and pushed her whole head underwater. Jenos and Ryalie didn't react. I watched until she came up for air. She turned, blinking at us, then shut her eyes and stretched her arms out for assistance. Jenos cupped her hand and led her back the way we came. I looked up at Ryalie for some insight, but he shrugged and walked away. I stared down at the water and fought the urge to dip my head in as well.

"If your eyes come into contact with that water, you'll go blind," Ryalie said, without looking back.

I turned and ran to catch up. "I wasn't going to. I was only curious."

"Curiosity will kill you, if you're not careful" Ryalie said.

"You mean curiosity killed the cat?"

"Cat?" Ryalie asked.

I laughed. "Never mind."

Outside, at the base of the small mountain, Shechire opened her eyes and revealed two deep obsidian eyes blinking to adjust to the sunlight. "I can see auras again," she sighed in relief. She then took a quick step away from me as if she realized something frightening for the first time.

I stiffened. I hadn't considered if my aura could give away my secret.

"What is it? My aura?" I asked, attempting to sound calm.

"The intensity rivals Ryalie's. Impatient and reckless," she said, glancing at the knight in question.

I felt like a vein in my head was about to pop. Did she say that because she wanted to insult me and use her so-called ability as an excuse?

Ryalie laughed and nodded "She's not wrong, but I don't think you need auras to figure that out."

"You've known me almost as long as her. How would you know she's not wrong?"

"You make a strong first impression," he said.

Shechire continued, "You've been through much. Strength, and compassion like this—" she reached her hand out to me like she could touch whatever she was seeing. "— is forged."

I smiled. "Wow, who would have thought?"

"Not me," Ryalie murmured.

I smacked his arm.

"There is something else," she said, sweeping her eyes over me. "You have a silver and gold lining in your aura, which usually signifies someone of high lineage." She narrowed her eyes at me. "Who did you say you are?"

Ryalie and Jenos looked at each other, then at me.

I shook my head. "I'm the sucker who saved a pretty boy's life, and now I'm paying for it."

"What?" She strained her eyes like she lost her sight again.

"It's a long story," I said.

I peeked up at Jenos in time to see him smile. I smiled at him with a sense of victory. It wasn't a competition, but I was winning.

Alix thought of himself as patient, but his limits were really being tested.

He had spent the day with his parents and Princess Aretia. He'd done similar things with many of the heirs of all the kingdoms to foster healthy bonds, but never for this long. Aretia would normally be one of his preferred guests but today he was not in the mood.

They sat at the table beholding a glorious feast. While they were all talking, Alix's mind kept turning to what Ryalie and Jenos were doing. He hadn't spoken much the whole day, and he couldn't keep still.

He couldn't help but wonder if this was a punishment for leaving the palace and procrastinating his many duties. His parents were once understanding of his tendencies, but in recent months they'd become far stricter.

His responsibilities had increased so drastically it was clear his parents were trying to suffocate all temptation out of him. He said nothing but Ryalie complained on his behalf.

"Alix," his father called.

"Yes, father," Alix said, attempting to focus.

"Are you alright?" The queen asked. When Alix looked at her, he saw no concern in her hard frown. He immediately sat a little straighter.

"I'm fine, mother. I'm tired. That's all."

"Alright. How are the preparations for the ball coming along?" She grabbed her glass, long, thin fingers gripping it like a weapon.

"I'm almost finished with the piece," he lied.

"Always a perfectionist," his father mumbled. He ate his meal but also kept an eye on the glass his queen gripped.

"Your sister will not be home this time," the queen said casually, but he heard her disappointment.

He couldn't sympathise. He was conflicted. Her absence made it both harder and easier to breathe.

Alix shrugged. "It's expected." His sister didn't come home much, and when she did, it was a fleeting whim followed by bouts of anger.

"Who will you be taking?" she asked.

Alix froze. Her words were suggestive. "I've made no plans with anyone," he said.

"Why have you not asked Aretia?" she persisted.

"I apologize, princess. I've been careless," he said, bowing his head in Aretia's direction.

He had no intention of asking her. He'd always gone with her, and she would be there regardless. Along with the other Crowns.

"It's all well, my prince, I will see you there, and I shall save you a dance," she said, her bright brown eyes twinkled as a whisper of colour adorned her cheeks.

Alix liked Aretia. She was everything expected of a princess and more. He'd tried to spark a flame between them. There were moments when he thought he'd succeeded but in recent days he realized how far they were from it.

"It is soon time you and Aretia wed," the queen announced nonchalantly.

It took all of Alix's control not to choke on her words. "I beg your pardon mother?"

"You have been together for so long, you may as well," she said and folded her hands, one on top of the other like she did when she had her mind made up. Not even his father could overrule her on a final decision.

"You want Aretia and I to get married?" Alix asked.

His parents nodded.

"Are you sure?"

"What do you mean?" the queen asked. "I thought you were fond of her. She has grown into such a beautiful young lady and will make a wonderful queen."

Alix couldn't deny this, but was that a good enough reason for him to marry her? He swallowed, unable to eat any longer. "We shall be engaged?"

Aretia smiled and said, "We're to be wed." Her eyes were as bright as her happiness. "Our engagement party will be grand."

"It won't be official until then." The queen nodded. "But behave as though it is now."

Alix's mind was spinning so fast he felt like he would lose his bearings and his dinner. He stood and headed for the door on the far end of the large dining room.

"Alix, where are you going?" the queen asked.

"I'm feeling unwell," he said in a weak voice.

"You have not excused yourself," she rushed her words in a higher pitch than usual.

He didn't care. He needed to get out, away from them and clear his head.

The walk to his room was silent. He couldn't get his head to stop spinning. It happened too fast, and he couldn't refuse. It was his duty and would be his honour to marry someone like Aretia.

When he reached his room, Ryalie and Jenos were walking his way. Their clothes were worn, tattered, and covered in dirt. Despite Alix's own pristine appearance in a gold embroidered, deep blue long-coat, he was envious.

"Alix, you missed out today." Ryalie pushed Alix's bedroom doors open and sauntered in like it was his own.

They were bruised from head to toe, Jenos's face was especially rough. But they were smiling. It brought back fond memories—memories he thought he would be able to keep making for much longer than he'd been given.

"Lilly was amazing," Ryalie said. "I like her."

"She did…better than expected," Jenos admitted.

Alix's eyes widened in surprise at Jenos's words.

"Alix," Ryalie said, putting an arm over his shoulder and leaning in like what he had to say was a secret. He gave him a funny look and asked, "Did you know she has a kiliabi?"

Alix couldn't comprehend it fast enough. "What?"

"Yeah, we saw her riding it. Jenos rode it too."

Alix chuckled. "A part of me isn't surprised."

"I'm starting to understand why you're so drawn to her," Jenos admitted less grudgingly than he would've a day ago.

"So, I can keep seeing her?" Alix asked.

"Even if I said no, you wouldn't stop."

"That's true, but it's always nice to have your blessing."

"Shechire likes her too. She won't admit it either," Ryalie said, giving Jenos a cheeky grin which earned him a scowl.

Alix folded his arms, a smile on his lips and envy in his veins. "Why were you so adamant about taking Lilly with you on this particular task? It was personal after all," he asked Jenos.

"I thought you said Alix made you take her," Ryalie said.

"It was a more believable lie," Jenos answered. He lowered his gaze and sighed. When he looked up, he answered, "I wanted to observe her, put her in a spot where she would have to reveal what she was."

"And?" Alix pressed.

"She's dangerous," Jenos said. "But not evil. I would dare to say she's even kind."

Alix smiled.

"But my instincts are warning me she's trouble."

Alix nodded knowingly. "Those instincts of yours has saved us many times."

"It would save us even more if you'd listened to me."

"Your instincts also take a lot of the fun out of everything,"

Alix retorted.

"Jenos's fun-sucking instincts aside, how was your day?" Ryalie asked, giving Alix a few playful jabs.

Alix pushed his way out of Ryalie's reach and strolled to his glass doors that lead to the balcony. A cold starry night looked back at him. He took a breath before he announced, "I am to be engaged."

The two fell into somber silence, then Ryalie erupted into laughter. "You...go-got- engag..." he couldn't even say the words; he was laughing so hard. "Don't joke like that."

"It's true. I'll be engaged to Aretia in a few months," Alix said with a straight face.

He stopped laughing as the truth of his words dawned on them. They looked at him in bewilderment.

"It's been decided? So soon?" Jenos asked, taking a step forward but then remained still. Alix was surprised to see him as lost as he was. Jenos out of all of them should have been the most mentally prepared for the news.

"Declared by the queen herself," Alix said.

"Do you approve?"

Alix rolled his eyes at Jenos. "Does it matter?"

"I suppose it doesn't," he said. "It's...so sudden. You're not officially crowned yet."

Alix shrugged. "It's bound to happen eventually."

"I always thought you two would get married, but..." Ryalie started. "Now that it's here, it feels wrong."

"And you can't refuse?" Jenos asked.

"You know the circumstances of my becoming Crown Prince

were…unique. I've been given many concessions until now," he said and glanced at Ryalie. "It's impossible to refuse."

There was a knock at the door. "Come in," Alix commanded. A maid opened the door, bowed, and shuffled into the room. She curtsied and handed Alix a piece of fine paper before exiting in silence.

"It's a wedding invitation," Alix said, tempted to tear the silver and gold lined paper into pieces but the image of the queen's hard frown stopped him.

"Already?" Ryalie said, sneaking a peek over Alix's shoulder. "How long has the queen been planning this?"

Alix imagined it had been from his and Aretia's first meeting, perhaps even before that.

"Well?" Jenos asked.

"Not a word of my engagement must leave this room." Alix placed the invitation on his desk, unwilling to look at it a second time.

Chapter 14

Fairy Tale

My body was as heavy as my eyelids.

"The sun is too bright," I groaned over my dry throat.

By what I can only assume was pure luck, I returned before Estell, and completely passed out in my bed. After hiking to the magical crystal cave, fighting mercenaries, and hiking back, I had no more energy to spare.

I pushed myself onto my back and stared at the ceiling, contemplating my life choices.

"What are you doing?" Estell asked, standing at my door. "Get up. Time for training."

My muscles ached and I groaned.

"Hurry up. Camerin is waiting."

I sat up. I'd almost forgotten that Cam would have come home. I jumped out of bed and raced down the stairs and into the kitchen.

My spirits deflated when I saw him. "Oh, Cam."

He looked exactly the same as the day he left, which reminded me of our real relationship. I'd remembered him through rose-coloured glasses while he was away.

"Good morning, Lillianett. I trust you've been well," he said.

"Hi, Cam."

"Camerin," he corrected.

Estell stood behind him and patted his shoulder twice. "I'm sure you're glad to see both of us since you didn't yesterday."

I stiffened. "Sorry. Yesterday was rough."

"You mean your training?" she asked.

I paused and bit my tongue. "Yes. Training."

Estell walked up to me. She lifted my arms and examined my skin. I hadn't looked in the mirror yet, but I knew what I'd see wouldn't be pretty.

"You look like you got into a fight," she said.

"I got a little rough. Fell a lot." Half lies were also half truths.

"Uh-huh." She nodded. "Anyway, get yourself downstairs. Time for a little training."

"Could you heal me up a little? I'm sore all over," I said.

She smirked at me and reached into her pocket, pulling out a pouch of small, dark green leaves, and placed it in my hand. I reached a finger inside the pouch, and I grimaced—they were furry to the touch.

"After training, chew and don't swallow until they're tasteless," she said.

"After training?" I asked.

"I can't have you drowsy while we train. It would place you

at a disadvantage."

I always felt at a disadvantage with Estell. "What about your needles?"

"You need to build up your tolerance for pain," she said.

Cam followed Estell down the stairs to the basement. I watched in exhaustion as they went on their merry way to ruin my morning. I placed the leaves on the table and followed them.

When I reached the training room, Estell was stretching out her limbs, and Cam stood at a distance like a wallflower.

"Is it two on one today?"

Estell laughed. "Do you want us to kill you? No. We're going to spar, and Cam is going to watch."

"I'm sure that's not as creepy as you made it sound," I said.

"By watching, he can see how far you are and take over."

I widened my stance and lifted my arms, lowering my centre of gravity. Estell lunged, forward and I just barely dodged her left hook by the skin of my teeth.

"Your reaction time has improved," she said with a smile. "Keep it up, if you can."

"You enjoy hurting me, don't you?" I panted, struggling to get to my feet.

I'd managed to keep up with her longer than usual, taking a few hard blows and returning a few of my own. But Estell was still faster and despite her size, her fists were heavier. The level of experience was also a glaring difference.

Between our bouts, Estell took the time to correct and teach me, with Cam chiming in from the wall. We stayed down in the basement for hours. Cam went upstairs for food and water once and tagged in on one of the sparing sessions.

No matter how much I pleaded, Estell refused to use her needles to ease the strain on my body, which made the hours tick on at an excruciating pace.

"You landed a few shots," she said between her laughter, which I had admittedly grown fond of, despite the conditioned pained it caused me. She offered me a hand. "But yes, it is fun."

"You've come a long way since I have been gone," Cam said. "How is your archery?"

"Show him," Estell said, slapping my back to push me forward.

I stumbled, stifling my yelp, struggling to maintain my balance. I looked back at them with an exhausted frown, but they weren't biting. I clicked my tongue and grabbed a bow, lining up the arrow with the target.

"Her form has also improved," Cam said. "Does she have an anchor yet?"

"She hasn't found a form that is quite hers yet," Estell said.

I shot the arrow, and it landed in the outer ring. "Translation: I still suck."

"That's why you practice," Estell said.

"Thanks for not disagreeing." I drew back the string. I shot another arrow and watched it hit the outer ring again.

"Keep your eye on the target. Try drawing the arrow further back," Cam said.

I nodded and drew the next arrow further back, biting my lip.

The string was tight between my fingers, ready to snap at any moment.

I released the arrow, and it hit the outer ring of the bullseye.

"Better," Cam said.

"I have a question," I said lining up my next shot. "What can weavers do?"

"That's a surprise. Why so curious?" Estell asked.

"Survival. 'Know thy enemy' and all that," I said.

"I was going to leave this part of the training to Camerin," Estell said, giving Cam a pointed look.

"Weavers use their *Arcania* to manipulate the senses. In essence, they can create illusions. The more skilled a weaver, the more realistic the illusion," Cam explained.

"How realistic?"

"They can kill you," Estell said.

I released the arrow and missed the target. "What?"

"Yes, but if you don't let them hold you long enough for their ability to completely overtake your mind, you'll be fine. You only need to be faster. When faced with a weaver, always go for the kill."

"Or knock them out," Cam said.

"Do they also have specialties?" I asked.

"Good question. They do. Sensory disruption and sensory manipulation."

"What's the difference?"

"One is a like having a dream and believing it's reality. The other is like being told lies and believing they're truths."

I paused, lowering the bow. "They can do all that?"

"Yes, but it's all temporary," Estell explained. "It's a good way to get information out of the enemy."

A shiver went up my spine. I couldn't imagine having my mind violated that way. It almost happened yesterday. I couldn't get the sinking feeling out of the back of my mind, like I was sinking in sands of darkness. If it wasn't for Ryalie, who knows what could've happened.

It wasn't supposed to have happened. I shouldn't have been in that situation to begin with. When I saved Alix, I never could've imagined where it would lead. I still didn't know where it could go. If they kept coming back, maybe even more knights would follow, less loyal and more hateful. Jenos still didn't trust me. Ryalie was a little trickier to read. Alix struggled for days before he came back, and he still wasn't convinced.

"Take aim," Estell commanded. I snapped my arm up and suppressed a whine. "Your arm is slacking. Straighten it."

I could tell Cam and Estell about the prince and his knights. I could expose my mistake and maybe they could do something. Maybe we could live in a different kingdom and this time I would truly stay hidden. Maybe Blaze could come with me. The thought of leaving her behind made my chest heavy. If I left, would the last few weeks become nothing but bad memories?

They weren't all bad.

I shook my head and focused on the target. The arrow cut through the air and struck the centre. I gasped, blinking in surprise.

"Now, if you can make that shot consistently, I will ease up on your training," Estell said.

I frowned. "I thought Cam would take over, since he's back."

"I can't let him have all the fun," she said.

My shoulders dropped. The exhaustion in my muscles came back with a vengeance at the thought of both of them handling my training. There was no way it ended well for me.

Estell's eyes analyzed me. "It must have been quite a fall."

I stiffened. She didn't know. Couldn't know. She was fishing. This was a good time to come clean and admit that I'd dug myself into a hole that could quickly become my grave. One I didn't have any hope of digging myself out of. It wasn't all my fault, even Cam had praised me for saving Alix. If I told them now, we could be gone in no time.

I'll have every able man in my kingdom find out who you are.

What if Alix came after me? There wasn't much of a chance of that happening and yet there was still the possibility that he would, and that would bring unwanted attention. People would be sent to bring him back, people who would ask questions.

Was the safest option to keep acting like nothing had changed? Hope he'd get bored of me and let me live the rest of my year in isolated peace.

"Can I go chew on the leaves?" I asked.

"Go," Estell said.

I was surprised she didn't argue but I didn't question it.

I went upstairs, took a seat, and started chewing. It took all my self-control not to spit and choke on the bitterness that burned as the flavour slid down my throat.

I sighed as I looked out at the sky that was easing into a deeper shade of blue as the sun set.

They hadn't come today. I should have felt a great sense of relief, yet there was an unmistakable emptiness.

Free running, senses open to their limit, was a thrill. The first, second, and third time were overwhelming. My heart raced so fast it was impossible to get air into my lungs. I'd lost my breakfast the second and third time as I blacked out on the forest floor.

Now it was a thrill, adrenaline in my veins expanding my mind. Like being on the world's fastest rollercoaster. I wanted to scream and laugh at the same time as the world passed me by in a sharp blur of colours.

Cam was with me this time. He ran at my side, easily keeping pace and watching me.

I stopped when he stopped. He picked up a plant. A stalk with round, light green leaves and tiny white veins. He held it in front of me.

I panted, searching my memory. "Edible."

He picked up another one: long reeds with reed tips.

"Inedible but can be used to disinfect wounds when made into a paste."

Another one: small blue flowers made up of balls of fluff.

I held my breath before saying, "Poisonous."

"Good," he said.

I nodded and leaned back on a tree. Cam wanted to make sure I hadn't forgotten what I'd learned in my first month. How could I when I'd spent more hours outside than in? I didn't exactly have a social life to keep me busy.

"How do you feel?"

"Good." I nodded. "You?"

He nodded.

Estell had left days ago. Cam and I were back to our normal routine. Estell was easier to talk to because at least she talked back. Cam's training was less intense, and he focused a lot more on my thought processes and movement.

Cam riffled through a bush and held out his hand to me. In his palm were berries, leaves and something that looked like a green mushroom.

I pointed at the berries. "Can be eaten but not the seeds." I pointed at the leaves. "Will leave me numb for hours, but if taken correctly can be used to ease pain." I pointed at the mushroom. "Edible, if cooked, otherwise, will kill me in less than a day."

He dropped them on the ground and gave me a nod.

The forest was my birdcage, and I knew it well after immersing myself in it every day. If I found something I wasn't familiar with, I brought it to Cam or I searched for it in the books he had. He'd used some of the plants on me often enough, and he'd brought home some of it to eat, so I knew at first glance what was and wasn't edible.

"Shall we continue?" Cam asked, dusting his hands clean. He didn't wait for me to respond and started running. I followed after him, pushing my body and lungs to keep up.

It didn't fail to amaze me what my body could do. How fast, and strong I'd become. Not to mention my senses: everything was brighter, louder, and even food tasted richer on my tongue. I never dreamed it would be like this. My father had hinted that the change would occur, but he avoided the subject. He wanted Glorus to be the furthest thing from my mind until the last possible moment.

Glorus had started out as a fairy tale to my young self, one my mother told me every year on my birthday until I became too old for bedtime stories. She called La-Muse the *Rose Princess*, as beautiful as any flower and sharper than any thorn. She always described her as brave and full of love, and what happened to her as unfortunate.

Unfortunate. I was a lot older when I realized that it was nothing less than cruel. She didn't deserve what happened to her. I didn't deserve to be treated like a monster. To have eyes turn on me with such hatred and fear. Alix, Jenos and Ryalie may be accepting now, but I could never forget how they'd looked at me when they first found out what I was.

Those eyes weren't anything new. A black girl with red hair and green eyes, in a small town that snowed for half the year, brought a lot of attention. Unwanted attention. The features were a family trait, something passed on to every female of the Halibel line, according to my father. He had the photos to prove it. Only the girls had red hair, but the eyes were a given, no matter the gender.

Knowing that put me at ease but it did nothing for the boys that pulled my hair and called me names.

My mother was more than happy to enroll me in a self-defence class and save herself the trouble of teaching other children how to act right. My father just wanted me strong enough to endure the real training that would be involved in my year in Glorus.

They both instilled in me an unwavering sense of self. When I broke down, hating that I was born from sin, they assured me that I was born from love, a love La-Muse chose above everything else and one I should uphold in everything I do.

And I did. I spoke up, shouted out, talked with my chest, and carried a well of pride inside myself. I never backed down from a fight, which got me in more trouble than my parents bargained for. My inability to just walk away was my downfall. My father warned me it would be, time and time again.

Cam stopped by the river and pulled out a pocrat reed. I inhaled deeply, catching my breath before speaking. "Suppresses bleeding, and roots can be used as a disinfectant."

"I would be disappointed if you did not know," he said, dropping the reed back into the water.

I could never forget. "I've used it enough times."

A shadow of a smile passed over Cam's features and he ran again. I sighed, already exhausted but I ran after him, struggling with every step.

Chapter 15

Legendary

My days were quiet. Everything had gone back to how it was before, as if nothing was out of place. But I felt out of place, like I'd seen the light and now longed to see it again, suffocated by the darkness of my isolation. I shouldn't have felt that way. But my heart ached harder and longed to see the world beyond the forest more than before.

I pulled the bow just as Estell walked into the basement.

"Five more shots and you can take the rest of the day off," she announced.

I lost my grip, and the arrow flew loose, striking the wall and bouncing back onto the floor. "Estell?" I gasped.

I hadn't seen her in over a week, but she walked in like she'd just come back from going upstairs for five minutes.

"Excuse me?" Cam asked.

"You heard me. I need to take you out shopping," she said. She grabbed him by the collar and fussed around playfully.

"Shopping?" I looked at Cam who wore a less than thrilled frown.

"The EverSnow Night," Estell purred. "I've been invited to the ball, and I'm dragging him with me."

I chuckled. "Sounds cruel."

"I'm dragging him to free food and a fun night out. It'd be cruel not to invite him," she said.

Cam looked at me like he wanted my help getting out of Estell's plan, but I didn't have a bone to throw him. Frankly, if it got them out of the house and cut my training session short, I would be willing to buy the outfits myself.

"Have fun," I said.

Estell grabbed Cam's arm and started pulling him out the door and up the stairs.

"Oh, he will."

Once I'd made my five shots, I plodded upstairs, relieved to have a peaceful day to myself. I wanted to sleep the day away or play the piano. It'd been a while, and my fingers were losing their flexibility.

Once I'd finished bathing and getting dressed, I decided to go into the forest. I hadn't seen Blaze in a few days, and I wanted to ride her before the weather got too cold.

A light, cool breeze greeted me as I opened the door and my body stiffened, shaking off the cold. Most of the trees were completely bare and the ground was layered with dry, brown leaves. It was quieter than usual, making the crunch under my feet loud which was how I heard the echo of another pair behind me.

I turned and faced Alix who was still walking towards me. A smile began to spread over his face, slowly, the closer he came. And the closer he came the harder my heart began to beat. A panic settled over me like a wet blanket. I'd wanted to see him again, but now that he was here, I was reminded why those feelings were wrong.

He stopped a few inches away. "Hello, Lilly."

I swallowed. "Why are you here, Alix?"

"I thought you'd be happy to see me." He inched even closer.

"Why would you think that?"

"I thought we were getting close," he said, tipping his head slightly to the side, his dark, brown hair shifted with the movement. He snaked his arm around my waist and pulled me up against him. His cream shirt was thick but cut low to reveal the outline of his toned chest. "I would like to get closer."

I stiffened. "Alix," I began to protest but lost the fight when I looked up onto his sun kissed face. The look in his eye made me swallow my words.

He hugged me. "I've missed you," he whispered into my ear

I gasped and quickly pushed myself out of his arms, turned and walked straight into something. When I looked, I found Jenos and Ryalie standing there. How had I not heard them?

My eyes looked back and forth between them, and I sighed in exasperation. "They're multiplying," I groaned, rubbing my eyes with my palms.

"What is?" Alix asked.

"My problems."

Ryalie attacked from behind, hugging me, his arms wrapped around my shoulders like warm steel bars. I stood at attention, bracing for him to squeeze the life out of me, but he softened against my back.

"I missed you too," he said. "Thanks for helping us."

My muscles relaxed, and I wiggled to see his face. He had a wide grin, and his cheeks were a little flushed. It was a stark difference from when we first met.

"It's no problem," I mumbled. "Now get off me."

"Ah, she's embarrassed," Alix said. He leaned on Ryalie with an elbow on his shoulder, and they both smiled at me with sly wickedness.

"What are you guys doing here?" I asked before I lost my composure again.

"Checking in on you," Alix said. "Jenos insisted."

"I did no such thing," Jenos said.

I shook my head. "I'm looking for Blaze."

"Your kiliabi," Ryalie exclaimed with child-like excitement. He darted his head around like he expected Blaze to come walking out of nowhere.

"Yes, I heard you have a kiliabi," Alix said. "I'd love to meet it."

"Her," I corrected. "And why?"

"The chance to interact with a kiliabi, without the threat of death is rare," Alix explained. "And Ryalie insists."

"I do," Ryalie agreed.

I rolled my eyes. "Okay. You can tag along, but I can't

guarantee the whole 'without the threat of death' scenario."

Alix's lips spread into a smile, and he chuckled. "And what makes you so fearless?"

"I didn't know I was supposed to be afraid of her," I said.

His smile dropped. The other two stiffened as a wave of realization hit them all at once. I shook my head, holding back my laughter.

They followed me, barely making a sound. I snuck a peek behind me just to make sure they were still there.

"I've been curious," Jenos said. "How did you tame a kiliabi? How did you even find one? They're rare, usually found in *Arcania*-rich areas. The Hollow Forests are said to be their homes."

"She found me," I said. "She used to watch me, always at a distance. I don't know if she was wary of me or hunting me."

"If she were hunting you, you'd be dead," Alix said.

"I guess you're right," I said. "Short story made shorter, she approached me, and we've been inseparable since."

"How touching," Ryalie said and fake-sniffled.

"Yeah, yeah. And what about you three? How did you come to be such close friends?" I asked. "A knight, a mercenary and a prince."

There was a joke in there somewhere.

"Where do we begin?" Alix mused.

"I hear the beginning is a good place to start," I said. "How did you meet?"

"Jenos belongs to a prestigious family of knights. We've known each other most of our lives, but we only got close once we met Ryalie," Alix explained.

"I snuck out to Calla Lanae, the capital city, to cause some trouble. I was seven—" Ryalie started.

"Eight," Jenos corrected.

"Oh, I never did tell you my real age." He smiled with a wicked glint in his eye when he saw Jenos's frown. "Anyway, I was stealing food and playing pranks," Ryalie said with a hint of nostalgia in his voice. "Alix had snuck out of the palace that day, and Jenos followed him to make sure he didn't get into trouble."

"It's been a life-long mission," Jenos said. "More than a decade later, and I'm still doing it."

"So, you've always been a worrywart," I said.

"It's a good thing I followed him because he befriended Ryalie almost immediately."

"How was that a bad thing?" Ryalie asked. "I'm a pleasure to be around."

"You were part of a mercenary family, and Alix is a prince," Jenos said. "How much pleasure you brought was inconsequential."

"So, you were friends from then on?" I asked.

"No. Five years passed," Alix said.

"Then?"

"We met in Syver Academy, the training school for Glorians," Ryalie said.

"Wait. You were a mercenary. How did you get in?" I asked. "Or can any Glorian get in?"

He shrugged. "I lied my way into taking the test and my

abilities did the rest."

"Disgraceful," Jenos said, shaking his head.

I chuckled. "So, you reunited. Was it love at first sight?"

Silence fell and their footsteps ceased. I turned back to find they'd all paused in their tracks to look at each other as though they'd forgotten each other's names.

"We hated each other," they said in near perfect harmony.

My mouth fell open. "What?"

"I couldn't stand how great Alix thought he was," Ryalie said pointing at him.

"Ryalie was an impulsive idiot. Not to mention a lying mercenary," Jenos said.

Alix sighed. "Jenos was a rule-following bore."

"So…" I dragged the word and absorbed the new information. "Ryalie disliked Alix because he was smug, Jenos disliked Ryalie because he was a hot-head and Alix disliked Jenos because he was too well-behaved?"

They nodded.

"Well, it doesn't sound like anything's changed."

They nodded again.

"So, what did change?"

Alix groaned, "Team training."

"Syver requires a minimum of three years. The first year focuses on the individual: building basic strength and skills. The next two years are completed in teams to train in more advanced skills," Jenos explained. "Age varies in the academy, as long as you're skilled and willing, you can get in at any age, how long you take to graduate can also vary, but those three years are mandatory."

"And you all happened to be in the same team? Quite the coincidence."

"No, we were the biggest troublemakers, so it was only natural," Ryalie said with a chuckle that turned into laughter.

I glanced at Jenos, who looked like he'd tasted something sour. I patted him on the shoulder, unable to hold back my sympathy.

"How long did it take for you all to like each other?" I asked.

"It was when we were sent on our first assignments," Alix said. "Students that are deemed ready are given small tasks to give them experience."

"All we needed to do was watch over the peace in a small town," Jenos said. "The simplest of tasks for a first mission."

"So, stop petty crime," I said. "You were basically beat cops."

They looked at me like I'd spoken Latin. I shook my head, urging them to continue with their story. Blaze was bound to show up any minute, she was close, I could feel it.

"We discovered the small town was being used by a mercenary family—not mine—as a base of operations to smuggle a poison," Ryalie said.

"Trouble loves to find us," Alix murmured.

"The right thing to do would've been to return and request assistance," Jenos explained. "But Ryalie, being who he is, got caught."

"I said we should help him, but Jenos said it was too risky and against the rules," Alix said. "So, I went in alone."

"I followed, against my better judgement," Jenos said.

"I distracted the mercenaries, while Jenos freed Ryalie. My distraction caused mass hysteria which helped us get the better of the mercenaries," Alix said, sounding mighty proud of himself.

"They were a tiny family. Barely anything to brag about," Ryalie said in a tone that made it sound like he was bragging.

"From that day on, we grew closer and closer. We took on more assignments, and we were soon talked about in all the kingdoms," Ryalie said. He jumped on Jenos's back and lifted his arms in triumph like he was expecting applause from an invisible audience.

"You two always take on more than you can handle," Jenos grumbled and dropped Ryalie on his backside.

"If it weren't for our efforts, we wouldn't be so close. Where is the gratitude?" Alix asked.

"Should I also be grateful for the several near-death experiences?"

"It never hurts to live a little," Ryalie shrugged.

"Tell that to my scars," Jenos said.

"We've apologized," Alix said.

"Is your apology worth anything if you never change your behaviour?"

Despite his words, Jenos's eyes held a warmth in them, and there was no grudge in his voice. I'd never seen him more relaxed, though he still looked stiffer than the other two.

"So, after training, does everyone become a knight? Or is that only for prestigious families and liars?" I asked.

"Hey," Ryalie protested.

"Knights are either chosen or assigned," Alix explained.

"Jenos and I were chosen by many kingdoms, but Alix wasn't having it, so he dragged us home with him," Ryalie said, shrugging with a hint of pride.

"Other kingdoms wanted an ex-mercenary?" I asked.

"This was before they found out," Ryalie admitted with a shrug.

"So, you both decided to work for Alix?"

"Work for him?" Ryalie asked. "No, we are his personal guards, elite knights, revered by all in every kingdom. Our accomplishments have made us *Legendary Lords*."

I folded my arms, amused by his boastful tone. "Yeah, but you work for him," I said. "You're glorified babysitters."

Ryalie paused, gob smacked.

"When will we see your kiliabi?" Alix asked. "How do you know where to find her?"

"I don't, not really," I said. "She finds me. I mostly rely on luck."

"Excuse me?" Jenos asked. "Luck?"

"Yup. Don't worry. I'm usually lucky."

He stared at me, speechless. Ryalie and Alix looked unfazed by my answer. They both shrugged and nudged him to keep walking.

"You're as bad as the two of them," he said.

I gasped. "Hey, there is no need to be so rude. Take that back."

"I agree. She's so much worse," Ryalie said. I elbowed him in the ribs.

"So, you three are pretty famous?" I asked.

"Us four are," Ryalie said, sticking his four fingers in my face. I crushed his fingers in my hand, and he whimpered, tugging at my grip.

"Four..." I paused, my eyes catching on something bright. "What's that?"

I broke away from them and approached a lone flower growing in a patch of dead grass. It was a large, brilliant pink blossom with several tiny purple filaments at its centre that were so dark they were almost black. It had a long, thin stem that somehow kept it upright, and its leaves grew high, almost cradling the shell-like petals.

I'd walked past the area many times but never noticed it before. I was confident I knew about most of the plants in the forest, but this one was new. I would have noticed it otherwise.

"They're blooming again," Jenos said. "Is this by chance or did something prompt the arrival?"

I ignored Jenos's less than subtle look in my direction and approached the pink monstrosity. "What is it?" I broke the flower from its stem and got a lung-full of a sweet smell that engulfed my senses.

"Lilly stop!" I heard Alix scream.

When I turned back, the world flipped upside-down, and I found myself staring at the sky. I blinked. Everything was spinning and my head felt like it was full of air. I couldn't move my limbs. They were sinking into the grass. Although my eyes were wide open, the world grew darker. I gasped for the breath stolen from my lungs, but my chest grew tighter. My senses faded. The last thing I felt were a pair of arms wrapped around me in frantic desperation.

I heard soft movements beside me. They stopped and I felt a shadow looming over my body. I tried to stay as still as possible, but cold fingertips yanked my right eye open.

"You can wake up now."

I didn't recognize the voice. I grabbed the stranger's hand and pushed it away as I sat up to look for a way to escape, but the room began to spin. I blinked a couple of times, trying to adjust to the light and tell up from down. A glass of water appeared, and I looked up at the stranger offering it to me.

"Who—"

The door flew open, and Alix stormed into the room.

"Lilly! Are you okay?"

My mind couldn't keep up with the series of events.

"Where—"

Ryalie and Jenos cut me off as they somehow pushed past each other to get through the door.

"Lilly, you're alive," Ryalie said.

"What—" I tried again, but then Ryalie grabbed me in a hug as if he couldn't believe that I was real. I grabbed the skin on his hand and started twisting. He yelped and jumped back. He retreated behind Jenos, who was holding back a smile.

"Who is she? Where am I? What happened?" I asked in one breath. I grabbed the glass and chugged down the water. I was so relieved to get all my questions out, a part of me didn't even care if I got answers.

"This is Alle, a friend of ours," Alix said.

"Alle, also known as the one who saved your life," she said and took the glass away.

Alle was short and curvy, with a high-puff of cloudy curls, full lips and deep brown skin. She held herself as though she towered above us all. The confidence she exuded gave Alix a run for his money.

"Saved my life?" I asked.

"Here," Alle said, placing a book on my lap. I looked up into her big black eyes framed by long lashes, and she nudged for me to look at the book. It said *Mara Prana* in big, bold letters. Underneath was a picture of the flower I'd seen in the forest.

"Arguably the most beautiful but definitely the most dangerous flower in Glorus. They don't bloom often. In fact, it's been three years since anyone has even seen one." She gave me a tight smile. "We just met, but I can already tell you're trouble."

My mouth fell open. "Thanks for saving my life, but where am I?" Everyone in the room avoided my gaze. A lump formed in my throat. "Alix?"

Alix smiled at me and started backing away towards the door. The closer he got to the door the louder my heartbeat sounded in my ears.

"Don't be mad," he said.

"Did you do something that would make me mad?" I asked.

He hit the door frame. "You're in my palace."

He was out the door before I could open my mouth. I looked at Ryalie and Jenos, and they both fled the scene.

I looked at Alle, but she shook her head. "I'm not leaving."

I sighed. "How did I get here?"

She started packing things into cupboards while taking other vials and bowls out, arranging them on a table near a host of plants, some of which I didn't recognize. She answered distractedly as she worked, "If they want to do something, nothing will stop them."

"They're unbelievable." I shook my head.

"Yeah, they are," she said with a giggle. "Oh, and they are hard to love." She shook her head, placing some things down on a table at the other end of the room.

I nodded. "Especially Alix."

Alle came closer, and her face softened into a smile, revealing a set of deep dimples in her cheeks. "But they're worth loving. Especially Alix."

"I don't see it," I said.

She chuckled. "Is it something in your blood that makes you funny?" she asked, walking away. "Never thought I would meet a *Renai*."

I froze. "They told you?"

"You think I would let Alix come in here with a strange girl I've never seen before and not ask questions?" She laughed.

"He promised he wouldn't," I said.

"I told him I wouldn't help if he didn't tell me," Alle said. "What good is a promise if you're dead?"

"You would have let me die?" I swallowed hard.

"No. And you wouldn't have," she said with a shrug. "But Alix was in a panic"

"I wouldn't have?" I asked. "But you said…"

She placed a finger against her lips and winked.

Okay, then.

"He told you and you still helped me?" I asked. "Why?"

"I was shocked," she admitted, "but the way he looked at you and begged me… I could never say no."

The panic that had begun to build started dying down into a lazy calm. A part of me gave up.

"Thanks again for helping me," I said.

"I did it a little out of curiosity too," Alle said. "How did you befriend Alix and two of his most loyal knights? At great risk to themselves, no less."

"I saved Alix's life," I said.

She shrugged. "That's it? I've saved his life dozens of times, and I'll be saving it dozens more before my days are done. Saving his life may be a reason to keep you alive, but not to keep you by his side."

I frowned. I knew that, and it always made me uneasy not only for my safety but for his as well. What would happen if people who weren't friends found out about us? Would he lose his right to the throne? Be banished from his kingdom? Would he be punished with me? It wasn't a big concern at first, but more and more people were finding out, and the risks were getting larger.

"Alix said trouble loves to find them," I mumbled.

"Well, that is half true," she said. "Those three love finding trouble just as much."

I smiled. That sounded right.

Alle grabbed my arm and stuck a healing needle in my wrist. "What's this for?" I asked.

"Post treatment. The poison wouldn't have killed you, but it would have made you feel like you were dying. It's mostly out of your system, but some effects will linger," she answered, sticking four more needles in me. "You need three treatments. I gave you an emergency treatment when you came in. I'm giving you your intermediate one now, and tomorrow morning I'll give you your final dose."

"In the morning? So, I should come back to the palace tomorrow?" I asked, massaging my arm to chase away the numbness.

"No," she said. "You could have an adverse reaction to the treatment. Maybe it *will* kill you. You're a *Renai*. I'm not sure how your blood or *Arcania* will react. You need to stay here for me to monitor you."

"What?" I exclaimed louder than I intended to. "I can't stay here. I need to go home."

"Well, you must stay or risk death," she said.

"I risk death by staying here," I argued.

"Don't be so dramatic."

"Did Alix put you up to this?" I asked.

Alle pursed her lips into a slight smile. "I'll never tell."

"I can't believe this," I said, getting down from the bed and walking towards the door.

"You're in good hands," she said. "I've saved Alix, Ryalie, and Jenos from their idiocy many times."

I held back a smile. "Don't you mean injuries?"

"Do you think I mean injuries?"

A chuckle escaped my lips, but a frown soon formed. The lump in my throat grew, and my stomach was unsteady, like a ship at sea during a storm.

"Will this be okay?" I asked, eyeing the door.

She smiled at me with a hint of pity. "If you don't let them see your mark, you'll be fine."

"And if they ask why I'm here?"

"Say, 'Prince Alixios.' They won't give you a second look," Alle said and pushed me out the door. I looked back and the door slammed shut in my face.

Chapter 16

Take Me Home

The hallway went farther than I could see. Marble floors lined with a single red and gold striped carpet lay beneath my feet. Small chandeliers hung on the arched ceiling. On my right, were floor-to-ceiling windows with pulled-back burgundy drapes. Between each window stood smooth cylinder columns. Washed in light, the corridor almost sparkled.

I walked down the hallway, looking for something that could be an exit or lead me to one of the three traitors that abandoned me. I turned a corner and stopped just as I was about to walk into two women going the opposite way. Panicking, I ducked and tried to make a run for it, but one of them grabbed my arm and pulled me back with a stern grip.

"Excuse me. Who are you?" the short one with a steely blue gaze asked. I immediately made note of the sword tucked next to her hip.

"Jimi, don't be so rough," the other said.

I blinked at the person who spoke. Her shiny auburn hair fell in soft waves over her shoulders and framed her young, porcelain face. Her lips were plump, and her brown eyes were big with a shine all their own. We were about the same height, but I couldn't shake the feeling that she was taller. Her deep blue dress—no, gown—had ruffles on the hem and hugged her waist like a corset, pushing her ample bosom high. The dress was so gorgeous on her that I found myself staring for a second longer than I intended. But her appearance was nothing compared to the way she held herself, with a grace and confidence I'd only seen in one other person. I'd no doubt she was a Crown.

"I-I'm s-sorry," I stuttered and bowed. "I'm lost."

"Who are you?" Jimi asked and released my wrist.

"I'm here because of Prince Alixios," I said, dodging her direct question.

"Oh," the princess said. There was a hint of confusion mixed with surprise in the word. She looked at me like she couldn't imagine I even knew Alix's name. Part of me wished I didn't. Her surprise then turned to a frown. "I see."

I avoided her gaze and spotted Ryalie in the distance.

"Ryalie!" I shouted to get his attention.

The princess and Jimi stared at me like I'd lost my mind. It felt like I would if I stayed a minute longer.

Ryalie turned in our direction. "You're okay," he said when he got close enough.

"Yeah, thanks for abandoning me," I grumbled.

"You looked like you were going to punch me again." He

paused when he saw the princess. There was a moment of shock before he bowed. "Princess Aretia."

The princess nodded. "Ryalie. Always a pleasure. So, you know this girl?"

"*Know* is a strong word," Ryalie said.

I pinched his back, and he jumped. "You brought me here," I hissed.

"Yes, I brought her here, and now I'll take her back." Ryalie grabbed my shoulders. "If you'd excuse us."

Ryalie pushed me down the corridor and we zigzagged through the palace, passing confused stares and bewildered faces that retreated if we came within a foot of colliding with them. Two minutes into our journey, I had a sneaking suspicion that he was as lost as I would've been.

"Ryalie," I said, digging my heels into the ground. "Where are we going?"

"We're looking for Alix," he said, already trying to push me onwards again.

I shook my head. "Take me home."

"Alle said we shouldn't," he said.

"I should have stayed in bed today," I whined. "I want to go home."

"And I want friends that aren't so troublesome," Jenos said, walking towards us. "I can understand your grievances."

"I want that for you too." I nodded. "Bringing a strange girl into the palace like it's nothing and…actually, how did you get me here?"

"Your kiliabi," Jenos said

"You rode Blaze?" I asked in disbelief.

"She found us seconds after you lost consciousness," he explained. "She allowed me to ride her with you in my arms."

"You're not scared of her anymore?" I asked.

"I guess I've learned that I don't need to be," he said and gave me a small smile.

"That's amazing," I said, patting him on the shoulder. "Now, take me home."

Jenos frowned, his brows pressing together. "We can't do that. Not yet."

"Sure, you can. Is Blaze still here?" I asked.

"Yes. I hid her behind the palace," Ryalie answered with an inappropriate level of pride.

"She's where?" Jenos exclaimed.

"Well, she wouldn't leave," Ryalie said. "And this way, I got to ride her too."

"How in the world were you not seen?" Jenos asked. The disbelief in his voice was undermined by his frustration.

"Who said I wasn't seen?"

I mirrored Jenos's flabbergasted expression. It was a miracle there wasn't mass panic in the palace.

Jenos pinched the bridge of his nose and sighed. It looked like he was trying to count back from ten.

"Are you okay?" I asked.

He groaned. "I have a mess to clean up, like always."

"Before that, do you know where Alix is?"

"Ballroom. Go down this hall and follow the music," he said. He walked away, dragging Ryalie along with him.

I walked down the hallway, passing several maids and workers who didn't even look twice at me. Then I heard a piano. The notes were delicate but disjointed, like whoever was playing was testing the pairing of different notes. I followed the sound, which led me to a pair of grand, white double doors. I pushed them open and stepped into a silver and white ballroom with walls that swept into a domed ceiling dripping in fine artistic finishes. A huge crystal chandelier hung low, lighting up the entire space. There was no natural light, but drapes lined the walls all the same. I had to take a deep breath because I lost mine as I walked through the room, twirling on the soles of my feet, trying to take it all in at once.

I came to a halt at the stage where two grand pianos stood together like pieces of a puzzle. Alix approached me with a smile on his lips. "You found me."

I glued my eyes on the pianos. My fingers itched to stretch over the keys. "You play pretty well. What were you playing?"

"A piece I've been working on." His eyes took me in and then settled on mine. "It's for the EverSnow opening performance, but it's incomplete."

"You composed that?" I asked. "You're going to perform?"

"It's a tradition that the heirs perform but since my twin is not here, it leaves me to do it alone," he said.

"You have a sibling? A twin? There are two of you?"

"A twin sister and an older brother."

I stepped onto the stage and glided my fingers over the smooth edges of the piano. I could see the age in the small cracks and chips, but they glistened almost as good as new.

"Do you play?" he asked.

I sat down and started playing the first few notes of Beethoven's *Bagatelle No. 25 in A minor*. It was one of the first pieces I'd learned, but it was still a nice challenge to get my fingers moving and used to the keys again.

Alix leaned in and I smiled at him. "I dabble."

"You are exactly what I've been looking for," he whispered. His eyes locked onto mine with an intense smouldering linger of desire. I'd never seen anyone look at me like that.

I fought against my need to squirm in my seat and cleared my throat. "Excuse me?"

"Help me finish my piece," he said.

I laughed. "I came here so you could take me home."

"That's not going to happen, so you may as well help me," he said. Although he chuckled, he wasn't joking.

I glared at him. "You can't keep me here."

"Create a piano duet with me," he said. "I promise you'll be safe in the palace, and I'll take you home as soon as we do. The piece is mostly done anyway."

I opened my mouth to refuse but then glanced down at the gleaming keys. I wanted to stay and play the piano a little longer. I'd missed playing on such nice equipment, and the ballroom's acoustics were great. A little longer couldn't hurt anything, and he said I'd be safe.

"Fine," I said. "Should I play the harmony?"

"Don't be so boring," Alix said and slipped in next to me.

"Use the other piano." I scooted down, but he scooted closer and bumped me playfully.

"Come on. Don't be shy now," he said.

"I'm not shy. Tell me what you want from this piece. You were playing in a minor key. Do you want to keep that?"

"I want to tell a story. Our story," he said.

I groaned. "It's been nothing but chaos."

"Perfect," he said and banged on the keys, making me jump. "Let's have fun."

I lost track of how long we'd been sitting together, talking about his piece, trying to decide on the melody, tempo, musical form, and theme. Sounds that didn't go together clashed and flooded the ballroom. The frustration felt exciting, like trying to find the last few pieces of a puzzle. I could almost see the completed score underneath Alix's mad scribbles.

"Let's run through what we have so far," Alix said. "After you."

I nodded and began playing. Alix was adamant that we lead with the harmony instead of the melody, which sounded disjointed and out of place. We chose to start in a minor key and a slow tempo. I made my way to allegro as Alix came in with the melody, playing over my harmony like a honey glaze. I chose a theme that went down in octaves as it went on and Alix played a variation which he took liberty on, slowing down and speeding up against my sound.

We stopped and paused for two beats, then I started again, playing at a higher octave in a major key, taking the melody. When I went into allegretto, repeating the same set of notes,

Alix matched my sound with his own with slower and bolder ones.

"That's all we have for now," I said.

"It sounds good," he said. "It needs a name. Any ideas?"

"Name it after yourself," I said with a shrug. "That sounds like something you'd do."

He chuckled. "Not this time. I'll get the credit, so why don't you name it? I'll let you have that. It's the least I could do."

"The least you could do is take me home," I said.

"I saved your life," he said inching closer.

"It wasn't in danger," I said with a shrug. "And besides, I saved yours first." I inched closer and he smiled. I smiled in response, unable to suppress it, but pulled away before I got swept up in his pace. "Anyway, get whoever is going to play this with you to name it if you're too lazy to do it yourself."

Alix's face dropped. "Someone else…"

"Hey, Lilly, I found him!" Ryalie's voice bounced off the walls. He sauntered into the room with an irritable Jenos at his side.

"I found him first," I shouted back.

"Finding me was a competition?" Alix asked and leaned in with a smile. "What's the prize."

I flicked his forehead and scrunched my face up teasingly. "Take me home."

"Ryalie, must you be so loud?" Jenos asked.

"I happen to like the sound of my voice."

"That would make you the only one," I said.

"Alix, what's wrong?" Jenos asked.

Alix was staring into space like he was trying to think his way out of a tricky maze. I was about to tap his shoulder when a new voice bounced off the walls. "Alixios!" It sounded like an older woman, and there was a bold power of authority behind it that made me sit a little straighter.

Alix rose from his seat and walked to the exit like a loyal soldier.

"What happened?" Jenos asked.

"I don't know. He was normal a couple of seconds ago."

"Forget about Alix. What was that song you two were playing? It sounded crazy," Ryalie said.

"Is that the piece for the EverSnow Night?" Jenos asked. "Will you be performing together?"

"Of course not. I'm not attending the ball." I watched as Jenos physically relaxed at the news. I'd put him through enough.

"What? Why not?" Ryalie asked.

"Because you're going to take me home, right?"

"We said no, so attend it," Ryalie commanded.

"Who do you think you are?" I gasped playfully. "I will not be ordered around like some commoner. I will have you know I am descended from royalty."

Ryalie staggered back and took a knee. "Princess, I meant no disrespect. Forgive me."

I lifted my chin up and smiled. "You are forgiven. Now, take me home, at once."

He jumped up to his feet. "That's still a no."

I shrugged. "I tried. So, how big of a deal is this ball?"

"One of the biggest in the world," Jenos answered, all

seriousness.

My jaw dropped in time to see Alix walk in with a spring in his step and a smile stretched wide over his face. He looked like he'd heard the best news of his life so far.

I trotted down to meet him. "Who was that? You look happy."

"That was Queen Miyra, my mother," he said. "She wanted to know who I was playing with and whether they could play with me during the ball."

"The queen asked—wait. You said no, right?"

He sucked his lips over his teeth. "Why would I say that? That would be lying."

"But I *can't* play," I insisted.

"Of course you can. You have no excuse."

I stared wide-eyed at him and felt my blood boiling. I didn't want to die yet, what better excuse was there? "What is wrong with you?"

"I want to play our song together. Is that so wrong?"

"When it puts me at risk, it is."

"You're safe with me," he urged.

"I haven't been safe with you since the moment I met you," I snapped, a new anger boiling in my chest. "It doesn't have to be me."

"There's no one else," Alix said, stepping closer, looking into my eyes. His sapphires doubled in size and gleamed with a gut clenching recklessness. "There will never be anyone else."

I folded my arms. "How did you explain my presence to the queen? I'm a complete stranger that came out of nowhere."

"I said I needed a temporary personal maid to help with the

final preparations for the ball."

"You said what?" I hissed.

"It's the perfect cover. No one will look twice at you, and I'll be by your side the entire time. Isn't that great?"

It did sound great. With a cover like that I could walk around, and no one would suspect me, and with Alix by my side and as my alibi, I'd be as safe as possible.

"How long?" I asked.

"The ball is the day after tomorrow."

How was I going to explain being missing for that long to Estell and Cam? "I can't. You need to take me home."

He grabbed my two hands in his. "I need you."

"I should go…"

"I need you, Lilly," he whispered. "I want to play our piece with you, no one else. It has to be you."

My face dropped. My heart raced in my chest and my breath caught. I wanted to play the piece too and hear the final product. I was finally out of the forest, something I always wanted, but I knew I needed to go back.

"It's easier to ask for forgiveness than permission," I mumbled to myself. My better judgement was telling me to refuse him, but the small part of me, that was always the loudest, tugged at my heartstrings. I sighed in defeat. "Okay, I'll stay."

Alix grabbed me in his arms. "You'll be safe, I promise"

I wrapped my arms around his back, and my head slumped against his shoulder. All three of them were good liars, but not good enough.

Alix's room was exactly what I'd expected. There was a king-sized bed with more pillows than one person could handle and a carved wooden frame with plush, merlot velvet cushioning. There was a lot of floor room and a sunken lounge with two large couches, a centre table, and a tea set. A beautiful spiraling glass chandelier hung in the middle of the room, and opposite from where I stood at the entrance was a glass door. Its curtains were pulled back to showcase a large balcony that looked over the palace grounds. There was also a dressing table with a large mirror.

The room was spotless. Nothing was out of place.

"Why do I have to stay in your room?" I asked.

"It's here or the workers' quarters, where the chances of you getting exposed are high. I, on the other hand, already know your secret," Alix said.

"This palace is huge. I'm sure there is a spare room."

He walked into another room, and I heard running water. "Yes, there are. They are periodically checked by knights during the night."

"What are you doing?"

"Preparing a bath for you. You must be tired."

"Thanks," I said with suspicion. "You're acting...princely."

"I am a prince you know," Alix said coming out of the room with a smile. He hadn't stopped smiling since I said yes. It was starting to creep me out.

I rolled my eyes. "I guess it slipped my mind."

He chuckled. "I need to go. You can sleep on the bed tonight."

"I can sleep on the couch," I said.

He paused to look at me through narrowed eyes and drawn brows. "You will sleep on the bed. Don't fight me on this. I'll take the couch."

"But—"

"I need to go," he said, waving back at me. "I'm already late. Sleep well. On the bed."

I frowned at his departing figure. I turned to enter the bathroom but froze at the door. "It's huge." I swore I heard my echo. There was a large shower and pearl-white bathtub, two sinks that stood on black stone, and under the sinks were white cabinets, and above them was a huge, framed mirror. Between the bath and shower hung large and fluffy robes, and the marble floor had two large black rugs.

A fragrance, that was intoxicating and rich, hit me, like grapes mixed with lilacs. I took in a big whiff and sighed as my muscles melted.

I immediately stripped down and sank into the warm water. My whole body became putty under the warmth. All my doubts were a distant memory. I didn't know what Alix put in it, but I'd never felt more comfortable.

After soaking for a bit, I grabbed a bathrobe and wrapped a towel around my hair. I was about to walk out when I glimpsed myself in the mirror. I turned my head to get a good look. At least it didn't *look* like I'd lost my mind. I turned away from the mirror and pushed down the robe. My mark was still there, rosebuds surrounded by sharp thorns and vines, twisting with malice down my spine. What else was I expecting?

I walked out of the bathroom and almost jumped when Alix entered at the same time. "What are you doing here?" I asked through clenched teeth.

"Giving you something to wear," he said, patting the clothing in his hand. He put them on his bed. "Did you enjoy your bath?"

"Yeah, it was nice," I said, trying not to focus on how I wasn't wearing anything underneath the robe. "Weren't you late for something?"

"I am, but I had to take care of you first," he said.

"Great. Thanks. Bye."

"Don't tell me you're shy," Alix said with a sly grin. "Remember when I found out your secret? You were wearing even less."

I grabbed the towel off my head and threw it at him. "Get out!"

He dodged it and ran out, leaving a trail of laughter.

He'd brought me a pink and white, polka-dotted satin nightgown that reached below my knees. I glared at the gown and couldn't help but wonder where he'd gotten it.

I went down to the sinking lounge and plopped myself on the largest couch. It felt like a sack of cotton and feathers. I yawned, trying to stretch my mouth wider than it could go, and my eyes fluttered to a close.

What a day.

Chapter 17

Poker Face

I couldn't remember the last time I'd felt so comfortable or warm. I turned to my side, pulled the blanket further over my body and snuggled even deeper into the pillow. My lungs filled with the bitter-sweet smell of spring, and I sighed it out, letting the slight buzz of the morning carry me back into a deeper comfort.

Pillow? I didn't have a pillow when I fell asleep. My eyes fluttered open, and I found Alix climbing into bed. We locked stunned eyes, and he smiled. "Good morning."

"Wha—?"

I shot up and fumbled around, tangling my limbs in the blankets. My body tipped toward the edge. I gasped, bracing myself for the crash but Alix grabbed me and pulled me into his arms

"Careful," he said.

"Why am I in your bed?" I asked, flustered, pushing away from his freshly showered body.

"Because that's where you slept," he said.

"I fell asleep on the couch."

"You did, didn't you? Do you like not listening to me?"

"Yes, I do, but that's beside the point. Where did you sleep?" I asked.

"On the couch, but that's beside the point. Why did you fall asleep on the couch?"

Ignoring his question, I climbed out of bed, stretched my arms up, and clicked my joints back into place. "Why were you watching me sleep?"

"So, you're going to ignore my question?" he asked, slipping out of bed to stand beside me. He swept his gaze over me and smiled like he was satisfied.

I frowned. "Yes. Why were you watching me sleep?"

Alix shook his head and half rolled his eyes. "I wasn't. I was about to wake you up, but you woke up before I could. It was bad timing."

"Bad timing?"

"The worst," he said. "Ready for breakfast?"

I brightened at the offer. My stomach was empty. "I could eat," I said.

Alix grabbed a fuzzy hooded robe from the bed and draped it over my head. He took my hand and led me out onto the balcony. The air was crisp and chilled against my face. The palace grounds were vast, an ocean of green with grey stone paths that created a perfect symmetrical pattern. Trees and flowers dotted the landscape, and a large grey wall contained it all.

On the balcony there was a table set for two with a breakfast buffet. Half a dozen plates held a variety of colourful choices. I almost drooled. I'd been eating nothing but mush and fruit for weeks.

"Sit. Enjoy," he said.

I didn't hesitate. Before I even sat down, I had food in my hands. I didn't know what I was eating, but everything tasted so good. The salty, sweet, and tangy flavours mingled on my taste buds. It was euphoric.

Nothing had been more torturous than the bland food I'd been eating.

I was keenly aware of Alix's eyes watching me, he even went so far as to push the food closer to my side of the table.

"Slow down. There's plenty of food," Alix said, taking a bite of bread.

"Who knows when I'll get to eat like this again?" I said, standing to scoop a pastry from his plate. I smiled teasingly at him before biting down.

"All you have to do is ask, and I'll bring you to the palace to eat your fill," he said with a chuckle. "I was going to eat that by the way."

"Sorry." I laughed. "It's not like I'm ever coming back here again, so let me indulge."

Alix frowned. His shoulders slumped as he avoided my gaze. The hand he'd been eating with lowered to the table, like he'd lost his appetite.

I picked up the fruit he held and shoved it against his mouth. "Eat. You'll be crazy busy today, and I won't be held responsible if you faint."

He grabbed my wrist and ate the fruit out of my palm. "Hmm, it's very sweet."

"Don't you dare lick my fingers," I grumbled.

He released my wrist. "I wouldn't dream of it."

I continued eating. "So, what am I doing today?"

"For the first half, you'll be composing with me, after that Alle will give you the last of your treatment and then you can start your maid duties."

I almost choked. "My what?"

He grinned. "The Night Ball is tomorrow. I'm going to be busy, like you said."

"I bet you will. I also bet if you hadn't bothered me all those days, you'd be less busy," I said.

"You sound like Jenos."

"So, we're both right," I said with a grin.

Alix chuckled and shook his head. "Are you done?"

"Eating or teasing you?"

"Both."

I shrugged. "Sure. For now."

"Great," he said, jumping out of his seat. "Time to get your uniform."

I frowned. "My what?"

My uniform was a bright blue dress that flared out at my waist. It had long sleeves that ended in white cuffs and a white apron. The button-up collar was high and had a simple lace trimming around the neck. The fabric was light and easy to move in, yet discomfort was all I felt.

"I like this. You should become my maid for real" he said.

I looked down at myself and sighed in defeat.

"So, you didn't sneak out of the palace and go home?" Alle asked when we arrived.

We'd spent the whole morning composing, and I was about ready to call it a week. My hands were still cramping. We'd made so many changes the piece was almost unrecognizable. We couldn't agree on how to start or end the song, and the ball was tomorrow.

"Yup," I said, hopping on the cot. "You can add that to the list of my recent regrets."

"Always good to see you," Alix said, kissing Alle on the cheek.

Alle patted him on the shoulder and shoved him aside so she could get to the other side of the room. "That's because I've saved your life more times than you can count."

"You get saved quite a lot, huh?" I asked.

"I save more than I'm saved," he said.

"I've yet to see that," I said.

"Same here," Alle said.

"This is not a fair fight," Alix argued. "And aren't you supposed to be treating her?"

"You don't get to tell me how to do my job, prince or not. I'll remember this the next time you're dragged in here on death's door." Alle brought out three needles. "Lilly, the last treatment eats up a lot of energy. You're going to feel very weak after I give it to you. Do not overexert yourself or you will faint."

"No one told me about this," I said.

"It wouldn't matter anyway. You must get treatment," Alle said and poked one needle into my arm. "Now relax." She grabbed my wrist and poked the second needle and then the third. "There," she said.

I hopped off the bed, and my knees almost buckled under me. I grabbed the bed frame, rapidly blinking to straighten my vision. "Okay, wow."

"Take care of her," Alle ordered.

Alix gripped the side of my arms and pulled me a little closer. "I always will." He spoke so close to my ear, a shudder chased his words down my spine.

Alle paused and stared. She looked like she had something to say but chose to keep it to herself. She waved us off.

Alix led me out of the room, where Jenos was waiting. He stood like a soldier awaiting orders, but then Alix manoeuvred me into his arms like he was passing off a package. I blinked in confusion.

"Jenos will take care of you until I finish my more pressing duties."

"He will?"

"I will?"

Jenos and I looked at each other with mirroring levels of confusion. Alix chuckled and started walking away.

"Your kingdom is doomed," I said.

"It's hard to argue with you." Jenos paused and raised a brow. "You're dressed like a maid."

"Oh good, you see it too."

"I suppose he wants you to hide in plain sight." Jenos placed his hand over his mouth pensively and took a moment. "Okay, come with me."

He led me to the smallest room in the palace—the smallest I'd seen anyway. The floor was carpeted, with a single table at the centre and five chairs angled to face each other, each with its own smaller side table. A chandelier hung low over the heart of the room and the light from the window to the left shone on it, creating a sparkling array of shimmers. Paintings hung on the light blue walls, complementing the collection of vases and lamps standing on the many cabinets clinging to the corners.

"What is this room?" I asked.

"A tearoom." Jenos reached into a cabinet.

"*A* tearoom. So, there's more than one?" I said and walked past a table with three tea sets.

"Here," Jenos said, handing me a duster with a long shaft.

I took it and held it like a weapon, playfully jabbing him. He didn't look amused.

"You need to lighten up."

"Have you forgotten your position?" he asked.

I sighed and started dusting the chandelier with a pout. "No. I'm sorry, milord."

"Milord?" He almost sounded offended. "Not that position. Being in the palace is dangerous."

I paused. "I didn't know you cared."

He frowned. "Why are you taking this risk?"

"You're the ones that wouldn't take me home," I argued.

"But you could go home now. Your treatment is complete. There is no danger to your life anymore, not if you go home."

I stopped dusting and I looked him in the eye. He wasn't wrong, I knew he was right. I needed to go home, but I couldn't, or I didn't want to, not yet. "Tell me about the EverSnow Night," I said.

He stiffened and his brow twitched. "What about it?"

"It sounds like a regular thing."

"It's the annual celebration of the first snowfall and the last day of the War of Bloods," Jenos explained. "It's considered one of the most important days in history."

"Wait, does it start snowing here at the same time every year?" I asked. Jenos nodded. "Only in Tamikar?"

"Yes, it only snows in this kingdom," he said.

"So, it will snow tomorrow. Before, during, or after Alix's performance?"

"After. I imagine you two will open the dance floor as well," Jenos grumbled with a thick layer of distaste in his voice.

"I have to dance too?" I asked. "You have me composing, performing, and dusting. Now you want me to dance? I should demand payment at this point."

Jenos snorted but composed himself. I was worming my way into his heart. The more he liked me, the less likely it was he would change his mind and turn on me.

I put down the duster and grabbed his hands.

"What are you doing?" he asked, flustered.

"Dance with me," I said and pulled myself against him. "I would hate to make a fool of your dear prince."

"You just don't want to work," he said.

"That too. Now spin me," I demanded, and he did. I twirled on my toes, and he swung me back into an impromptu waltz. He danced me around the room, leading me into his pace. He knew exactly how to move without overwhelming me. He twirled without missing a beat, and our rhythm increased until finally he dipped me. When he pulled me back up, I hugged him.

I was already out of breath, lightheaded.

"You're wonderful," I breathed.

He pulled away from me and kissed my hand. "It was a pleasure, princess."

"You knights and your charm." I laughed, picking up the duster. "Did you and Alix learn to dance from the same person? Your styles are similar."

Jenos opened his mouth, then paused. "When did you two dance together?"

I laughed. "You are weirdly overprotective."

"He's the future king. The future of this kingdom. There is no such thing as being overprotective."

"You say that like he's the only heir. He has siblings. If something were to happen to him, the kingdom would continue, right?"

"It's not that simple," Jenos admitted.

I started dusting the chandelier. "It never is. Well, go on. Simplify it."

"His eldest brother gave up his right to the throne, and his sister left years ago and doesn't come home often." He did a poor job of hiding his disdain for Alix's sister's choice, but there was more under his tone, sadness maybe. "She left Alix alone to deal with running the kingdom. She was a prodigy, like Alix, and could've been the next queen, but she made her choice."

"I imagine being a royal is suffocating," I said.

"She made her choice," he repeated. "But Alix couldn't abandon his kingdom, and so he stayed. After training in Syver, even Crowns would take a few years to explore the world and grow as individuals, but Alix had to return and be groomed for greatness."

"Groomed for greatness," I mumbled.

"A lot happened, compromises had to be made," Jenos explained. "Ryalie was one of them."

"Oh, so that's how a former mercenary becomes a prince's knight. Emotional blackmail. Can't say it isn't effective."

"A lot of his past transgressions have been forgiven but things are changing. Decisions have been made." Jenos's lower lip stiffened, and his eyes softened. If I didn't know better, I would think he was looking at me with pity. "I don't think Alix will be easily forgiven for involving himself with you."

I put down the duster and looked down at the cream-coloured carpet. I'd convinced myself that it'd be fine since Alix was so confident, but I couldn't expect to rely on him, especially since he would be caught in the mess if it blew up in my face.

The door clicked open, and I froze.

Princess Aretia walked in with another lady by her side. It only took a second to recognize who she was. Alix was the male version of his mother. They had the exact same eyes, her brown hair was sharply cut at her shoulders and although her features were softer, they were equally well-sculpted. She wore a long sleeved grey and green dress that flowed to the ground. Compared to Aretia's extravagant red and black gown that was made up of lace and bows, Queen Miyra looked plain in comparison but somehow the simplicity of her clothes outlined her finely aged beauty. From the way she held herself to the confidence in each stride, I could see where Alix got many of his traits.

Jenos bowed. "My queen."

I followed suit and curtsied, lowering my head to avoid her gaze. I needed to sneak out.

"Jenos, it's always a pleasure. It's rare to not see you at my son's side," Alix's mother said. "And who is this?"

I stiffened. Jenos put his hand on my shoulder. "This is Alix's personal maid, the one that will be performing with him tomorrow night."

"Oh," Aretia gasped. "I met you before. So, you're a maid. I had the wrong impression before. It's lovely to meet you."

"I-I'm honoured," I stuttered, keeping my gaze down.

"Why are you with her, Jenos?" the queen asked.

"Alix asked if I would help her get accustomed to the palace," he answered. He squeezed my shoulder, and I started eyeing our escape route.

"We have other maids that could do that."

"Yes, but he's worried that she would be uncomfortable around strangers."

"How considerate," the queen murmured giving me an

assessing look that sent shivers through me. Her eyes were cold and stern, nothing like Alix's, yet I could see the Alix I first met in them.

"Yes. Now, if you would excuse us," he said and bowed again. I curtsied and walked to the door, my salvation.

"Before you go, tell me…" the queen started. "I never got your name."

I froze and glanced at Jenos. "Her name is Rosette," he said.

"Rosette, who taught you to play piano? You were wonderful yesterday."

"Uh…" I started but I was coming up blank.

"Rosette doesn't speak," Jenos said. "It's another reason Alix asked me to help her."

Great. Now I was mute.

"That's odd, I heard her speaking the other day," Aretia said. "And just now."

I shut my eyes, kicking myself.

"The severity of her condition is unstable," Jenos said.

The queen and Aretia looked at me, and I nodded, hoping my refusal to look them in the eye would be perceived as shyness instead of guilt.

"I see. My apologies," Aretia said.

I didn't know if she was sweet or gullible.

"Rosette, make us some tea," the queen ordered, taking a seat.

I looked up at Jenos for help. He interjected, "She's new and wouldn't know how to make the tea to your liking."

"Not to worry. I will show her," Aretia said and pulled me to the tea sets. "I've seen it done many times."

I mouthed the word "help" to Jenos, but he shrugged. It was out of his hands.

"Always use this set when serving the queen. I like it as well." Aretia started to make the tea. Her long, slim fingers poured a delicate amount of leaves into two small sieves laying over each teacup. While the water boiled over what looked like a slab of slate, she squeezed a round red fruit over the leaves and set the tray.

"I'm sorry for my behaviour yesterday," she said. "I thought you were something else to Alix, but I should have known you were a maid."

I knew she didn't mean anything by it, but it still came across as snide. She looked at me to gauge my response, and I smiled with a nod.

"The water should be ready," Jenos said, stepping in. He grabbed the pot off the slab and placed it on the tray and then took the tray and placed it on the table closest to the queen. I'd noticed her stealing glances at me since she walked into the room, and I couldn't help but feel as if my mark was somehow exposed.

"Always the perfect gentleman," Aretia said. "Snacks. We forgot about snacks."

"I'll be sure to tell a maid to bring some. For now, I should get Lil-*Rosette* back to Alix," Jenos said. He took my arm and led me out of the room. "Please excuse us." He offered a quick bow and closed the door.

We walked through the palace, quickening our pace, then stopped when we turned a corner. I took a sharp breath. The world was spinning underneath my feet.

I could no longer hold back my laughter. I snickered at him, pounding my fist against the wall, unable to contain myself. "Rosette? Unstable mute?" I asked between laughter. "Why were you so scared?"

"One of us had to be," he said.

"Oh, no, I was terrified. My poker face is just unbeatable," I said, trying to suppress my laughter.

"Poker face?" he asked.

"An unreadable facial expression," I explained. "Is it too late for you to take me home?"

"Yup!" Ryalie said, swinging around the corner, making both of us jump in surprise.

I looked at Jenos, feeling the weight of my decisions hit me with a new vengeance. "Take me home."

Ryalie grabbed my wrist and started dragging me away. "I'm taking you to Alix."

We zig-zagged through the palace, passing many curious gazes. Finally, Ryalie burst through a door.

"I found her," Ryalie announced and escorted me inside.

Alix sat at the opposite end of the room behind a large desk that looked like it had the world's supply of paper on it. Books lined the bookcase to my right, beside a bay window, and above my head was a simple chandelier. The floor was cold tile, but a thick carpet gave the room a hint of coziness. Between Alix and I, was a royal blue couch and a table with a tray of snacks.

I strolled in and sat on the couch, helping myself to the plate of cookies. "Oh, these are good. I've missed this."

"I admit, I was worried," Alix said. He looked past me, at Jenos. "How was it?"

"I've had a name change and now I'm mute," I said.

Alix jerked his head to the side and pulled his brows down. "What?"

"We crossed paths with the queen and Princess Aretia," Jenos explained.

Alix nodded in understanding. "What's your new name?"

I swallowed the cookie. "Rosette."

"Rosette," he repeated. "How are you feeling, Rosette?"

"Sluggish but fine," I answered. He eyed me and I smiled, biting down on more cookies.

"Ryalie, I've been meaning to ask. How have you been looking after Rosette's kiliabi?" Jenos asked.

"She's secured in the old stables, deep in the South Forest," Ryalie said. He sat next to me and took a share of the treats.

"Your palace has a forest?" I asked.

"It's a garden," Alix quickly corrected. "What about her food?"

"Food?" Ryalie asked.

"Yes, what are you feeding the kiliabi?"

Ryalie turned his gaze to me, searching for an answer. I shrugged. I called Blaze my pet, but it's not like I ever took care of her. She was more like a fast, self-sustaining motorbike with a heartbeat that I talked to on occasion.

There was a knock at the door, and the room fell silent. Alix cleared his throat. "Come in," he commanded.

A beefy young man with shocking blond hair and blue eyes

to match, opened the door. He walked with his chest out and wore a blue shirt one size too small. As soon as he took his first step into the room, he bowed. "My Legendary Lords, it is an honour."

"Rise, Kais. Your flattery will get you nothing," Alix said, standing from his chair.

"It's always worth a try," Kais said.

Ryalie and Jenos greeted him with firm, knowing nods. For a moment, I felt like an outsider looking in. It was so easy to forget that I didn't belong in their world.

Jenos grabbed Raylie, dragging him off the couch. "We would like to catch up, but Ryalie and I need to see to a hungry...pet."

"Pet?" Kais asked.

"Big pet," Ryalie said, barely holding back his laugh.

Jenos and Ryalie left the room, and I stared after them, dumbfounded. Did they forget about me? What was I supposed to do now? Alix and Kais were standing at my only exit.

I glanced back at the window and let the thought of escape cross my mind.

"And who is this?" Kais asked, walking towards me. "Is your maid unwell? Why is she sitting and eating?"

I jumped up and scurried to stand behind the couch. I'd forgotten how I appeared to other people.

Alix snickered. "This is my new personal attendant, Li— Rosette. She's new and unwell. We're close, which is why I give her so much freedom."

"You've always been soft," Kais said, eyeing me. "Can she

not speak for herself?"

"She's mute," Alix explained.

"Really? What caused the condition?"

"Family issues, going back generations." Alix's eyes were alight with laughter. I had to remember to kick him in the shin when we were alone again. He continued, "She'll be performing with me tomorrow."

"I look forward to that," Kais said and took a seat.

Alix joined him. "As you should."

"Make us tea," Kais ordered me. I was half-tempted to smack him over the head with the pot.

"The same for me, please," Alix said and smiled like a fox.

I had to remember to kick both his shins.

Biting my tongue, I walked to a table in the left corner of the room where the tea set sat like a decorative piece. I started making tea, mimicking what I saw the princess do, and even set the tray in the same way.

"This is a surprise," Alix murmured when he saw me coming.

I bent forward to put the tray down, but suddenly felt a hand slide up the back of my thigh. A sickening shiver jumped through my limbs, and I dropped to my knees, spilling the tea everywhere. I flinched as droplets of scolding hot water hit my skin. The adrenaline went straight to my head, and the room began to spin. The exhaustion I felt after having my treatment was hitting me with a new vigour.

"Are you alright?" Alix asked, pulling me up from the floor.

I nodded.

"Look at what you've done," Kais shouted. The hot water

soaked his shirt, and his arms were bright red.

My eyes widened and I felt Alix's hand tighten. He sat me down after giving me a once-over. "I'll get towels and call a healer. Stay here."

When the door clicked shut, I felt the full weight of Kais's glare. I wished Alix hadn't left me alone.

"I hope you play better than you serve," Kais grumbled and sat down in a huff.

Apologizing would've been the best course of action, but he'd made it difficult to feel any kind of remorse. Luckily, he thought I was mute, so I didn't have to say anything. If only he thought I was deaf too, so he wouldn't talk to me either.

"Help me remove this," he said, tugging at his shirt.

I stared at him, raising my brows like I hadn't heard him correctly because I couldn't have.

He tugged more aggressively at his shirt. "Come on. Your accident injured my hands."

If it were any other time and place, I would have punched him. But I wasn't in any condition to start a fight. I was in Alix's palace, and worse, I was pretending to be a maid, and Kais was somebody important. The odds of punching him and walking away weren't in my favour.

I shuffled closer to Kais and started to unbutton his shirt. My fingers fumbled, and I bit my lip to keep back the frustration. His shirt slipped off, but before I could shuffle back, he grabbed my wrists and squeezed. I bit back my scream.

"You may be useless, but you're pretty," he whispered in my ear.

My body stiffened before I started fighting to break his grip. He laughed and pulled me against his body. The more I struggled, kicking, and pushing, the heavier my heartbeat became and tighter my lungs felt in my chest. My muscles ached, and exhaustion clouded my head.

Kais chuckled. "You're not much of a fighter."

Before the scream building in my chest could burst out, he grabbed my face, and I felt his lips on mine. I bit down as hard as I could. He jumped up, hissing. His pale blue eyes glared down, and I glared right back.

I got onto my feet and tried to run for the door, but he snatched the back of my collar. I chocked as I fell forward, and the dress ripped. The sound was painfully audible in my ears, and the feeling it left made me shiver violently.

He stopped and started backing away from me.

I turned to find him wide-eyed and trembling. "You..." he started, but then the door swung open, and Alix walked through.

It took him a second to piece together what was happening. He rushed to my side, went down on his knees, and searched my face. He raised his hands as though to touch my cheeks, but they trembled, so he clenched them into fists.

"That girl! She...she's the *Renai*. She's..." Kais shouted. That's when I realized he had ripped the part of my clothes that hid my mark. It was my turn to be wide-eyed and trembling.

Alix rose and faced Kais with an expression I had never seen before. Now I could see the queen in him. He always looked smug, but I'd never seen him look down on someone. His lips were set in a firm frown, and his chin tilted upwards. His eyes were cold and distant, like Kais's existence was a mere nuisance.

"Keep silent," Alix commanded.

"But, she—"

"Do you want to stay in my good graces? Keep your mouth shut, or you and your family forfeit all you have."

Alix pulled me into his arms and carried me out of the room. He walked in complete silence, and I felt something I'd hoped to never feel again when I was around Alix—fear. It was like an instinct warning me that my life was in danger.

He took me to his room and placed me on the bed. I crawled to the centre and rested my head down on the plush sheets. And that's when he punched a wall. I was so shocked I sat up, shaken by his burst of anger.

He murmured something I couldn't hear and walked to the foot of the bed. His eyes were alight with rage. Then, right before my eyes, his face melted with grief, like something within him broke.

"I'm so sorry," Alix whispered, pushing two hands through his hair. "I'm such a fool, and he…he…" Alix looked at me through pained eyes and crawled onto the bed. "Lilly." He whispered my name like a plea. He stared in silence, then looked away in shame. "It's all my fault. I shouldn't have done this. Bringing—forcing—you into my world. I'm as bad as he is. I should have taken you home." He avoided my gaze. "I'm sorry."

Did he think I blamed him for this? I lifted my hand towards him with all my strength and touched his cheek. "It's okay, I'm okay."

His eyes widened and he put his hand over mine.

"He hurt you," Alix said. "Where?"

I showed him my wrists, tainted with Kais's fingerprints.

Alix glared at my wrists and took hold of them but let go like the act burned him. His eyes widened with panic, and he manoeuvred away from me.

"Alix…uhm…" Words tumbled in my head.

"I failed to protect you," he whispered.

"I'm fine," I said. My vision was getting cloudier. I couldn't keep my eyes open.

Alix climbed onto the bed and reached his hands out. The tip of his fingers reached my swollen lips. I looked up at him, and he snatched his hand away, pulling it into a tight fist. He shook his head as though to rid himself of a thought and turned away.

"I'll do better. I'll protect you," he said, but it sounded like he was saying it to himself.

My body hit the mattress, and I sighed out my last whisper of consciousness.

Chapter 18

Promise

W hen I opened my eyes, the morning light had flooded Alix's room and steam was wafting in from the bathroom.

I sat up and flinched at the sudden headache buzzing at my temples. Thirst ravaged my throat, and the room began to rock back and forth in a nauseating rhythm.

There was a knock at the door. I jumped to attention but calmed down once I saw Alle stroll into the room. She smiled at me when she reached the bed.

"You look terrible," she said.

"Thanks," I grumbled. "Can you help me look not-terrible?"

"No. That's all on you, but I can help you feel not-terrible," she said. She climbed onto the bed and pushed my head forward. It was so sudden I couldn't get a word in before she stuck a needle into the base of my skull and pulled me upright.

"Better?" she asked.

I rubbed my neck. The buzzing went silent, and the dizzying

rhythm my body had been twisting in ceased. "Yeah, better."

"Good. My work is done. Alix is in the ballroom waiting to practice the piece you'll be performing tonight."

"Tonight. The ball is…tonight." Reality was beginning to sink in. Memories of yesterday's events flashed in my mind like party lights.

"Are you having second thoughts?" Alle asked.

I sighed and rubbed my temple to stop my better judgment from screaming so loudly. "Second, third, and fourth thoughts."

"What happened yesterday?" she asked.

I searched her face to gauge how much she knew.

"You passed out and had a few marks on your skin. I know Alix would never do that to you, so who was it?"

"Do you know Kais?" I asked.

Alle made a face like she smelled something foul. "Kais Lancerez. He's like Jenos. He comes from a long line of knights, but unlike Jenos, his family isn't humble about it," she explained. "The Lancerez family is well known for trying to marry one of their own into the royal family."

"Are they trying to get Kais and Alix together?" I laughed.

Alle laughed too. "No, not that they didn't try, but Kais has a sister, Violitt"

"And Alix refused her?" I asked.

Alle shook her head and shuffled off the bed. "He refused to marry her, but he didn't refuse her. Charm isn't the only thing he uses his mouth for."

I rolled my eyes. "He'll kiss anyone, won't he?"

Alle paused and looked back. Her lips curled into a smile.

"He kissed you…"

"I didn't say that," I said quickly.

"Yes, you did. I said nothing about kissing," she said.

"It was implied," I said.

"Yes, you did imply it." There was no winning against her. "That explains why Alix has been daydreaming and mumbling to himself."

"Does he do that often?" I asked.

"When he's flustered, he doesn't have an inside voice," she explained.

"But he didn't kiss me," I said.

She smiled like she heard something juicy. "He didn't? Not even a little peck?"

I shook my head. "No."

Alle's eyes softened. Her lips tipped into a budding smirk. "You should kiss him," she said.

"No, never." I pushed the blankets off, jumped out the bed, and walked into the bathroom. "I'm going to do what I need to do and go home."

"Why? You don't want to kiss him?"

I didn't answer her. I couldn't say that the thought had never crossed my mind. I liked Alix, and I kind of wanted to know what all the fuss was about.

"Your silence is lovely," Alle said.

I frowned at my reflection and splashed water over my face. My head was in turmoil. Where did I even begin when I saw him?

Either way, this had to be my last day of freedom. After

tonight, I had to say goodbye to Alix for good.

There was a knock at the door when I'd finished changing into a new maid's uniform. Ryalie's head popped into the room. "What is taking so long? Alix is waiting for you."

"Okay, I'm coming." I walked up to the door, but Ryalie refused to open it wide enough for me to walk through. "I thought you said he's waiting."

He crossed his arms over his chest and gave me a scrutinizing gaze. "What did you do to him? He's been mumbling to himself."

"So, I've heard," I said. "And why do you assume it was me?"

"Wasn't it?" he asked. "It was you last time."

"Last time? I didn't do anything."

He glared with enough force to make it playful, then pushed me out the door by the shoulders. "You did something to him. Fix him."

"You're his babysitter—knight—whatever. You do it," I whined, trying unsuccessfully to shake him off.

We arrived at the ballroom. I stared at the doors. It was like they were beckoning me, tempting me—daring me to open them. I didn't want to run away. The exact opposite. I wanted to burst through the doors and perfect our piece. My desire to rush straight ahead scared me at times.

I stepped back into Ryalie. He was like a brick wall. He didn't flinch but stood steady, almost dependable. I rested some of my weight on him. "Do you think I'm making a mistake?" I asked.

He said nothing at first. When I looked back, he looked

comically confused, with pouted lips and a furrowed brow. He shrugged. "If you're having fun and you're happy, then it doesn't matter. Deal with the consequences after you've squeezed as much pleasure from it as possible."

"Is that what you did?" I asked. "When you left your family, I mean."

"Yeah. Turns out it wasn't a mistake," he said and walked away.

His simplicity was a comfort.

When I opened the door, I heard Alix slam the piano, releasing a barrage of jumbled notes.

"What did the piano ever do to you?" I asked.

He paused, startled by my entrance. "You're here."

"You called," I said.

Alix squirmed in his seat and avoided my gaze. He stared at the keys. His fingers hovered over them with uncertainty.

I sat down next to him and slammed my fingers onto the keys, making him jump. I caught his eye and smiled. This thing between us was never awkward before, it didn't need to be now.

"Shall we begin?"

He composed himself in seconds. "After you."

"Of course."

We played our piece for hours, pausing whenever a maid arrived with sustenance. We argued about what adjustments we wanted to make, from the pacing to the rhythm. Alix was surprisingly stubborn. We both kept hitting the wrong notes and then getting into frustrated grumble matches about it, not to mention our hands cramped up between practices

When we finally agreed on how to open the piece, everything flowed like breathing. For a moment, we forgot everything that was wrong while trying to fix something that wasn't even broken.

"I'm still not satisfied with the end," Alix said, whimsically skipping his fingers across the keys. "Thoughts?"

"How about a sudden end, as the song builds, we break into silence?" I suggested.

"Silence? Just end it out of nowhere?"

I nodded. He said this song was our story, so I couldn't imagine a more fitting end to the piece. There was no better way to end it. "Silence," I said with a final nod.

He frowned. "If that's what you want."

"Great," I said, standing up. "I'll leave you to your last-minute tasks."

He grabbed my wrists but released me, pulling his hand away like he'd been bitten by a viper. I turned to him questioningly.

"What makes you think I have last minute tasks?" he asked, avoiding the awkward exchange.

I followed suite. "Call it a hunch."

He cleared his throat and held out his hand. "May I?"

I placed my hand in his and he pressed his lips against it. My stomach clenched.

"I look forward to playing with you tonight, princess."

I took my hand back, ignoring how my skin tingled at the softness and heat that had made contact. Alix took a healthy step away from me, watching me closely.

"I'm not a princess," I said. He stared at me for a long minute.

"What?"

"I'm remembering the day you ran," he said. "Will I ever get you to stop running from me?"

"You need to stop chasing me for that to happen."

"Lil—" he started, but the sound of the doors opening interrupted him.

Jenos walked forward. "Alix, you still have many things to…" He paused. "Is something wrong?"

"No," I answered and escaped from Alix's reach. "I was telling Alix that I need to go home after the ball. I'm sure Cam and Este—" I gasped, sucking in air hard and fast as I remembered. "I can't perform tonight."

I was about to run out of the room, but Alix grabbed my arm before I could get far. "Where are you going? You can't disappear and miss the performance."

I pulled my arm out of his grip. "Oh, yes, I can. Cam and Estell are going to be here for the ball tonight. I don't know how I'll explain being missing for two days, let alone why I'm performing with a prince."

"Who are Cam and Estell?" Jenos asked.

"My caretakers," I explained.

"You have caretakers?"

"You will perform tonight. It should be fine as long as they don't know it's you, right?" Alix asked. "It's no problem."

"Since you have all the answers, how do I explain being missing for the past two days?" Something I'd avoided thinking about.

"I'll think of something," he assured me. "I promised I would protect you, remember?"

"I almost believe you," I whispered.

Alix flinched. "Take her to my room. I'll go see Alle, and then see about getting to my many duties."

"Your room? Alle?" I asked.

"*See* about getting to your duties?" Jenos asked.

"You two need to learn to trust me," he said. Jenos and I gave each other knowing looks of unease "Trust me," Alix insisted.

Jenos nudged me. I followed him out of the room and down the hallway. There was a moment of silent tension. A panic eased into my nerves, making my shoulder bunch up. Was this a mistake? Of course it was, I knew it was but…

There was no but.

"You and Alix looked close," Jenos said.

"You think so?" Nervous laughter escaped my lips. My shoulders slumped down and I groaned. "This was all a big mistake."

"Saving him or coming to the palace?"

"I was brought to the palace. I didn't come here," I corrected. "And the mistake was somewhere in the middle."

"You don't regret saving him?"

"No," I answered without hesitation. "I'll never regret that."

"Despite your current situation, you have no regrets?"

"Oh, I have regrets. Like not packing up and moving kingdoms the moment I saved him." I paused, the clicking of our steps against marble the only sound between us. I took a breath before I said, "My mom used to say, 'You should do what's right, not what's easy, so you have less regrets.' Saving him was the right thing to do."

Jenos stared at me. "You were raised to love and be loved, weren't you?" he said like a confession.

"You didn't expect that from a monster, did you?"

Jenos clenched his jaw and tipped his chin up. "Knowing you has contradicted everything I knew before. I struggle to make peace with what I believed and what I know now. It's still…difficult."

"Must be tough," I said.

"Ryalie adjusted well," Jenos said. "Alix adjusted too well… What is happening between you two?"

"I don't even want to think about it," I said.

We reached Alix's room, and Jenos opened the door for me. I walked in and collapsed on the nearest couch, pushing down all my anxiety. I'd stored it all in the back of my mind, but I felt seconds away from a breakdown. What was I going to tell Cam?

I groaned into a pillow and flipped onto my back. Jenos stood by my feet, looking down at me and I frowned back at him. "There is nothing going on," I insisted.

"Are you sure?"

I jumped up. "No, I'm not. This is why you should have taken me home when I said so, but you had to listen to Alix."

"You decided to stay," he argued.

"Yes, and why did you let me?"

Jenos sighed in exasperation and collapsed onto the couch with all his weight. He slumped back in surrender. "Alix wanted you to stay. It's always been hard to say no to him."

I patted his shoulders. "You've had it rough too."

He looked at me and laughed like something in him cracked.

I smiled. "You need to do me a favour and promise me you will."

"Depends on what you ask."

I meet his dark brown eyes, solid and attentive. "After the ball, when Alix finally takes me home, keep him away from me. No matter what, do your job and keep him away from danger."

"I thought you said you're not dangerous," he said.

"Oh, now you believe me," I said. "I'm not. But Alix is dangerous to me. He's starting to get under my skin, and it scares me."

"It sounds like I'm protecting you," he said.

I gave him a tight smile. "It's better this way."

Jenos searched my face. "What happened?"

I shook my head. "You need to keep him away from me."

"I can't—"

"You have to. You know what I am and who he is. It's too risky," I said. "You only have to do it for a year, less than that. I'll be gone by then, and you'll never see me again."

The blood drained from his face. "What?"

"Please, Jenos. Promise me," I begged.

He hesitated. "Alright."

The door clicked open. Alix walked in with Alle close behind. She had a box in her arms and was smiling like she'd just gotten a promotion. The way she smiled rounded her face and made her look years younger, especially with the dimples.

"Jenos, you're still here?" Alix asked. "Come and assist me. We only have a few hours."

I squeezed Jenos's hand, and he gave me one last glance before walking to Alix's side.

"What's happening?" I asked.

"Alle is here to change your appearance, so you can perform tonight," Alix said with a reassuring nod in my direction.

"Excuse me?" I asked, not at all reassured.

Alle walked up to me and grabbed my chin, lifting it. She smirked down at me. Her eyes twinkled with a mischievous glee that made me want to run and hide.

"You're in the best hands," she said.

"Your dress should come later tonight," Alix said and walked out with Jenos before I could ask any more questions.

Alle started taking out small cylinders and thin paintbrushes, along with an assortment of velvety cases. She lined them up on the table with precision and knelt in front of me. "How are you feeling?" she asked like a nurse.

"Better," I said with a nod. Now that I'd made that deal with Jenos, I felt a sense of security. I couldn't be sure he would do what I asked, but knowing I was bound to leave Glorus must have been some motivation. If he listened to me, this was my last night of freedom before I returned to my birdcage. There was nothing I could do but squeeze out as much pleasure as I could from it, as Ryalie put it.

I closed my eyes to let Alle start working and replayed the last couple of days in my mind. I had to find the courage to say goodbye.

I'd looked in the mirror so many times that I never thought twice about my appearance. Since I'd gotten my mark, I took a few more seconds than usual to linger. But after Alle finished my disguise and I put on my dress; I couldn't stop staring. It was me, but not the me I'd seen before.

The royal blue, silver laced halter gown began at my neck with a cluster of blue gems that separated into five lines flowing down to the sweet-heart neckline. From the centre of my waist, a deep blue cascade of silk began with layers of silver lace on the sides.

I pressed my fingers against the mirror to get a closer look at my new image. Alle used eye drops to change the colour of my eyes so that the only trace of green was closest to my pupil. My red hair had a layer of a gel-like substance that defined my curls and turned my hair black. The gel was something Ryalie apparently concocted which explained his hair. Alle had pinned my hair up high with silver ornaments that dripped down like falling stars. She also painted the skin around my eyes black and stuck on several gems of different sizes and shapes to create a spiralling mask that hugged my cheekbones and framed my eyes.

There was no way Cam and Estell would recognize me. I couldn't recognize me.

Alle smiled at her work. "You may be my masterpiece."

"I'm going to stick out looking like this," I said, moving my freckle-less face back and forth in the mirror.

"Exactly, no one would suspect you're trying to hide," she said.

"You're amazing," I said, still unable to look away from my reflection.

"I can't take all the credit," she admitted. "Alix chose everything."

"Alix? Everything?" I failed to hide my surprise.

"He has good taste. He even found a dress to hide your mark." I turned to confirm her words. She was right. There was no sign of it.

"If that's all, I'll take my leave." she opened the door in time for Ryalie to come strolling into the room.

Ryalie's shiny black shoes squeaked to a halt. He wore black pants folded up at his ankles, and a crisp white shirt with thin black stripes that hung past his hips, and a sharp silver necklace. The coat he wore on top had silver patterns on the lapels and cuffs. His hair was now a silvery white and pushed back, giving him a more mature look.

It took him a second to take in me in, but then he smiled. "This is going to be fun."

I shook my head, laughing under my breath. I had to agree.

Jenos strolled into the room next in a pressed, deep black, three-piece suit. A red waistcoat hugged his torso, and his silver embroidered blazer held his frame to perfection, hanging loose at his thighs. There wasn't half an inch of him out of place. Even his Eldridge tie knot was perfectly assembled. His usually tied hair was loose, and his curls were fluffed to one side of his face.

Somewhere in the world, a magazine was missing its model.

"Are you ready?" Jenos asked me.

"What do you think?" I asked, twirling to give a three-sixty-degree show, almost entangling my legs in the process.

"Alix has excellent taste," Jenos said and offered me his hand. I took it and he kissed the back. "And yes, the dress is wonderful too."

I laughed and hooked our arms. "Oh, you flirt."

Ryalie trotted to my other side and hooked his arm with mine.

They led me through the palace: down a corridor I'd never been before. With every step I took, I heard my heartbeat steadily get louder in my ears. My legs moved me forward as though I belonged. It was a ten-minute walk to the double tinted glass doors.

We paused and I stared at the faint lights on the other side.

"Are you ready?" Jenos asked.

"No," I said. "Open the doors."

Ryalie peeled himself away and threw the doors open. I stepped forward without letting myself take a second to rethink my decision. My better judgement told me to run away, but everything else pushed me into the light. The cool breeze was the first thing to hit me, and then the dozens of lights twirling like stars.

"Welcome to the East gardens," Jenos said.

We walked down a column-lined stone walkway. Each column dripped with tiny blue gems, which hung on a string so thin that they were almost invisible. Many paths crossed and diverged from each other through patches of grass and flowers, while small trees dotted the area like soldiers. The trees had no leaves, and instead, naked branches reached for the sky, holding many tiny lights. The stage stood at the centre of the garden, with a grand piano, identical to the one in the ballroom.

People filled the wide, open grounds. There were rows upon rows of tables stacked with food. The chatter became more audible the closer we got to the party, but they quieted down and stared at me when I walked past.

My heartbeat was deafening.

"We have to wait for the sun to set," Jenos said.

I peeked at the last dying embers of daylight. "What happens when the sun sets?"

"The young Crown of Tamikar makes his entrance," Ryalie said.

Jenos handed me a glass of something clear and bubbly, which I couldn't taste, no matter how many sips I took. I couldn't stop glancing at the sun like a count down.

As the light faded, more people arrived, talking amongst themselves, the anticipation building. Jenos and Ryalie were talking, and although I chimed in occasionally, I stole glimpses at the full moon that was forming in the distant skies. Stars dotted the heavens, clustering together and growing across the horizon. The darker the sun's light turned, the more vibrant the East gardens became.

Jenos looked to the pathway we'd walked down. My eyes followed, waiting. My blood rushed in my veins as I searched for his face. Then it went silent.

Chapter 19

Ever Fall! Ever Rise!

A man walked forward and bowed to the guests. When he straightened his back, he swept his eyes across the crowd then announced: "His Royal Highness, Prince Alixios de Valor."

Alix sauntered into the gardens on cue and, immediately, our eyes met. My breath caught. He smiled, coming my way despite the many guests staring at him in anticipation. His eyes never left mine, and I couldn't look away. He wore a deep, navy-blue suit with a long jacket that adorned him like a cape. His pants were tucked into a pair of black boots, and the vest he wore was a dark, shimmery grey, contrasting the bright white ascot around his high-collared neck. His dark hair was mostly pushed back with a few strands falling loose, pulling focus to his jeweled blue eyes.

He looked princely, true to his title.

Ryalie and Jenos bowed to Alix. I awkwardly followed suit with a quick curtsy.

Alix's smile turned to a grin, and my chest tightened.

"Are you ready?" he asked

I held my hand out, not trusting my voice. He took it, leading me through the crowd, which parted like curtains, towards the piano.

"Are you sure you're not going to regret this?" I whispered.

"Never," he whispered back.

Alix guided me to my seat, and I spread my fingers across the keys. My heart was a jackhammer against my chest. He faced the audience, and I peeked at him. There wasn't even a hint of tension on his face, let alone his body. It was too easy for me to forget who he was, but I realized it again, that this was his element. He was a prince, and seeing how the people stared up at him, willing to listen, they adored him.

"Good evening," Alix greeted. "On this glorious day, my talented partner and I shall perform a new piece: *Flowers for your curse*."

I held back a smile and shook my head.

Alix sat down next to me. I'd played for audiences before, but this was different, everything was different. But as with any other performance, after the first note, everything would fall into place, and my fear would melt away.

It began like raindrops falling into a pond, hitting the water, rippling out one after the other. Slow and almost sad. Lonely even. There was a hint of hesitation before the tempo picked up by half a beat. I repeated the first few notes twice. Then Alix came in like a playful sprite in the forest, chasing the raindrops. It went on like this, with Alix playing after me, his footsteps over mine.

We glanced at each other.

The sound changed. Alix took the lead, playing whimsical high notes. There was a pause for a beat, then he continued. I followed onto his second note but stopped abruptly, while he continued alone. The opening of our piece was like chasing elusive winds, as delicate as snowflakes blown past the horizon. Our sounds collided with one another in a dizzying waltz up and down the scales, with a powerful melody that spread a smile across my face. Alix stopped playing, and I hit a solo that challenged his previous whimsical sound, spinning circles around him with the keys before descending back into the slow raindrops. Without pause, we both broke into a harmony of sounds.

Then my sound faded out, melting away from his. I waited for the sudden end.

But he continued.

My hands froze as the piece proceeded, as though starting a new chapter to the symphony of child's lullaby, gentle with a hint of playful hops. I closed my eyes to take in the music with a steady breath in my lungs. An unfamiliar sound that made my heart clench in anticipation.

He took my hand in his and played the final note with his finger on top of mine. The sound vibrated through my body like a promise.

I looked to see him lift my hand and kiss my finger.

"It's only right we do it together," he whispered.

The audience erupted into cheers and applause. I almost

jumped out of my skin in surprise. I'd forgotten they were there. Alix stood and pulled me with him all the way to the edge of the stage. He lifted his right hand and raised his head with a bright smile glazed across his face. I followed his gaze and saw the queen on a balcony above. My back instinctively became stiffer, and my heart almost stopped when I realized the man next to her was Alix's father, the king. I felt Alix tug my arm as he began to bow, and I melted into a nervous curtsy, dropping my head low.

Alix released my hand and presented me to the crowd, clapping along with them. I stood stunned, unsure what to do. The audience looked up at me, their applause resounding for me. Their cheers were like rushing water, deafening and continuous. I stared in disbelief, then straightened up, lifting my chin with pride.

I had to take it all in. After tonight, I would be back in the forest, isolated, hiding away like a scared beast. But tonight, for a moment, I was in the spotlight in front of the same people who would persecute me at a drop of a hat, and they weren't looking at me like I was a monster.

I turned to Alix and mouthed, "Thank you."

Alix offered me his arm. I took it and we walked down, melding into the crowd. Ryalie was the first to come up to us, grabbing me in a bear hug.

"Ryalie," I whined breathlessly, patting his back in surrender.

"You were great," he said, squeezing me before letting go.

Jenos nodded. "It was an honour to hear you play."

Joy swelled up in me. I smiled, unable to put my appreciation into words.

My smile faded and I straightened up when I glimpsed Alix's parents walking toward us. We all bowed to them. I struggled to keep calm.

"A brilliant performance, son," the king said. "It reminded me of when you would play with my mother."

"Thank you," Alix said with a nod. "This is...Rosette, my partner. She deserves a lot of the credit for tonight's performance. Rosette, King Alpan and Queen Miyra"

I peeked up at the king, and his sharp brown eyes softened towards me. His hair and beard were salt and pepper against his tanned skin, which wrinkled around his eyes when he smiled. His body language was stern, and he held himself like Alix and the queen, with an air of importance.

"It's a pleasure," he said. "You have my thanks for helping my son."

I nodded.

"Rosette is an unstable mute, dear," the queen explained. "Though, she looks very different from the last time I saw her."

"Yes, she wanted to hide her identity. She'd rather keep from drawing too much attention after tonight," Alix explained.

"I see," the queen said. There was a hint of suspicion in her tone, but she didn't press the matter any further. "Enjoy the ball to your heart's content. You've earned it."

Alix bowed. "Thank you."

They walked away and I released a breath of relief.

"She's right. Your performance was spectacular."

We all turned to find Alle standing behind us, wearing a pure white dress that hugged her curves and flared out at her knees. The top half had a layer of silver lace, and half a cape hung across her right shoulder. Beside her, Shechire stood wearing a simple black dress but an extravagant amount of red jewellery. Her black hair was even spikier than I remembered, and her pale skin glowed in the lights of the garden.

"That was certainly a good show," Shechire said. Her obsidian eyes held mine. She smiled. "Good to see you're still the same."

"Did my aura tell you that?" I asked.

She half shrugged. "You never did tell me who you are."

"I have to keep a few things to myself," I said with a grin. "How are you?"

"Fine." She nodded. "Better."

The stage began to fill up with performers and instruments. Music filled the night air and the energy in the garden shifted. I smiled as the enchanted symphony played on my muscles, itching for me to move along to the sound.

"May I?" Alix asked, offering me his hand.

"I don't think—"

He took my hand and led me to the dance floor, where we stepped into each other's arms and swayed to the music.

"You don't play fair," I said.

He chuckled, sweeping me across the dancefloor. "I can't play fair with you."

He was right. I didn't play fair either.

"Thank you for doing this," he said. "I promise after today, I won't be so pushy."

After today, I didn't plan on seeing him ever again. I squeezed the hand that held mine, pushing down the longing in my lungs. "You'd better keep that promise."

Alix dipped me, swinging my body in a crescent, then pulled me close against his chest. I couldn't count how many times I'd clung to him. I didn't know when I'd became so comfortable in his arms, when it had started to feel easy. Every moment spent with him was getting more dangerous.

I had to get away.

"What are you thinking about?" he whispered.

"I'm thinking how lucky you were to have met me," I said with a teasing grin.

"Me? What about you? I'm the one who saved you from a life of boredom, brought you to the palace, fed you the best food, and even made you the star of the ball. I gave you a dress worthy of a princess—no, a queen—introduced you to life-long friends, and even kept your secret."

I smiled up at him. I couldn't help it.

His eyes softened and he kissed my forehead. "I'm the luckiest man in the world," he murmured

Ryalie suddenly appeared behind Alix and tapped his shoulder. "I'll take it from here."

"She's my dance partner. Find your own," Alix said.

"No." Ryalie grabbed him. "*Your* dance partner is waiting for you."

We followed Ryalie's gaze to find Aretia staring at us. I couldn't make out her expression. She looked neither upset nor happy. She looked on like the saint of patience, like even if it took all night, she would wait there for Alix to come to her.

"Well, that's not creepy," I murmured and pushed Alix away. "Go make her stop."

"But—"

"Go," I commanded and stepped into Ryalie's arms. "I'll be fine."

Alix hesitated, then sauntered to the other side of the garden. Ryalie looked down at me with unease, his new hair shimmering in the light. It was a nice colour on him.

I lifted a brow, and he nodded. "Be gentle with me."

I snorted. "Let's go eat."

We walked to the tables of food, and my eyes lit up in anticipation. I didn't hesitate and started sampling everything that crossed my eye. Sweet, savoury, spicy, there was every flavour my heart yearned for.

You're going get sick," Ryalie said, but his cheeks were just as stuffed as mine, making his words muffled.

"Let's see who gets sick first," I challenged.

"Are you two incapable of dignity?" Jenos asked, coming up from behind us. Alle was at his side.

I swallowed the food and shook my head. "Don't talk to me about dignity when all I've eaten is mush for months. Who knows when I'll eat like this again?"

"I'll sneak you into the kitchens next time you visit," Ryalie said.

I met Jenos's gaze, which flinched with uneasiness. I'd thought he'd be pleased with our deal—relieved, even—but he looked hesitant. I was hesitant too, but I couldn't let that part of me win. Not this time.

"What kingdom is Princess Aretia from?" I asked.

"Revena, the kingdom to the West," Jenos said. "She's the youngest of three, like Alix. I'm sure her siblings are somewhere."

"Other Crowns are here?" I asked.

"I'm sure Alix is with them. Peace doesn't maintain itself," Alle said with a slightly condescending tone.

"How have you maintained peace for so long? I mean, it's one thing to say you won't fight, but it's another to commit," I said. "Was the War of Bloods really the last war?"

"It was," Jenos said. "It was so devastating that the Glories forbade war. Any kingdom that incites war will be stripped of its title and will be brought to ruins. That's what happened to the kingdom of Halibel. They tried to incite war after their queen was…lost."

"What?" I hadn't heard anything like that before. All I knew was that the kingdom of Halibel no longer existed as punishment for what La-Muse did, but that had only been an assumption. "So that's what happened."

"Without war, all that was left was cooperation," Alle said. "No matter what the issue is, kingdoms have no choice but to sit down and talk until an agreement is reached."

"Wow, you cracked the code on world peace," I said. "Doesn't anyone complain that it's a little tyrannical?"

Alle laughed. "War can be tempting, I suppose, but everyone remembers. The scars are still there. The lives lost to bloodshed and plagues. Decades upon decades later, and we're still trying to heal."

The War of Bloods had always been just a story to me. It played a part in my family history, but it was a world away from my reality, not so different to a fairy-tale. I was only interested in the aftermath, the fall of my ancestor that'd burned the curse into my blood. But La-Muse had lived through the war and suffered the loss of her family. Was the War of Blood's the true beginning of everything? Was there more to my fairy-tale?

"Enough talk about war," Ryalie said, shoving more food towards me. "This is a ball for peace and fun."

Alle snagged a bite and smiled. "To peace."

The ball was a spectacle of light and music. There wasn't a moment I wasn't dancing or eating. Ryalie eventually danced with me, but he was as lively on the dance floor as he was with everything else. He moved me with wild abandon that was elegant in its own way.

Several guests came up to me to introduce themselves and congratulate me on a successful performance. I bowed and smiled so much my neck and cheeks were beginning to ache. Thankfully Jenos explained that I was mute which made the interactions brief.

My heart hadn't slowed for a second. The world was brighter in every way.

"Are you having fun?" Alix asked, offering me a drink.

I took a sip of the minty sweetness and nodded. "I am."

He smiled and his hand reached for mine, but then someone cleared their throat. We jumped and faced Cam and Estell.

I froze.

They were both dressed formally, Estell in a champagne satin dress and Cam in a simple black suit. He always looked clean and proper, but there was something off about him. His usual statue-like face had a few cracks. He looked sad, like there was a heaviness on his chest and it kept him up at night.

"Your Highness, we wanted to greet you before we go," Estell said. Her speech was reserved. It didn't even sound like her.

"Already? Before the first fall?" Alix asked. I saw him glance at Cam. He must have recognized him. I hoped neither of them recognized me.

"It can't be helped, I promised to make an appearance, but I must get him home."

"I believe we've met," Alix said. "In the forest."

"Yes, my prince." Cam bowed. "It's good to see you in good health."

"Thanks to that young woman...what was her name?"

I resisted the urge to glare at Alix. Why was he making light conversation about me?

"Lillianett," Cam said.

"Yes, her. How is she?" he asked.

"The prince has met Lilly?" Estell asked.

"Yes, she saved my life. I'm indebted to her. I only hope that one day I can repay her kindness."

"That is benevolent of you, but I am afraid she is not with me at the moment," Cam said. "She's been gone for a few days now."

I felt a sting of guilt pierce my chest. I couldn't look him in the eye. I wanted to walk away. Better yet, I wanted to tell him it was me and live with the consequences.

"She's a capable girl. I'm sure there's no need to worry," Alix said.

"You may be right, but it was my duty to watch over her, and I failed. How shall I face her family?"

"She's fine," Estell said, rubbing his arm. "You worry too much. She'll come home soon."

I peeked up at Cam and found him staring at me. I flinched, praying he didn't see past the disguise. "My apologies. I failed to greet you," he said and bowed his head. "Your performance was beautiful."

My mouth twitched, wanting to thank him, but I held my tongue.

"Rosette doesn't speak," Alix said. "But thank you."

Cam nodded. "Lillianett often played the piano."

I grimaced. I messed up. I shouldn't have disappeared without a word. I should have gone home the moment I woke up.

"I swear on my title you will hear her play again," Alix said.

I looked up at him. He looked serious.

Estell and Cam stared at him with confusion. I couldn't blame them. That was a strange thing to promise since they thought he had no power to promise that.

"Thank you," Estell said. "We will take our leave."

"Thank you for your time," Cam said and took one last glance at me, lingering. I broke away from his searching eyes. I couldn't face him. I still didn't know what I was going to tell him when I got back.

When they were out of sight, I grabbed Alix. "You promised,"

I said. "You'll take me home."

Alix didn't say anything. Instead, he took my hand and led me through the crowd to stand with Ryalie, Jenos, and Alle who handed us drinks.

"What is it?" I asked, but then the king walked up to the edge of the stage with his own drink in hand. The garden lulled into silence.

"We will never and must never forget the War of Bloods, which ravaged this world for a decade. It was the decade of broken lives and shattered hearts. A stain on every kingdom. Today we honour the end of that war, the day the people raised their arms for mercy and snow fell like an answered prayer," he said. "And every year, snow falls on the same day to remind us of our peace and remind us of our promise. Never again."

"You didn't know about that, did you?" Alix whispered to me.

I shook my head. "What started the war?"

"What starts every war? Greed." he answered.

The king raised his glass, and the crowd mimicked the action. "To the first snow, the first fall, and the ever-rising peace of the four kingdoms."

"Ever fall! Ever rise!" the crowd shouted together in harmony.

On cue, snow began to fall. I arched my head back in disbelief to see snowflakes hover down, one by one, like angel feathers. I'd seen snow dozens of times, but this was different. There was something magical about it, like the snow was glitter dust.

"This is the end of the night," I said. My chest was tight. I didn't want it to end, but I needed it to.

Forever was never an option.

"It is," Alix said. "It ends as it did all those years ago."

"Thank you," I whispered. "It's so beautiful."

He placed his hand on my cheek and looked into my eyes. "It was my pleasure. If you ever want anything, just ask."

I took his hand in mine and bit my lip, hating the words I was about to say. "Take me home, please."

His smile dropped and the tenderness in his eyes became pained. He tried to smile but ultimately failed. "Of course," he said.

This was for the best.

When Alix stepped into his room. He could hear running water from his bathroom. Lilly was still removing Alle's artwork. He hadn't expected Alle to be so extravagant with the disguise, but he'd still spotted her the moment he walked into the garden. Everyone else melted away into blurs of muffled voices and distant figures. When she'd stood in front of him, in that dress that looked like it was made of starlight and the night sky, even Jenos and Ryalie had disappeared. She was all he could see. All he wanted to see.

Lilly stepped out of the bathroom and Alix leaned against his door, clicking it shut. He didn't know what it was about her that made him want to hold his breath. She sauntered forward with a bounce in her step; the pleasures of the ball made her glow. Her thick, damp red hair bounced along with her, and her skin was cool against the moonlight. She walked up to him and grinned from ear to ear, and his heart jumped into his throat.

"Ready to take me home?" she asked, gesturing at the closed door.

He started. "Tonight?"

"Yes, tonight. As soon as possible," she said, trying to reach around him for the knob.

He took her hand manoeuvred her away from the door, careful to make his touch gentle. He pulled her along and she followed with furrowed brow and pouted lips. Alix wanted to laugh at her or maybe kiss her. He wasn't used to not knowing what to do. She had that effect on him,3 his maddening princess.

"You must be tired. Why not rest for the night?" he asked.

"I'm not tired. I'm fine," she insisted and pulled against him to make him halt.

"In that case—" he swept her into his arms and started dancing her across his room "—why don't we take this time to finish our dance."

By the time she got her bearings, she was moving in time with him. Alix guided her around the room with ease, and she followed along like they'd danced dozens of times before and not just twice. He smiled down at her, and she looked up into his eyes. Her eyes hadn't quite returned to their original colour, they were still mostly brown, but the green was beginning to show through.

Her eyes were the first thing he'd seen when he started to regain consciousness the day she saved his life. He remembered thinking how bright they were. Now, they shined up at him with a joy he'd longed to see. He would give so much of himself to see them like that every day.

"Alix" she said and placed her feet firmly on the ground.

He hesitated. He knew that look. "Tired already, princess?" he teased, hoping she couldn't hear the trepidation in his voice.

"I like dancing with you," she whispered, "but we can't dance forever."

"Then let's talk," he said and pulled her to the couch. He took her hand and kissed her knuckles. She was so warm, and her hands were rough yet delicate within his.

"Talk about what?" she asked in exasperation.

"Talk about you. Your childhood," he said. He saw a flash of pain cross her face, with anger in her eyes, but it quickly faded.

"My childhood…was normal," she admitted.

Alix wanted to pull her into his arms and ask her why she made that face. He knew there had to be a reason she was so strong against the hatred shown towards her. Had she had to learn to be strong? Was he just like everyone else that had hurt her?

"Tell me about your parents, your friends, your home, your world, the things you miss, the things you love about this world, the things you want to see. I'll make it happen. I can give you so much, show you so much. Just tell me about yourself. Tell me…tell me…" his babbling trailed off as he looked into her eyes that held no small amount of sadness. His heart deflated and he pressed the hands he held to his face. Her fingertips were cool against his skin "Tell me you'll stay with me a little longer. Please." Had he ever begged anyone like this?

"We need to talk."

Alix's head snapped up and he felt the last remnants of air squeeze out of him.

She continued, "It's not that I don't want to stay with you—"

"You want this too," he breathed. He felt alive again. There was hope, a sliver of a chance that she wouldn't run from him.

She sprang to her feet. "Stop hearing what you want to hear."

He flinched.

Lilly forced air out of her lungs in a long exhale. "This isn't right. You should be begging me to leave. You should want nothing to do with me."

Alix wanted to laugh bitterly at the thought. He wanted everything to do with her. He brought her into his palace—his home—the heart of the kingdom. The queen would have his head if she ever found out. But Lilly had already become a part of his life. Ryalie adored her, Jenos respected her, and Alle approved of her. And Alix—Alix could barely let a moment go by without thinking about her. His past self would say he'd lost his mind. There was so much he needed to do and even more he needed to be.

Alix stood up and lightly caressed his thumb over her freckled cheek. He'd thought before how he would love to kiss her freckles; they made her so beautiful. Everything about her was beautiful.

"Stay with me," he said. *Not just for tonight, maybe not forever, but for a little while longer.*

Her voice trembled when she said, "Shouldn't you be seducing a princess, like Aretia?"

"You are a princess," he said and slid his hand down her arm until he found her fingers.

"I'm a *Renai,* princess of a ruined kingdom. I don't count."

"I will never deny your crown." He went down on one knee and pressed her knuckles to his lips. "You're my princess."

It was becoming harder to breathe. Alix offered me everything I wanted. I could stay hidden and still experience the world.

I stared down at him, unable to form thoughts as he looked up at me with those sparkling blue eyes. I pressed my hand against his face. He was so warm, and his eyes widened, shinning even brighter.

He kissed the inside of my hand. "Lilly," he breathed my name like a promise.

I swallowed. Ryalie's words came to mind, and I hardened my resolve. I was going to squeeze as much fun from being out of my birdcage as I could.

Before I could stop myself, I went down to my knees and pressed my palms against his sharp jawline. I leaned into him and pushed my fingers into his soft hair. My eyes flickered up, and I pressed my lips against his.

For a second he didn't react. Then he kissed me back. Electricity hit my body in waves, and heat rushed through my veins like wildfire. My mind went blank, and my body moved on its own. My hands searched his broad back and slid over his chest. There were no thoughts in my head, just the sensations, the way his skin felt against mine, and how our laboured breathing mingled together. He tasted intoxicatingly sweet and addictive.

Alix wrapped his arm around my waist and pulled me against his fevered body. His hand pressed against my back, tracing my spine, chasing my shivers. The sensation spread through my body in static tingles. I pulled away, catching my breath. He grabbed my arms and tugged me like he was afraid I would run away. We searched each other's eyes. I wasn't sure what I was looking for, but I clearly saw his desire. He pulled me in closer and kissed my collarbone, then slowly made his way up my neck.

"Stay with me," he breathed while he pressed his lips against my jawbone, just below my ear. My body tightened and melted all at once.

His raspy voice and the feeling of his hot breath against my skin made me shiver. My mind was going blank. I couldn't win against the way he touched me.

I didn't want to.

Chapter 20

Did You Know?

My eyes fluttered as I dug myself deeper into the plush blankets and closer to the warmth in front of me. The sweetness I felt spread through my body was like warm honey and I never wanted to part from it.

knuckles softly caressed my cheek, and my eyes shot open.

Alix's lips stretched into a wide grin and his eyes softened.

"Your face is creeping me out," I grumbled.

He chuckled and continued to stroke my face with his knuckle. "What a rude thing to say about the face of the happiest man in the world," he said in a whisper.

"Happiest man," I scoffed. I tried to sit up, but he pulled me down and hovered, entrapping me between his arms.

"How about you spend one more day with me?"

"One day becomes two," I murmured. "Two days becomes a week, and a week becomes forever."

"Sounds great," he said and gave me two pecks on the lips. "Let's do that."

"We can't." I pushed him back so that I could sit up. "I need to leave. I can't be your maid forever."

Alix took my hand and kissed it. "We can think of a more suitable arrangement, I'm sure."

I laughed. "Suitable arrangement? Like wha…"

I lost my train of thought when I noticed something on the index finger of the hand he kissed. The silver ring was shaped like a small rose in bloom, and inside the rose were several tiny, deep blue gems. A lump formed in my throat, made of pure fear. I stared at Alix, speechless.

"Do you like it?" he asked.

"What is this?" I couldn't hide the horror in my voice.

"A gift. Dresses, jewels, and kisses." He smiled and his eyes gleamed with laughter, but I didn't understand the joke. "I had it made for you. The gems are jaxixe. It's one of the rarest gems in the world, and it's lovely on your hand."

I looked down at the ring, then up at Alix. The gems matched his eyes. "It's beautiful. But Alix—"

"No buts. If you don't accept it, I'll find an even more outrageous gift."

I bit my lip. I knew he would. "Fine. Thank you."

"You're welcome." He kissed my forehead.

I pulled away from him and jumped out of bed. The sooner I showered, the sooner I could leave. With any luck, Jenos would keep his promise. The ring would be a souvenir of our time together, and that would be enough. It had to be.

"Are you sure you don't want to spend another day?"

I turned on my heels to face him as he sauntered towards me, shirtless, low hanging pants and something in his eyes that made my stomach clench. "I'm sure."

"Oh, come on," Alix purred and draped his arms over my shoulders. "Do I need to bribe you with food before you give in?"

I paused at the thought of eating the palace food again but shook my head free of the temptation. I pulled him off me and started backing away. "You made a promise. I expect you to keep it."

"And I will, but you didn't say I couldn't try convincing you to stay longer," he said.

He backed me into his desk. "Alix…" I tried, but he leaned into me, shadowing my lips with his. We were a breath apart, daring each other to close the distance.

"You know you want to," he said with a wolfish grin.

There was a knock at the door, and I sighed in relief. I was inches away from agreeing to stay against my better judgement. "You should get that," I said.

"Or they could leave," he said, but the knocking persisted. "Fine. But we're not done."

Alix walked away. I turned, calculating how I could slip away from him. I glanced down at the mess of papers on his desk and noticed one had slipped out from the pile. I grabbed it off the ground and flipped it over.

You are courtly invited to the wedding of Prince Alixios de Valor of Tamikar and second Princess Aretianna vi Fantassia of Revena.

I looked down at the print as each word landed its blow. I smiled bitterly. I felt like such a fool, but at the same time, I felt relieved. I had an excuse to leave and never come back.

I walked to the door, ready to confront Alix, but once I saw what was on the other side, my mind blanked. I couldn't quantify my emotions. All I could do was watch Alix and Aretia kissing. He held her in his arms like I'd imagined he'd held me. The part of me that should have felt rage felt icy and numb.

"Oh," Aretia said when she saw me, face flushed a dainty pink. "Rosette, you're here…out of uniform…"

Alix turned to look at me like I was a ghost.

"I never told you how amazing your performance was yesterday. Do you think you could play at our wedding? Could you compose something new?"

I ignored her. I didn't even look at her. All my focus was on Alix, who was struggling to speak. I didn't want an explanation. I wanted to make sure he understood the weight of the situation. This was reality, and I was done trying to escape it.

"Princess," I bowed. "I must take my leave."

"Oh, you're speaking. That's good. Do you have to go? I would love to get to know you more," she said.

There was an innocence to Aretia that passed for elegance. It could have been the way she stood like she was balancing porcelain on her shoulders, or the gentle glint in her brown eyes. Or even the way she smiled like the world was beautiful because she didn't know just how ugly it could be. All hidden by the maturity in which she held herself.

"Sorry, but I must go." I bowed again and was about to walk away, but Alix grabbed my arm. I tugged against his grip, but it was firm. "Prince Alixios, please let me go."

"Lil—"

"Please."

Alix's fingers unfurled, one at a time. The second my arm was free of his hand, I walked away. I wasn't sure where I was going. I was looking for something familiar that would show me the way out.

"Lilly," Ryalie called, walking toward me, with Jenos not far behind. "It's great you're still here. I was thinking today we could—"

I cut him off. "Take me home."

"What? Why? Stay a little longer. We could have some fun today," Ryalie said.

"Did you know he was getting married?"

They stiffened and went as silent as death.

I nodded. "Take me home."

"Lilly." Ryalie tried reaching for me, but I continued walking down the hallway.

"Please wait," Jenos called out. "It's complicated."

"It's not. I shouldn't be here, I never should've come here," I said. I could taste the overwhelming regret in my words. I shouldn't have been greedy. "Keep your promise, Jenos."

Ryalie jogged to catch up to me and kept pace. "We can get your kiliabi, and she'll take you home, okay?"

I nodded. That's all I wanted.

The morning air was crisp with the new winter chill that bit into my skin, and white snow that blanketed the world. My body broke out in goosebumps, and my toes retreated, curling up. I grasped my forearms and caught my breath before releasing a white mist.

"We should go back and get you warmer clothes, maybe a coat," Ryalie said.

"I'm fine. Blaze will warm me up," I said.

Ryalie hesitantly gave in, and we continued through the parted snow, deeper and deeper into the rear gardens. The snow sat on the deep green trees and shrubs like frosting, and the skies were clear, allowing the sun to shine down to create a sea of diamonds.

"Lilly," Jenos called out, jogging to catch up to us. "Wear this." He placed a thick wool hood over my shoulders and started adjusting it. "I'm sorry."

"Don't be," I said. "Keep your promise."

He pressed his lips into a thin line and nodded.

"You can't leave!" someone out of breath shouted.

It wasn't Alix's voice. I would never forget this voice until the day I died. It made my skin burn in anger, and yet I was happy to hear it.

I turned. Kais trudged through the snow towards us. The sunlight made his bright blonde hair glow, and his pale skin was practically luminescent.

He grabbed my shoulder, pressing his nails into my skin. "I won't let you leave until you—"

"Clench your teeth," I said. I drew back my arm and punched him in the face, then swung my foot into his shin. Kais cried out, dropping to his knee, hissing what I imagined were curses under his breath. His hand covered his face as he glared up at me with tears in his eyes.

"Don't look at me like you didn't deserve that," I said, shaking out my hand. That was another broken nose to add to my record.

"What just happened?" Ryalie asked.

"He assaulted me the other day," I explained.

Ryalie and Jenos's eyes widened, and they turned their gaze toward him. Kais panicked and pointed his finger at me. "She's a liar and a monster."

"Oh, yeah, and he knows my secret too." I was at pique frustration.

"He knows you're the *Renai*? Why didn't you say something?" Jenos asked.

"A lot happened," I said, shaking my head. A lot was still happening.

"You both know," Kais said, getting up off the ground, hopping to keep balance. "You knew and did nothing. Has she threatened you? Bewitched you?"

"Threatened..." Ryalie started like he was considering it.

"Shut up, Ryalie," I grumbled. "I haven't done a thing. I'm leaving anyway. You'll never see me again. Blaze!"

I heard a low grumble and the slow crunch of her paws against the snow.

"You're all traitors," Kais said and started backing away. "All of you." He turned and attempted to run but wobbled towards the palace.

"This isn't good," Jenos said.

"We outrank him. I'll can beat the silence into him later," Ryalie said with a little too much enthusiasm in his voice.

"I would prefer if you didn't make a bad situation worse," Jenos said.

Blaze cuddled into me from behind, and I brushed my hand through her warm fur. She was what I needed most in the world. Now that she was here, my urge to leave was even stronger.

"You're all very noisy this morning," Alle called out, strolling towards us. She stopped and stared at Blaze and then looked back. "I just saw Kais limping, and now there's a kiliabi on the palace grounds. Is there something you need to tell me?"

"Long story," I said and jumped onto Blaze's back. "I'm going home. Thanks for everything."

Blaze took off in a sprint towards the horizon. I closed my eyes and tried to get lost in the feeling, to not think of anything, especially the hurt that ached like the brisk wind on my face.

Alle wouldn't have believed it if she hadn't seen it herself. She'd seen kiliabis before but never so close and never ridden by a person.

"What do you need to tell me?" Alle asked but then the breeze cut through her and made her shiver. "No, wait. Tell me inside, where it's warm."

They all walked back to the palace. Alle could tell Jenos was struggling to find the words to explain. He wasn't much of a talker to begin with.

"Alle, did you know that Alix is to be engaged?" Ryalie asked.

"What?" She laughed. "This is no time for jokes, Ryalie."

"He's not joking," Jenos said. His frown was grim, twisted with regret. "The king and queen have arranged for him to marry Aretia."

Alle was too stunned to respond. To think Alix's parents would take this route. Granted, she understood why they felt the need to secure the lineage and create a stable reign.

"So, then…" Alle started to say. Everything started to fit into a puzzle, and she needed one last piece. "How long has he known? And when did Lilly find out?" she asked.

"Alix has known for a while," Jenos admitted. "It seems Lilly found out a few minutes ago, and I doubt he was the one to tell her."

Alle quickened her pace towards the palace. She raced through the hallways and up the flight of stairs and headed straight for Alix's room. Ryalie and Jenos were on her heels.

When they arrived, she swung the door open to reveal Alix's slumped figure down on one of his couches, with Aretia's arms draped over him.

"Aretia, we need to speak with him," Alle said.

"Alle, Alix seems to have come down with something. He won't even look at me."

"I'm aware and I'm here to help," she said. "But we need to speak to him alone."

Aretia's face fell. She hesitated to leave his side. Alle understood why Alix couldn't break off their engagement.

Aside from pressures from his family, Aretia deserved better.

"I understand," she said and quietly left the room.

"What happened, Alix?" Alle asked, towering over him.

Alix wiped his face and groaned. "She left. I couldn't stop her."

"What made her leave?" Alle asked. She needed to hear it from him.

Alix unclenched his fist. Inside was a crumpled wedding invitation. "This and then a visit from Aretia," he said. He wasn't talking to them anymore. "I couldn't suddenly reject her, but why did Lilly have to walk out at that moment?" He shook his head. "No, this is my fault."

"You kissed her," Jenos said.

Alix nodded. "I kissed her like I have dozens of times."

"How did you think this was going to end?" Alle asked. "Did you think she would play your maid forever, even after you got married?"

"Of course not," Alix snarled.

"Then what?" Alle demanded. "How did you think bringing her here was going to end? You know what she is. Who you are. You knew all of that."

They stared each other down.

"She was just something to pass the time, wasn't she? Another pretty face to relieve the pressures of being the perfect prince. The queen's perfect, second choice."

"Enough!" Alix shouted, snapping to his feet. He shut his eyes tight, overcome with too many emotions, from regret to anger.

Was Alle right? Did he think of her that way? He'd never hurt like this before. It was just too complicated. He needed a minute to think.

"You can never see her again," Jenos said.

"I must. I need to explain everything," Alix said. "Beg—"

Jenos shook his head. "It won't matter."

"How can you say that? If I just—"

"No," Jenos barked. "She made me promise that once she went home, I would make sure you never go looking for her again. It's what's best for the both of you."

Alix clenched his jaw. "You would betray me?"

Jenos grabbed him by the collar. "I'm doing this *for* you. And her. Staying away from each other is for the best. She could see that. Why can't you?"

"I can't," Alix said and threw Jenos's hands off him.

"Why not?" Alle asked.

"It's impossible!" he shouted. Alix collapsed back onto his seat, combing his hand through his hair. "Whenever she ran from me, I chased after her. Even after I found out what she was, I chased after her. Even knowing that the only thing waiting for us in the end is pain and heartache, all I want to do is chase after her."

Silence.

"I get it," Ryalie said. Everyone looked at him, stunned. He smiled and shrugged. "She's your favourite feeling."

"How would you know that?" Jenos asked.

"It's how I felt when I met you all," he explained. "Going against my family and entering a completely new world. It went against everything I'd ever been taught. But I did it anyway because some things feel too important."

"That's right," Alix said and stood. "She's too important." He started for his door, and they went after him.

"Wait, don't listen to Ryalie," Jenos said.

"Yes, this is a little more complicated than becoming a knight," Alle said, trying to pull Alix to a halt.

"Is it though?" Ryalie asked.

"Shut up," Jenos and Alle hissed.

Alix opened his door. In front of him stood a messenger and five knights, standing tall behind him like stone pillars.

"Your Highness, you've been summoned," the messenger said with the firmness reserved for the worst of times.

"I'll heed the summons at another time." Alix tried to push past them, but they grabbed him. "Release me."

"We are under orders from the king to detain you." He motioned for the other knights to come forward.

Alix froze. "Excuse me?"

The knights grabbed Jenos, Ryalie, and Alle. None of them struggled, looking for direction from Alix.

"Alright," Alix said and shrugged off the knights' grip. "Take me to my father."

I stood in front of Cam's door, trying to muster up the courage to open it. I couldn't think of an excuse for where I'd been the last couple of days. My mind hit a blank the moment Blaze dropped me off and strolled away. I wanted to run and hide myself in some cave for the rest of the year, but I knew I could never do that.

"Here goes."

I took a breath, then knocked on the door. I waited a few seconds and heard footsteps.

I braced myself. The door opened.

"Mom?" I gasped in horror.

"Lilly!" My mother grabbed me in her arms, but I was too shocked to hug her back. It was my mom, messy locs in a bun and all.

"Lillianett, you have returned," Cam said.

Estell was beside him and looked just as surprised to see me. She searched me, her eyes lingering on my coat.

My mom released me, and I stared wide-eyed at the three of them. "You told *my mother* on me?" I asked.

"Don't take that tone with him. From what I've heard you've been missing for days. They thought you were dead. I thought you were..." My mother caught her breath and stopped herself.

My gaze dropped, and a numbing rush of remorse hit me at the base of my stomach and burned my chest. "I'm sorry," were the only words that escaped my lips.

"Where have you been this entire time?" Estell asked. She grabbed the hood and used her thumb to caress it. "This is high-quality. Were you kidnapped by a wealthy family?"

"Close," I said with a nod. "Prince Alix."

They all stared at me. I could feel their questions piling.

"The prince kidnapped you, but you're still alive. No, he had nothing but praises for you yesterday at the ball. What happened?" Estell asked.

"I'll explain," I said and walked in, pulling out a chair. "You may want to sit down."

I started at the beginning, from when I'd saved the prince and how he'd become more and more entangled in my life. Disbelief shadowed their faces. Cam had his face in his hands the whole time I spoke, and Estell had her arms crossed over her chest, shaking her head. My mother listened the way she always did whenever I messed up.

"…And now I'm here," I concluded.

Silence. I waited, and the tension built, choking me.

"You were at the ball." Cam said in disbelief. If I hadn't told him, he probably wouldn't have believed it. "You were right there, next to the prince."

For the first time, I heard anger in his voice, and it scared me. My spine shook, and my throat had a lump of spit trapped inside.

"They all know who you are, what you are, and they still befriended you?" Estell asked.

"Somehow," I said.

"Just tell me one thing. Did they make you do all that against your will?" My mom asked.

I bit my lip and closed my eyes. I knew exactly what she was asking. "No. It was me too. I have to take some responsibility."

She smiled at me. "As long as you understand that. You're safe, and that's what matters until you get home."

I should have thought harder about running away.

"Well, now that I understand the situation, we need to leave.

Now. As soon as possible," Estell said.

"The farther away, the better. A different kingdom," I said. "Mom, you should…" I stopped. Something was off. I felt something coming our way, like spiders crawling up my back.

"Lill—"

"Shh." I crept towards the window to see outside and saw a small army of people coming towards the house. "You all need to hide."

"What's wrong?" Estell asked, already taking a defensive stance, and reaching for her needles.

I watched their movements for a few more beats, confirming there were too many for all of us to take on. "People have come for me. You three need to hide downstairs and stay quiet. As soon as it's safe, send my mom home," I said. "My mom needs to get home."

"How? Why?" Estell asked.

"I left a few things out of my story," I said.

"What about you?" my mom asked.

"If I hide, they will search and find us all and take you. They don't know about Cam and Estell, least of all you, so if you hide, you'll be safe."

"We could fight them, and go on the run," Estell said.

"No, there's too many," I said sternly. "And even if there weren't you'd be on the run for the rest of your lives, and I won't do that to you. I've been enough of a curse in your life."

"Lilly, you're not…"

The sound of their feet shuffling against the snow grew louder. It was like they were moving to the same rhythm of my heart, or maybe my heart was just that loud.

"No time. Hide," I hissed.

My mom grabbed me. "No. Let's just go home. Away from all this. I'll find a way to explain it to your dad."

"Mom, let go," I said.

"No!" she screamed through tears. "I'm not letting you die. No, no, no. I want you back home, safe with us. Please."

I gripped my mom's hand and released a shaky breath, holding back my tears. I couldn't let her see how scared I really was. "I have to take responsibility."

"Not like this. Please," she cried.

"Estell, please take her," I said. "Make sure she gets home."

Estell stuck a needle in the back of my mom's neck. Her eyes became heavy as she collapsed in Estell's arms. "Are you sure about this?"

"This way, my dad gets at least one of us home safely."

"You could escape with her," she said.

I shook my head. "Who knows what mess that could create? Look on the bright side, the curse ends with me."

"I cannot support this decision," Cam said.

"I'm not giving you a choice," I said and pushed him to the training room. "I'm sorry about everything until now. I hope you live a good life."

"I cannot let you face this alone," he said, standing his ground.

I hugged him, crushing my cheek against his chest, His heartbeat was frantic. I was sorry for everything. I was nothing but trouble, and I could never make up for it.

"How will I face your father?" he whispered.

"Tell him I love him and that it was my decision," I said. "He'll understand." *I hope*.

There was a knock at the door.

"Go. Now," I whispered.

They retreated downstairs. I stared at the door and let the thought of escaping cross my mind and slip away. I took three deep breaths and walked to the door. When I opened it, I was face to face with Kais's broken nose.

"Of course, it's you," I said.

"No escape for you now, monster."

"You're the monster," I said. "How did you find me?"

"We tracked your beast. Fitting that a monster would keep a monster."

"Say another word about Blaze and your teeth will match your nose," I warned.

I walked forward and one of the knights restrained me. A woman slipped behind me and stuck a needle into my neck. My consciousness slowly began to ebb.

Just before my light was snuffed out, I caught a glimpse of Blaze at the edge of the forest. With my last breath, I whispered, "Stay, girl."

Chapter 21

Blood Does Not Lie

It took a second to get my bearings once I opened my eyes. I was laying on my back in a small, damp, stone cell with rusted bars and a single barred window too high for me to reach.

"You're awake."

I sat up at the sound of Alix's voice. He was sitting next to me, his weight completely against the wall behind him.

"At least in here, you'll stop running from me."

I shook my head. "You're unbelievable. Why are you here?"

"I heard they detained you." He pushed himself off the wall and fully faced me. The red mark on his face gave me pause. It looked like someone slapped him, someone with nails. The look in his eyes made me wonder if he cried recently, they were so tired.

I stored away my worries and sympathy. "Does your fiancée know where you are?"

"That's a misunderstanding," he said. "I can explain."

"I find a wedding invitation, and five seconds after that I find you kissing the girl you'll be marrying," I said. "What is there to misunderstand?"

He buried his face in his hands and groaned. "I don't want to marry her."

"But you're fine with kissing her? Leading her on?" I asked. He flinched but held my gaze. I shook my head. "It doesn't matter."

"No, I can fix this. I can still—" he said.

"No! Look at where we are," I said gesturing to the dark cell I'd had nightmares about ending up in. "If this isn't a wake-up call, I don't know what is."

"This is all my fault," he said. "I should have done…more. I can still—"

"It doesn't matter," I said through clenched teeth.

Alix frowned. "It should."

"It doesn't." I stood up and walked to the edge of the cell. "You're still a prince, I'm still the *Renai*, and our time together has been a mistake. It was all one giant mistake."

He stood up, shaking his head like he was trying to erase my words. "You don't mean that."

"Leave, Alix," I whispered. "Just this once, do it."

"I can't. I won't."

"Look at where we are! What other option is there?" I laughed and smacked my palm against the steel bars. The rust bit into my palm but I was too riled up to notice the pain. "I'm a lost cause. You could lose everything because of me, and I'm not that selfish."

"I wish you would be. I am."

I stared at him in silence.

"I'm selfish enough to make you mine no matter what you stand to lose," Alix said. "I would do everything in my power to make up for what you lost, everything and anything, until what you lost can't even compare…" He entrapped me between his arms, "…to what you have."

I shoved him away and glared. "Talk is cheap."

"She's right." Kais walked out of the shadows and up to the cell, escorted by two knights that stood a step behind him. He opened the cell doors, and his escorts grabbed me. They tied a blindfold over my eyes and tied my wrists together. I didn't struggle.

"I'll never forget this, Kais," Alix said.

"That doesn't matter. I'll be celebrated as a hero after today, the man that found the *Renai*. And you, Prince Alix, will be known as a traitor."

Someone pushed me forward. I walked, turning my back on Alix. The less they associated him with me, the better. If there was any way to salvage his reputation, it would be to play the bad guy and treat him like something I used.

A hand pushed me down onto my knees and removed the blindfold. I blinked, blinded by the sudden light. When my eyes adjusted, I took note of the half a dozen knights in the room each with a weapon at their hip. Then I was looking up at the king and queen. I avoided their gaze and instead stared down at the tiled floors. In the corner of my eye, I saw six unfamiliar figures. They wore identical deep purple robes with intricate silver lining and patterns. There was something about them that held my attention and yet made me want to look away.

"Rosette?" The queen said. "Do you mean to tell me that my son's maid is the accursed *Renai*? I don't enjoy games, Kais."

He bowed. "I assure you, my queen, she is the *Renai*. I saw her mark with my own eyes. We've been played for fools by her and Prince Alix."

"Are you certain my son knew who she was?" the king asked. "And said nothing?"

"Yes, he threatened me to stay silent once I discovered the truth," Kais said. "But I couldn't."

"How did you see her mark?" one of the figures in the robes asked. She had long black hair that fell in soft curls against her rich, brown skin. Her features were as delicate and thin as her frame. She stood with a strong spine, her chin raised and her dark eyes stern.

"I happened to see…"

"He ripped my clothes off," I said before Kais could paint himself in any gallant light.

There was stunned silence as all eyes fell on me before turning back to Kais in question.

"How did you suspect she was the *Renai*?" the queen asked.

"He didn't," I said and glared at Kais.

"Is this true?" the dark-haired woman asked.

Kais fell to his knees and pressed his head to the ground. "Forgive me. I was a fool, but I've reflected on my actions."

His voice was low, and it shook along with his body. His nails scraped against the tiles like he was trying to brace his body against something I couldn't see. He didn't only respect her, he feared her, which affirmed my suspicions. They were the Glories, the ones who had cursed my family, the most powerful beings in Glorus. I had no hope. But I refused to cower, even if I was afraid. I was going to look my demons in the eye.

A door swung upon with a dramatic bang and the sound was followed by frantic steps. "Stop this! That man is a liar and traitor."

I closed my eyes tight, cursing Alix under my breath.

"Better that I'm a traitor to my prince than to all the people I swore to serve." Kais smirked, reveling in Alix's behaviour.

"I'll have you forfeit everything, even your life," Alix threatened. I knew he meant it.

"Silence," the king commanded, the room obeyed. "Alix, if what he says is true, then he did as you failed to do."

"And that is?"

"Abide by the law," the queen answered. She gave him a withering look, one that made me question whether she was his mother at all. "You've brought a cursed creature into our presence—our home."

"She's done nothing wrong," Alix stated.

"Her very existence is wrong," one of the Glories, the one with silver hair, said. He stepped forward and glared at me with brown eyes so bright they were almost red. If his face wasn't so stern, it would have been pretty, with his sharp nose and porcelain-white skin. He was shorter than the other Glory that spoke but exuded the same pressure.

"Why?" Alix asked.

"Alix, stop," I pleaded.

"You dare call my son by name? And without the title no less," the queen sounded enraged, ready to rip my throat out with her bare hands.

"It's fine," Alix insisted.

I waited to make sure I could speak. "It's okay. I understand."

"You understand?" the dark-haired Glory asked with a self-righteous gleam, and yet there was something somber in her tone.

"I scare you, don't I? I'm not like you, so I must be evil because you think you're good. People don't like what's different. That's a constant no matter the world."

No one knew I was a *Renai* back home, but I was different enough to warrant their scorn. Bullying and bigotry wasn't anything new, but it stung all the same.

There was a profound silence as they all stared at me. The Glories especially looked taken aback.

"You know nothing, *Renai*," the silver-haired Glory sneered, breaking the silence.

I looked him in his red eyes. "And why not? Is it because *I am* a *Renai*?"

"You're quite brave," another Glory said. This one had wavy brown hair, deep tanned skin, and a bored expression on his face, not unlike the look Cam often wore. He was the tallest of them and brawny. He gave off an unmovable feeling, like a mountain.

"Am I wrong?"

"You are unnatural," the ginger-haired Glory said, though she managed to say it tenderly. She was the smallest, with big brown eyes. She looked almost like a small animal in the way she was covered in white flowers and stood like she was trying to take up as little space as possible.

"I've done no harm in the months I've been in Glorus. If it weren't for Alix, you probably would never have known I was here."

I was a lot calmer than I thought I would be facing them.

"What is your relationship with the prince?" the dark-haired one asked, taking a step forward.

"He was attacked and dying. I saved him," I told her.

"Why? He was a stranger," she said.

"Why?" I asked. "Do I need a reason to save a life?"

She smiled a wicked smile, and there was something else, something akin to pride. "What have you done since arriving in this world?"

I couldn't tell them my long-winded story and implicate everyone I'd tried to save, but I couldn't lie either. The closest to the truth I could tell, the better.

"I kept to my cage for a while. Then one day I saved a life, and when I was given a chance at even a breath of freedom, I squeezed as much fun out of it as I could." I swallowed. "Then, I said goodbye to my mother."

They all fell silent, contemplating my answer. I thought of the pile of laundry I kicked into the corner of my room. I would never get to clean it up. More things to be sorry for.

"Interesting," the Glory with bright, honey-blond hair said. He had a slender figure and stood like he was balancing a halo above his head. His dark blue eyes had been carefully watching me from the beginning, but now they held mine. "And was it fun?"

I smiled, but I couldn't shake the sadness in the truth. "It was."

"And the ring?" the dark-haired Glory asked.

"I gave her the ring," Alix said before I could think of a way to explain away the extravagant piece of jewelry.

"Why?" the honey-blond Glory asked. He looked neither surprised nor interested, but like he was looking for the full story.

Alix hesitated and yielded a quick glance in my direction before answering, "I was expressing my fondness of her."

"In other words, you proposed," the dark-haired one said.

"You proposed to her!" the queen shrieked.

I sucked my lips over my teeth and didn't dare look up at her. Judging from the way she screamed, if I looked at her now, her glare would kill me.

"What is your name?" the honey-blond Glory asked me.

I hesitated. "Lillianett."

"More lies," the queen hissed. "You've brought disaster into my home—into my kingdom. Alix was already betrothed. Death is too good for you."

"See the trouble she's brought?" the silver-haired Glory asked.

The dark-haired Glory walked up to me. "Stand," she commanded. I began to rise. "Tell me... Lillianett, was it?" She started to walk around me like I was her prey. I lowered my centre of gravity, wary of her movements, fully aware I could die at any moment.

"Everyone calls me Lilly," I offered, attempting to dissipate the tension in my limbs.

"Lilly, is there any reason you should *not* be put on trial for your sins?"

"Because my only sin is existing," I replied.

She let out a boisterous laugh, which echoed off the walls. "When you put it like that, it makes it seem like we're the monsters instead of you. Doesn't it?"

"That's how I've always seen it," I said.

"Repeat that." She stopped in front of me and grinned wide. Her face was so close to mine I had to take a step back. "We're the monsters?"

I swallowed, my heart hammering in my chest. "You're the monsters," I repeated, loud enough for everyone to hear me.

They stared in stunned silence once more. If I were to die, I would die defending myself. I would be a fighter to the end. Just like my mom taught me.

Alix then began to laugh. The dark-haired Glory turned back and stared at the silver-haired Glory, who was glaring daggers but also looked hurt by my words.

"I demand her head!" the queen screamed.

"Mother!" Alix shouted, breaking from his reprise of laughter.

"My pleasure." Kais brought out a sword and charged toward me, arm raised for the swing. I found my legs too late. He folded his arm over my collar and held the sword to my neck.

Being in his arms was as pleasant as the last time.

"I should have done this sooner," he breathed in my ear, which made my whole-body heave in disgust.

"Stop, Kais," Alix warned. He kept a careful distance. His body jerked forward, but he kept his feet firmly on the ground.

"I'm sorry, but I must fulfil my duty to the Crown," Kais slurred.

"Well, this has escalated," the dark-haired Glory said.

"Any last words?" Kais asked.

I clenched my jaw and tried my best to stop my body from shaking uncontrollably from fear. I'd managed to act calm and collected so far, and thought I could do it until the end, but now that Kais was pressing a cold blade against my neck, I couldn't bring myself to pretend any longer. My body shook, tears were choking out of me, and my bones became putty.

"You really are monsters," I managed to croak out.

"Abomination," Kais hissed.

I felt the sword move against me. I let out a scream that shook me to my core. I wouldn't go quietly. I would burn the sound of my screams into their memories so that they would never forget.

Monsters.

A sound came roaring in from outside, swallowing my screams. It was a howling roar that tore through the air and made everyone in the room gape out the nearest window.

"Blaze," I gasped, my voice raw.

"What is that?" Kais shouted. I threw my head back against his broken nose, he cried out and I escaped his grasp stumbling into Alix.

"Untie me," I demanded, trying to shake off his arms.

As soon as I was free, I headed to the closest window, ignoring the protests that followed. I jumped out into the palace grounds. My feet hit the snow, and I gasped as the cold air stole my breath.

I found Blaze in an instant. Before I could step towards her, a knight grabbed me from behind. I thrust my elbow into his stomach and ran forward, avoiding the reach of others who tried to hold me back.

Snow crunched underfoot as I ran straight into one of the men trying to stab Blaze with a sword and successfully knocked him off his feet. I hit the ground in time to avoid another knight's sticky fingers and kicked his legs out from under him.

I scrambled to my feet, shuddering as the icy shards made my skin tingle, and grabbed the fallen sword. I swung it at a knight who was trying to wrap a chain around Blaze's neck. The sword clashed against the chains, taking the man by surprise, and giving me an opening to kick him in the gut. I turned as a woman swung her sword but couldn't react, causing my weapon to fly out of my hands. I hissed, shaking out my stinging fingers. I turned and ran, and the knight gave chase. I turned on my heels and kicked the sword out of her grasp, then began a barrage of quick jabs to keep her off balance. When she stumbled back, I swept her leg from under her, and she hit the snow.

"Stop her!" I heard the queen scream, but I didn't have the luxury to look for where she shouted from.

My attention was on Blaze, serene Blaze, who stared at me as though she were waiting for me to be done so that we could leave. She gave no indication that she would fight back. I nodded and she bowed her head. I ran and leaped high, landing on her back, and flipped off to the right, kicking down two more knights.

"One more," I puffed and ran around Blaze. I jumped to grab one of her tails, then swung off of it, launching my foot into a knight's face.

As I was about to mount Blaze, the biggest of the lot came from my blind spot. I dodged his punch by the skin of my teeth, but I was too slow to dodge his backhand. I hit the frost rolling and screamed out as the pain shot through my body in waves but gasped at the cold that burned on my skin. I huddled into myself, trying to gather the will to get on my feet.

The giant towered above me, about to stomp down. I scrambled desperately, just managing to escape, but ended up rolling across the snow-covered ground again.

I got up quickly, shaking the fluff off, but winced at the ache in my ribs, and the taste of blood in my mouth. I silently thanked Estell for being so cruel during training.

The large knight attacked again. I dodged cleanly this time. I aimed for his joints and tried to knock him off balance. My fist got him square in the jaw, which left him disorientated, then I aimed my fist at the centre of his chest. He gasped and with that opening, I kicked his knees.

I'd pacified all the guards. The moment I let out a relieved sigh, the cold hit me with a vengeance. I gasped as the ice tightened my chest and stung my ears. My clothes were soaked through and heavy.

Blaze snuggled up to me and wrapped herself around my body like an oversized coat. Her warmth seeped into skin, making my lungs lighter.

"You know, you could have helped," I said to her.

Blaze breathed into my palm and wrapped herself even tighter around me. My beautiful, dangerous beast. She came for me.

"You tamed a kiliabi," the dark-haired Glory said.

I hadn't noticed everyone that was inside had come out. How long had they been watching?

"It's been a long time since I've seen that. A huntress Crown of *Arcania*." She smirked, her eyes glowing. "Blood does not lie."

"She is, without a doubt, a princess of Halibel. The Blood has maintained potency through the years," the silver-haired one said with a hint of regret in his voice.

"You weren't sure, but you were going to let me die?" I said, more horrified than surprised.

"Of course not," the honey-blond said. "We would never have allowed it. Even now, we won't be killing you. But we will be taking you. Kija, if you would?"

"With pleasure," the dark-haired one said.

"Wait, wha—" I gasped out, but it was too late. A shadow of consciousness was all I had left before everything went dark.

I shot out of bed with a terrified gasp and immediately started coughing, only to wince at the pain in my limbs. Most of my body felt raw and heavy. I was choking in my skin. A bead of sweat escaped down my cheek, and my breathing came out hard. I looked around at an empty, unfamiliar room with nothing but a bed and two doors.

The dark-haired Glory came through a dark corner.

I gasped, stifling a scream.

"You can wash up in there, then meet me in my study."

She walked out the door.

I didn't know what was more surprising: the fact that I was still alive or that she told me to wash up and meet with her.

I walked into a spa-like washroom and gawked at the audacious space. This room was larger than Alix's bedroom and had a bath that took up more than half of the space. The water was steaming with a sweet floral scent, and near the door was a cabinet full of big, fluffy towels.

I took off my clothes and stepped into the water. I winced as it touched my tender, bruised skin, then felt all my pain and aches vanish with every passing second. My body became so fluid and relaxed that I forgot where I was or why I was so sore to begin with.

I closed my eyes and sank into the waters.

Once I began to prune, I decided that it was time for me to exit. My body was no longer aching all over. I rolled my shoulder and stretched my neck, not even a click in my joints. When I walked back into the room, there was a white t-shirt-like dress waiting for me. I put it on and, without looking in a mirror, could tell it was unflattering.

I stepped out of the room and went across the hall. I found the dark-haired Glory—Kija— sitting in silence with a book in hand. I hesitated, then entered with all the courage I could muster.

I stared at her and asked the only thing that came to mind. "What is this place?"

"You are in the palace of the Glories," she answered without looking up from her book.

I froze. "Where?"

She looked up with an amused half-smile and nodded. All I could do was stare in both awe and dread. Kija sat on one of the plush single couches, and she motioned for me to sit in the one opposite hers.

"I can't believe I'm in the Glories' palace, and alive."

"Yes, neither can Rion," she said. "He's the one with silver hair and scary eyes."

"Oh him. The one that hates me the most."

"He's always been such a stiff," she said and shrugged.

I paused, surprised by how nonchalant she sounded. "You are not what I expected. You're so normal."

"Should I be offended or honoured?"

"What I mean is, well, I imagined all the Glories to have a disposition similar to Rion's."

"Please, Lilly, don't insult us." Kija shook her head like she hated the very idea. I laughed. She was nicer than I ever could have hoped. I smiled at her, and she smiled back with a tender fondness. "You remind me so much of her," she said.

"Who?"

"Queen La-Muse." She closed her book. "That could be why Rion doesn't like you."

"He disliked La-Muse?" I asked.

Kija grinned. "No, he was very fond of her."

"He was?" Now she wasn't making sense.

She nodded, still grinning, but then she frowned, and her eyes became downcast. "He was...very fond," she said. I couldn't understand the sadness in her voice. It ran deeper than regret. There was pain.

I tilted my head at a loss. "I don't understand."

"It's not something meant to be understood," she said. "Have you learned a lot in your stay? I imagine this world is different from yours."

"It is. We're not big on kings and queens anymore, and we don't have gods roaming around making laws. Did you really forbid war?"

"Gods?" Kija asked. "I think there has been a bit of a misunderstanding. We are not gods. We have great power, but that is because we are a part of this world."

"Isn't everyone kind of part of this world?" I asked.

Kija pursed her lips with a hint of frustration between her brows. She looked like a parent trying to explain something that wasn't meant to be complicated to a child. "We have been here since the beginning, but we are not the beginning."

My eyes widened as her words began to make sense. "So, when you say you're a part of this world..."

"I mean that literally. We are physical manifestations, a part of the world given consciousness. Though we hold great power, we rarely use it unless the world itself is in question.

That sounded pretty god-like to me. "So, the War of Bloods

threatened the world?"

She paused, assessing me for a long minute. "*Arcania* is life," she began. "War is full of despair, and it ruins lives. It isn't heroic, like the kings of old believed. Men become monsters on the battlefield. They do cruel things. And with time, *Arcania* became corrupted. Death walked in its wake. That despair threatened to swallow the world, and it took years to undo. Even now there are still remnants all over of that corrupted *Arcania*."

The scars are still there, Alle had said. How literal was she being?

Kija wasn't looking at me. She looked into the space between us, reliving the darkness. It was like she felt the corruption encroaching, and it paralyzed her. Her eyes darted up. It frightened me, but I managed not to blink.

"This world will never heal."

I knew so little of Glorus, even outside of the forest, my birdcage, my world was still so small. There was more to the story, more to the war—I could feel it.

"How rare," someone new spoke and I gasped.

I looked toward the door and saw the one Glory that hadn't spoken at my mock trial. She had dark auburn hair in a pixie cut and steady, olive-coloured eyes. Her smile was playful, and she wore her robe more loosely than her fellow Glories.

"Gracing us with your presence, Siehrra?" Kija asked.

"It is Lilly who is gracing us with her presence," Siehrra said with a wink.

Kija nodded. "Yes, you're right."

Siehrra scoffed. "What topic did I walk in on that had you two so somber?"

"We're talking about Rion's fondness for La-Muse," Kija answered.

"We were all fond of her," Siehrra said, resting on the arm of my chair. She looked down at me and smiled.

Kija glanced at me and gestured at the door. "You may leave."

Where was I supposed to go?

Hesitantly, I got up and left the room. I was about to go back into the room I woke up in, but then my curiosity got the better of me, and I took a detour down a hall. I was lucky enough to find an open window and climbed down into the garden. It was an ocean of green, with waves of colourful flowers. Trees lined the outskirts of the garden, and at the centre was the largest tree, with many twisting branches and large green leaves that sparkled like emeralds under the sun. I manoeuvred my way through its uproots and pressed my palm against the trunk.

"This world will never heal," I mumbled Kija's words to myself and wondered what she meant by them.

I started climbing up the tree, pulling myself higher and higher, through the branches, dancing around the edge, until I could see past the wall. An ocean spread out before me, vast blue with white diamonds.

I never did find that tree to climb, better late than never.

"What are you doing up here?"

The sudden question made me jump, and I grasped a branch to save myself from falling.

The honey-blond Glory was standing beside me, staring with curiosity.

We stared at each other. I couldn't form words.

"Lillianett, how are you feeling?" he asked.

I hesitated. He didn't look hostile towards me either. His question seemed genuine. "Fine," I blurted when the silence stretched on even longer than before. He kept staring, like he wanted me to continue. "I—I…don't understand what's happening. I thought I'd be dead or…something, by now."

He frowned. "You would think so, I suppose."

He went silent, staring down at the branch he stood on. Of all the Glories I'd met so far, he seemed the most detached, like his mind was constantly racing to be somewhere else.

"What's your name?" I asked.

He was taken aback by my question, and I was taken aback by his surprise. "My name is Lucell. It's been a long time since I was asked."

"Yeah, I guess you're pretty famous."

His curious eyes were on me now, big and filled with pity but also a hopeful wonder. I felt like I was made of crystal, and he was afraid to break me.

"Looking back, it never made sense," he mumbled, but his words didn't sound like they were for my ears. Before I could question it, he asked, "Why are you up here?"

It took me a second to find the words to respond. "When I was a kid, I used to climb trees," I said. I looked out at the ocean that stretched past the horizon. "My mom joked that it was my way of running from my problems."

"Is that why you do it?"

I shook my head. "When I climbed high, everything seemed

317

small, even my problems. It's been a while since I had a problem big enough that needed me to climb this high."

"What's your problem?"

"I don't know," I admitted.

"I suggest you go higher," he said.

"That's not it," I said. "I don't know what's going on. It's not meant to be this way. Everything's all wrong. When I was found, I was supposed to die, or be punished, or *something*. I've been found but I'm still alive. I'm being treated like a guest. What does this mean? Why do all of you seem just as lost and confused as I am?"

"You weren't meant to get caught," he said with a hint of frustration.

His answer did nothing to ease my confusion. "What is going to happen to me?"

There was a long silence. He had a tired look on his face, like he didn't want to answer me. My heart sank, no answer felt worse than I thought it would.

"What do you think of Rion?" he suddenly asked.

I rolled my eyes before I could think better of it.

Lucell's laugh danced on air. "He has the best intentions. He's doing what he thinks is right."

"How is demonizing me right?"

Lucell sighed, all signs of laughter gone. There seemed to be an unbelievable weight in that sigh. "He sees it differently than you do. We've seen more than you have."

"You should all get your eyes checked." I bit my tongue hoping I hadn't overstepped.

But Lucell laughed again.

I looked down. "Kija says I remind her of La-Muse." I looked up at him. "Do I remind you of her?"

He stared at me, unblinking and his face softened. "You do remind me of the *Wild Rose* of Halibel."

"The *Wild Rose*?"

"Her nickname when she was younger." His smile widened, but like Kija, his smile became a frown. This close, I could see a well-aged sadness.

"After the incident, people called her the *Cursed Rose*," he said. "Much like your curse mark."

I became very aware of the rose pattern imprinted on my spine.

"It is not a curse you bear alone, Lillianett."

There was a storm in those words, restless and unsettling. I thought the same thing when I learned how Cam and Estell were related to my family. This curse was not mine alone to bear. But Lucell meant something different. The look in his eyes made me question everything I knew.

Chapter 22

Yellow Eyes

W e haven't made a decision," Lucell said, looking out into the horizon.

His words snapped me back to reality. "Decision?"

"We can't reach an agreement about what to do with you," he said. "You've made this difficult for us."

I was certain they'd decided many years before I was even a thought. This was like finding out the world was flat—it just wasn't right.

"You said you see us as monsters for putting this curse on your family." He spoke no louder than a whisper. If I didn't know better, I would think he was close to tears.

I wasn't sure how to respond. They were the monsters in this story from the day I learned about the curse. "I did—I do," I said with a single nod. "But from your perspective…was it the best thing to do? Was her crime that bad?"

He closed his eyes as though to…as though for the first time, considering the answer to the question. He opened his eyes and answered, "It was the best we could do."

"What do you mean?"

"Until we reach a decision, you'll be sent back to your caretaker. Once we've decided, we'll summon you back," he said, changing the subject and his tone.

"Hey, don't change…you're sending me away?"

He stared at me for a moment. "Your presence might…sway decisions."

"This all feels weird. It's like everything I've believed until now is a lie," I said.

It wasn't sitting well with me. They were treating my existence as a mere inconvenience, while everyone else had treated me like my existence was a curse. The Glories made the law. They started the cycle. They're the reason I was labelled a monster. What was I missing?

I stared at Lucell trying to gauge his expression and maybe uncover a truth, but I couldn't read his face. Was it unease? Was it uncertainty?

"Are you afraid?" he asked.

"Yes," I admitted.

My previous reality was scary, but there was a security in knowing what to expect. Not knowing brought out an existential fear, like walking in darkness and waiting for something to jump out. There was a pit in my stomach, like I was falling from impossible heights. I couldn't handle the feeling that the world could give way at any moment. There was something wrong. Something none of them were telling me. Maybe something they never told anyone. My mark itched the more I thought about it.

"I will send you back," Lucell said.

"Wait…" I started, but he stepped forward and covered my eyes with his hand.

When the darkness was lifted, I stood in front of Cam's cottage. Snow crunched under my feet and the cold air whistled sharply.

I walked up to the door and stared at it. What would I say? What could I say? I didn't understand anything.

The door suddenly opened, and Cam stared, stunned by my presence. "Lillianett?"

"Hi," I said.

"You are here, alive," he gasped.

"Don't sound too surprised," I said. He hesitated, gripping the doorknob while carefully examining me like I was a bomb. "I'm here, I'm alive," I assured him.

He opened the door and let me inside. "How?"

"I'm still working that part out," I mumbled. "Did my mom make it back safely?"

"She was devastated," Cam admitted.

My heart sank. "I'm not sure what's going to happen next, so let's not tell her anything until it's over. I don't want to get her hopes up."

Cam handed me a glass of water. We sat at his small table, which we rarely did together. There was a stretch of silence as I tried to figure out how to begin. I sipped the water, trying to buy some time.

"Where's Estell?" I asked.

"She left. She was summoned back to Syver."

"Training school place, right?" I asked.

"That is correct," Cam said. He shifted in his seat and adjusted so that he faced me. "Something has bothered me ever since you told us what happened. It overwhelmed me before, but now that you're here, I must ask. Did you trespass into the Exiles' Forest?"

I blinked. "A mission to a cave for a blind seer, being poisoned, basically held captive, playing the piano at the EverSnow Ball thing, taken, nearly killed, then set free, which destroyed all previous beliefs...and you're focused on the part where I lost my temper and *accidently* went where I shouldn't. Typical." I rolled my eyes at him.

"I had warned you many times to stay far away from that area," he started, ignoring my mini-rant. "It's forbidden to everyone."

"Yeah, and I never really understood why until I got there," I said, cutting him off. "Anyway, that's not what's important."

He pressed his lips into a tight line.

"What do we do now?" I asked.

"We leave," he said. "Pack your things."

His words startled me. "Can we? Can we leave, hide from the Glories?"

"No, but we can leave this kingdom at the very least. That should put your mind at ease and remove any temptations," he said.

I frowned. He wasn't wrong. I should have left the day Alix spotted me. There were many times I should have told Cam or

Estell, and disappeared, but I couldn't bring myself to do it.

"You're right," I said and stood to my feet. "When?"

"Tonight," he answered.

He wasn't wasting time, and I didn't have it in me to argue. I had no right to argue. I was the reason we had to leave in the first place. "Where will we go?"

"A new home, in a different kingdom," he said.

"Can I go out into the forest?" I asked. "One last time? Everyone probably believes I'm dead. It should be safe."

Cam looked like he was about to refuse, but then he looked at me and his face softened. He nodded.

My feet crunched over the dead leaves and snow that marked my path. I could see my breath and taste the cold as it caressed my skin. There was a new lull. The frosted wind mimicked the signs of life that were once there. It looked different, but I would know my birdcage anywhere. I complained about it, but at some point, it had become home. I was almost sad to leave it. There were so many memories.

"Oh Blaze," I whispered in realization. I had to trust that Alix had found a way to protect her, but I knew she could protect herself in the end. I was going to miss her most.

I walked down the path I'd run through dozens of times, the one that cut through the spiderweb of trails and parted at the river.

I stopped.

Before I could recognize the face in front of me, my mind was already asking the question: *How? How was she here?*

"It's good to see you again. I've been waiting," Zalia said.

Her ragged clothes fluttered in the wind, as did her hair. Her skin was mostly bare, which was what gave me pause. Her skin was clear. There was no sign of the strange black sickness I had seen before.

She approached me. Although I wanted to step back, I couldn't move my feet from where they dug into the snow. She stood a foot away. I stared into her eyes, peering from one yellow eye plunged in darkness, into the other, a deep but worn blue. She smiled.

My mind reeled.

"Come now," she said. "He's waiting."

Run.

I had to run. I turned on my heels and my feet kicked up the snow. I'd run many times through my birdcage. I ran when I needed to get away from Cam. I ran when Estell trained me. I ran from Alix, Jenos, and Ryalie. I'd run just because I needed a taste of freedom. But I never ran like this, so desperately and full of fear. I didn't understand the danger, and that made it so much more frightening.

Cam's cottage came into view and relief rushed over me.

A hand snaked around my wrist, and then another over my mouth. The moment I felt the warmth of flesh, I also felt a sharp sting, and I lost the strength in my legs. I forced myself to push forward, but it was like running through a pool of water.

Her hands felt like poison.

I was so close to the cottage, but I fell to my knees. I widened my jaw and bit down on the hand that silenced me. With a quick gasp, I shrieked as loud as I could, "Yellow eyes!"

Zalia's hand shut my mouth and the last of my strength faded with my scream.

"Was it wise to sneak out of the palace at this time?" Jenos asked. "I shouldn't need to remind you that tensions are high. The courts have demanded you stand before a tribunal."

Alix shook his head, breaking the twigs that stood in his path. He'd intended to go alone to see Lilly's caretaker, but he couldn't manage to convince Jenos and Ryalie to leave him be. He kept replaying the image of the Glories snatching Lilly from his reach and disappearing right before his eyes. His body failed to react. Whenever she'd walked away from him, he'd felt like she would disappear. He preferred it when she was in reach, or, better yet, when she was within his arms. That's where he could see her, protect her, like he'd promised.

But he failed.

"Alix, listen to me," Jenos said, grabbing Alix's shoulder.

"No," Alix said, swatting his hand off. "This is my fault. Lilly is…" He couldn't bring himself to say the words. He shut his eyes, banishing the thought. "The least I can do is apologize."

"Your kingdom demands an apology," Jenos argued.

"This comes first," Alix stated. "She didn't deserve this. I should have protected her. I swore that I would, but I got too greedy, and now she's…" Words were failing him. He kept seeing it in his mind, but the words refused to manifest on his lips. He didn't want it to be real.

"I miss Lilly," Ryalie said with a pout. "I wanted to fight her again."

"Simple-minded, as always," Jenos said. He couldn't deny that he felt her loss as well, but he couldn't let himself feel it. He swore to protect Alix, and by allowing him to continue his relationship with Lilly as long as he had, the kingdom had branded him a criminal. There was no doubt Alix would survive the ridicule, but he wouldn't come out unscathed. It would take years before his people would learn to trust him again.

Ryalie draped himself over Jenos. "Don't feel bad. There was nothing you could've done for her in the end." Jenos shook Ryalie off. He hated when Ryalie did that—spoke simple yet painful truth. He was simple-minded, childish even, but he managed to be sharp about the things Jenos struggled most with.

"That's not an excuse I will allow myself," Alix said. "I should have done more for her."

"You can't keep blaming yourself," Jenos said.

Alix stopped and his body slumped. He turned to face his oldest friends with a look in his eyes they'd seen only twice before: when his siblings left him and when the king's mother died.

"Did you know I was the first friend she made here? She asked me to be her friend in exchange for saving my life. No one but Ryalie has ever asked for something so absurd," he said. "And because of me, the Glories found her, took her, and now…" He still couldn't say it. "Maybe she was right. Maybe we are the monsters."

Someone came running up from behind them. They stood at attention but were confused by the tall man huffing, out of breath, before them. His blonde hair was dishevelled, and his clothes were wet and dirty from running in the forest.

It took Alix a minute to realize it was Lilly's caretaker. They had only met twice, but he'd always been stoic and composed.

"Prince Alixios," he huffed. He grabbed Alix's arms, gripping them, wide-eyed in desperation. "Lillianett. Have you seen Lillianett?"

Alix frowned. "She was taken by the Glories." He bowed his head. "I came to apologize. It is my fault that she—"

"No," he cried. "She came back. She was with me moments ago, but then I heard her scream, and now she's gone again. Someone took her."

"Lilly's alive?" Jenos gasped.

Alix couldn't breathe. He reached out to the caretaker and hesitated to place his hand on the man's wide shoulders. "Is it true? She came back?"

The caretaker paused and then nodded.

"You said she screamed," Jenos said. "Was she in pain? Did she fall? Get attacked?"

"No, you said she was taken," Ryalie said. "What did she scream?"

The caretaker swallowed. "'Yellow eyes.'"

"The Exiles," Jenos said grimly. "But that's not possible. We're far from their forest."

He was right. There was no one else that had yellow eyes except for the Exiles, but their forest detained them. It made no sense for Lilly to scream those words unless it meant something.

"Is it impossible?" Ryalie asked.

"Is what impossible?" Alix asked, breaking from his racing thoughts.

"Is it impossible for one of them to escape?"

Alix held his tongue before he spoke the obvious answer. Was it? What kept them confined to the forest was unknown. Presumably, it was the power of the Glories, but what if they found a crack? What if somebody slipped out?

Alix shook his head, unable to make sense of it. "But why would they take Lilly?"

"She's been taken?" They all turned to find Rion standing with a fierce look in his eyes. His frown was heavy, and his eyes scanned each of them with scrutiny. "Who took her?"

"We think it was an Exile," Jenos answered.

Rion's frown deepened. "That's not possible."

"Isn't it?" Ryalie asked.

Rion opened his mouth to reply but he paused as a thought came to him and made his very bones shudder.

He composed himself and asked, "Why do you believe she was taken by an Exile?"

"She screamed 'yellow eyes' before she was taken," the caretaker responded.

Rion closed his eyes in surrender, as though moments away from collapse. "So, she's gone. I told Lucell not to let her go. Making the same mistake twice. The fool."

"Do you know where she is?" Alix asked.

Rion stared at him in contempt. "The Lost Isle."

"The Palace at the edge of the world? The island lost to

history?" Alix was taken aback. He'd told Lilly he would take her there, but to think that is where she would be. Everyone knew where the Lost Isle stood but it was not on any maps. He couldn't begin to fathom why anyone would take her to a place no one had set foot on in decades. But before Alix could ask any more questions, Rion was gone.

Ryalie clapped his hands together in excitement. "The Lost Isle. I've always wanted to go."

Chapter 23

Innocent

K ija sat in her seat at the Court with the other Glories. The Court was housed in the centre of the world within a cave of *amerine*. The crystals lined the walls, floors, and ceiling of the large spacious room where the earth protruded to form a large table and chairs. There was nothing refined about their surroundings, but the natural splendour of light and pale stone did manage to hold its own kind of simple beauty.

Rion had informed the other Glories of the situation, and they all gathered without delay. The Court was traditionally where they discussed matters of importance, but now there was silence. An age-old fear had taken hold of their voices.

"He has Zalia. This is the worst-case scenario."

Kija shook her head. She knew Rion would be the voice of doom. True as his words rang, they were made bitter by his being the one to say it.

"Yes, Rion, but what do we do about it?" Lucell asked.

"We need to decide quickly," Zell said, stroking her ginger hair and ruffling her flowers.

"This was preventable. We should have imprisoned the *Renai* on the spot," Rion said.

Kija beat her fist against the table. "No."

"Why not?"

"We made a promise," Dalves said loud enough to break the tension. His bored expression became firm, unmovable.

Rion grated his teeth. He did not enjoy being reminded. "So, you want havoc to reign freely?"

"She is not the cause. We cannot punish her for a crime she did not commit," Siehrra said. "We tried that, and it was a mistake."

"What do you propose now?" Rion asked. He looked each of them in the eye, gave each of them the challenge of creating a solution. The *amerine* caused his silver hair to shine and turned his eyes to fire.

"The unbinding has already begun, and we cannot stop it. All we can do is keep the world from completely shattering from the backlash," Lucell said.

"Do you believe it will be that intense?" Kija asked.

"A rusted key makes noise," he replied, barely hiding his flinch. Rusted keys were also easily broken.

"And afterwards?" Rion pressed.

Lucell closed his eyes, hating the helplessness he felt. "We deal with that when it comes."

"That's not good enough. If it wasn't for—"

Kija beat her fists against the stone table and stood to her feet.

"It was a mistake. When will you except that and stop trying to look for someone to blame?"

Lucell stood. "It was also our mistake."

They all hung their heads, shamed by the truth.

"The storm is near," Lucell said.

"You realize that no matter what happens, if we let him win, we all die," Rion said.

Lucell stiffened and lifted his head in defiance of the fear in his throat. "I'm aware."

I lifted my head and opened both eyes, trying to focus, but the buzzing in my ears made me flinch in pain. I shut my eyes waiting for the ache to subside and I bowed my head again in an attempt to focus my thoughts. Ropes restrained my wrists and stretched my arms up like wings as I knelt on a hard floor. I wasn't cold, but there was a salty draft coming into the room, tickling my skin. I couldn't sense anything familiar, but there was nothing hostile either.

Complete silence.

I lifted my head again and this time froze, wide-eyed. Zalia was crouching down, smiling at me with a twinkle in her mismatched eyes.

"Hello," she said.

"Where am I?" I asked.

"Is that any way to greet your host?" she asked and stood up. "You're as rude as I remember."

She was different from the last time I saw her. There was a

confidence in the way she stood, and she moved with more ease. It was as if whatever had weighed her down was no longer there. She was free.

My eyes swept across the large, dark-grey marble floor. The room opened into a dome. The whole wall in front of me comprised of rows of glass doors leading to a large balcony that looked out onto the ocean. I could hear the turbulent crashing of waves and the eerie wailing of the wind, like the beginnings of a storm. Aside from Zalia and myself, there was no sign of anyone having been in the room for a long time.

Zalia grabbed my face with one hand, digging her nails into my cheeks, and made me look at her. "I asked a question."

"So did I," I growled.

"You did," she said and released me. "Are you ready?"

"For?" I asked.

"For your gift," she said. "Oh, yes, you asked where we are. This is the Lost Isle, known as the palace at the edge of the world. Abandoned by everything, even time. It's the Glories' former home. They abandoned it after the War of Bloods."

"Why?" I asked.

"Turns out, even the Glories run away from their problems," she said. "But you can only run for so long."

That's when I noticed she was holding a small box. She opened it and took out a deep red crystal the size of a golf ball. It gave off a faint light from the inside and reminded me of the crystals I'd seen in the caves with Jenos and Ryalie.

"*Amerine*," I said.

"Close. *Ameris*."

My mark burned like the day it appeared, scorching my flesh. Every cell in my body was screaming. I pulled at the restraints, arching my back, struggling to break free, but they didn't budge.

"What is that?" I asked through gritted teeth.

"What if I told you this was a lock, and you were a key?"

I stared back at her, confusion mingling with the pain.

She frowned at me. Pity shrouded her eyes. "I feel sorry for you. You are innocent. It's a shame. I'm…sorry."

"Then don't do whatever you're about to do," I panted.

"It must be done." Her eyes glazed over with an empty coldness that made me shiver. Her voice lost all warmth, "You see, unlike you, we were guilty. But he said our sins would be forgiven if I do this."

Zalia knelt in front of me. Both her eyes were now a deep, worn blue. She tore my shirt and placed the crystal on my sternum. The crystal sank into me. My chest felt like it was caving in, sinking deeper, and deeper. The deeper it went, the hotter it became, until I couldn't breathe. It overwhelmed me, stole my breath, devouring me whole from the inside.

"Za-li-a," I gasped out and then I heard a crack. My whole body stopped. I couldn't feel my heartbeat.

"I just want our freedom," she said. "You're the price I have to pay. Forgive me."

Something was coming. It pulsed against my spine and reached out towards my chest, slowly creeping like thorny vines wrapping around my heart. I felt something break inside me, and then, I heard my screams shatter my world.

The (True) Curse

We purge your tainted blood from our world, never to
return. Never again will it cross our own. With this curse
you are sealed. Your freedom, your life, your
existence…forsaken, for all eternity. This the punishment
for your sin. For your betrayal. For your greed. Should this
seal be broken, war shall reign, should this line be lost,
blood shall flow. A Curse of Roses is the scar borne upon
your prison, for the sake of life.

A fierce spark accelerated into a wildfire that rampaged throughout my body. As suddenly as it was lit, it escaped. It tore through me and consumed all my warmth.

I was so cold now, as if I was floating in a pool of ice water. It was impossible to breathe, but at least it didn't hurt anymore. My body was numb.

The sound of feet rushing roused me to a clearer consciousness. I heard voices, but they were so far away. I didn't want to open my eyes yet. I was so tired, so cold.

My body was falling, and then, someone caught me.

So warm, like sweet springtime. I knew these arms.

Alix held me close to his chest, and my breath came in like a gasp. I'd never realized how comforting it was to be held. I opened my eyes and looked up at his stricken face. I touched his cheek and caught a tear, confused by its presence. I followed his gaze down my body and found the jewel was breaking apart—and the cracks had spread across my body, like a rash.

No wonder my chest felt so hollow.

"Lilly," he choked through his tears.

Jenos, Ryalie, and Cam were there. I could sense their helplessness and confusion.

"Don't be sad," I whispered, though my heart was breaking.

Jenos shook his head. "Don't do that," he said.

I craned my head to look at him. Those stern brown eyes were shaken.

"Do what?" I asked.

"Smile like it's all okay when you know it's not. You know what's happening."

I didn't know I was smiling, but I felt what was happening.

With every passing second, I was losing hold of my consciousness. The further the cracks went, the colder and colder my body became. It was terrifying, I didn't want to feel this nothingness. There was so much more I wanted to feel.

"You'll be okay, right?" Ryalie said in a small voice.

My jaw dropped and my heart squeezed. His words drew tears to my eyes. "Yeah, everything will be okay."

Ryalie forced out a laugh. "I want a rematch, remember? So...be fine."

"Don't fake a laugh, Ryalie." The sound cleaved my heart in two. "It's so unlike you. When you laugh, you have to mean it," I said and reached out to him. He took my hand and squeezed it. "It's okay to be sad too."

"Was there any way I could have prevented this?" Jenos mumbled to himself, barely loud enough for me to hear him.

"You just can't help yourself, can you?" I wanted to laugh, but my chest was too heavy.

"What are you talking about?"

"Always trying to avoid the mess, but always there to clean it up," I said. My voice was starting to sound even further away, trailing into a whisper.

"That's my duty," Jenos said.

I nodded, trying to smile. "Yeah, you're a good friend."

Jenos knelt down and bowed his head to me. "I'm sorry. I'm so sorry." His voice shook violently, and I could almost taste the regret in it. I didn't want that, not his apologies nor his regret, but I accepted them, for his sake.

"I'm sorry as well," Cam said. "I failed to keep you safe. I failed as your teacher and caretaker." I'd never seen him so disheveled, damp, and dirty. His usually perfectly tied back hair had fly-aways and his eyes were alive with all the wrong emotions.

I shook my head. "I'm the one that's sorry," I sobbed. "I failed you. Thank you for taking care of me. Thank Estell for me too."

"What do I tell your parents?"

"They already think I'm dead. Don't break their hearts a second time," I said.

The thought of my parents made my eyes burn and my hollow chest ache. I was so sorry for the pain I'd caused them all because of my selfishness. My heart couldn't bear the weight of their grief. The image of my mother's tearful, fear-stricken face flashed in my mind, and the hollowness in my chest grew painfully.

"Alix?" Jenos whispered.

I looked up at Alix, who hadn't moved or said a word. He held me in his arms so desperately, as if it would piece me back together.

"Alix…"

"I can't, Lilly." He croaked and held me closer, burying my head against his shoulder. "I can't do it."

"You have to," I whispered. "Let me go."

"No!" he cried. "How can I let you go? I'll never let you go. I still have so much to tell you, to show you, to learn about you…and I never got to say how sorry I am."

"It's okay. I forgive you for everything."

"It's not okay. Don't forgive me," he breathed. "Stay mad at me, hate me, but don't leave me. I promised to keep you safe. I swore that you would be safe with me. You can't die. Please Lilly, I promised. I'm sorry! Please be okay."

Tears streamed from my eyes and sobs escaped my chest. I wanted to be okay, but I had to face reality this one last time. I'd been running from it for too long, but it had caught up and had me cornered.

I couldn't feel anything anymore, and my vision was beginning to fade, along with my consciousness.

"Please, please..." Alix pleaded. I couldn't feel his arms around me, even though he pulled me even closer to his chest.

"Alix," I whispered. He pulled back enough for me to look into his eyes. "I need to tell you something."

Fresh tears clouded his eyes. "What?"

I kissed him. He kissed me back with a desperation that could only come from pain. It was slow and deliberate, as though he was trying to make it last a little longer than it could. For a second, I thought I could feel his familiar warmth.

I pulled away. He pressed his forehead against mine. Soft sobs in the shape of my name escaped his lips.

"Alix," I whispered.

He opened his eyes, and I had one more look at his beautiful sapphire gems. They seemed as lost and pained as the first time I'd seen them. I lifted my hand to brush my fingers over his eyes, covering them like that first time and whispered against his lips. "Thank you."

Chapter 24

Mercy

The cracks had seeped into her eyes, but she never looked away. Even as she fell to pieces, red crystals hitting the ground in a shattering melody, she continued to cover Alix's eyes as though to shield him from the sight. A smile rested on her lips. In her final seconds, her hand fell, and she was gone. Everything she was broke apart.

A single sob escaped Alix's lips as he grasped her empty, tattered clothes.

Then there was silence.

They bowed their heads, weighed down by the loss. It was too heavy for any of them to move against.

The Glories appeared.

Alix didn't look up, and Jenos couldn't imagine he ever would.

"So, she's gone," Rion said.

"You don't have to sound so pleased," Zell said. She plucked a white flower from her ginger hair and let it fall to the ground like a prayer.

"Do something," Alix said, barely louder than a whisper.

"What?" Rion asked.

"Do something!" he shouted. "Put her back together again. Bring her back."

"Alix, the Glories can't bring back the dead," Jenos said.

"We can't," Kija agreed. "But she's not dead."

"What?" Jenos gasped.

Siehrra nodded and picked up one of the crystals. She held it close to her deep olive eyes. "She's right. She's not dead. Her body is in pieces, but her soul is intact."

"How is it possible that she's not dead? She's lying in pieces," Jenos said, gesturing at the dozens of shards.

"Yes, her body has been turned into *ameris*. You all know *amerine* occurs where there are strong pools of *Arcania*. It solidifies and is given form. *Ameris* is *amerine* that's been manipulated," Lucell explained. "Red *ameris* is *amerine* with a soul."

"She's alive," Alix breathed, holding on to that one piece of news. Everything else was background noise. "You can bring her back?"

Lucell nodded.

"Then do it," Alix demanded. The desperation stirred in his eyes, making them wilder.

"There is no reason why we should," Rion said.

"But she did nothing wrong. She didn't deserve to die like this," Alix contended. He fell to his knees and pressed his face to the ground at Rion's feet. "Please, save her."

Jenos, Ryalie, and Camerin all followed his lead and begged. The Glories stared down at their humble figures. It was not a new sight for them. Many had pleaded with the Glories over the years—centuries—for both profound and trivial matters. Some even bowed out of pure fear, and yet this surprised them.

"Why would you go so far?" Kija asked.

Ryalie was the first to sit up and speak with a spark in his eyes. "I don't want it to end. There was still so much to do, and I want to do it all."

It was a simple response which didn't fit the gravity of their request. Yet, no one else spoke, as though those were the perfect words, like his child-like plea was the only one fit for the moment.

Kija smiled in amusement. "I'm convinced."

"What?" Rion exclaimed.

"Well, it's only fair, since they asked so nicely."

"How their request was made is irrelevant," Rion said, his red eyes flashed in anger.

"Let's do it," Lucell said. "We owe too much."

"Yes, it wasn't supposed to be this way," Zell said, frowning at the shattered *ameris*.

"Have you ever thought that this outcome was perhaps a mercy?" Rion asked. There was desperation in his eyes, and deeper still, there was fear. It wasn't as though the thought hadn't crossed their minds. It certainly had, but they'd taken the easy way out before, and it led to them standing over the shattered remains of an innocent girl. There was only so much they could ask the Halibel bloodline to sacrifice for them.

"We made a promise. We need to do better, Rion," Lucell said. "Maybe get it right this time."

"What if you're wrong?" Rion hissed, grabbing Lucell before he could step forward.

"You should do what's right, not what's easy, so you have less regrets," Jenos said. "That's what Lilly once told to me."

Lucell removed Rion's hand. "She's right. I have a lot of regrets from the decision we made all those years ago, which must mean we were wrong. I know you feel the same."

Rion bit down on his lip. "We did the best we could."

"Perhaps," Kija said. "But as Lucell said, we must do better."

"And you all agree?" Rion asked.

They stood before him a formidable wall, unshaken by his hesitation. There was doubt, they didn't know where to go from here, nevertheless, they wanted to move forward.

Rion shook his head. "Do it without me."

"We can't do this without you," Kija growled.

"I know," he said and vanished before their eyes.

"What now?" Camerin asked. "Will Lillianett stay like this?"

"No, we can restore her body. It will be as though she's sleeping, like a piece of her is missing," Kija said. "I'm sorry."

"Do it," Alix said. "Please."

They cleared the way for the Glories to circle the crystals. Each of them stood with their arms stretched out in front of them, as though reaching out to a higher being for benevolence. They all stood in pristine stillness, and as they spoke, each voice weaved into echoed unison.

The hairs on Jenos's arms stood. The *Arcania* in the air grew thick and heavy. He'd read of the Glories abilities to channel and control vast amounts of *Arcania,* but he never imagined it was true.

They chanted:

> *Life and death begin with the breath*
> *The breath is the purest Arcania*
> *Arcania is the breath of the world*
> *The world is the vessel of all things*
> *In all things, life and death is one and the same*

Rion stared up at the old, framed painting that hung in a hall of portraits, covered in dust. A cloth clung to the frame, shrouding most of the image in darkness, save for a slither of eyes that seemed on the brink of tears.

"I still think it was a mercy," Rion said when he felt the Glories' presence behind him. They stood at his back like an army, and he was the enemy.

"For you or her?" Kija asked. When he didn't answer, she shook her head. "You have to stop running eventually."

Rion clicked his tongue and turned to glare at Kija. "You've all gone mad."

"Rion, you may be my equal, but I will not hesitate to strike you if need be," Kija said, her eyes wide and threatening.

Rion lifted his chin refusing to let her shake him.

Lucell sighed in defeat. "In hindsight, this was all unavoidable."

"He's free. What do you think will happen now?" Rion asked, resigning himself to stare at the painting.

"Chaos and corruption," Kija announced. "In due time."

"Do you not see the problem with his freedom?" Rion asked.

"We are aware," Lucell said.

"How do you propose we find him?" Rion asked, glaring as though to challenge them.

"We can't," Lucell said. "All we can do is wait. We have less than half a year."

"Until he comes to us, there is no point dwelling on it," Kija said. "We should allow Lilly to return home."

"You should have left her. He'll come for her now. And you know we can't…" He paused, swallowing his pain, eyes widening at his thoughts turned nightmares. "We can't protect her."

"The future is uncertain," Lucell said. "Perhaps we should leave it to Fate?"

Kija scoffed. "Fate is too fickle."

"Then Queen Ibis?" Zell suggested.

They all paused. That was an option. She was the rarest and most sacred of the Crowns. If she were born during the War of Bloods, maybe things would have turned out differently.

"I suppose we must," Rion said.

"And do you know what else you *must* do?" Kija said placing her hand on his shoulder, digging into the flesh below his collar bone. "Wake Lilly up."

He smacked her hand away and glared in response to their disapproving gazes. He turned his back to them and looked into the sad eyes of the painting that seemed to beg him to listen.

Alix had laid Lilly on his bed three days ago. He sat by her side, looking for some sign of life. Flickering eyes, a twitch, or even a deeper breath. But she hadn't changed for three days.

He placed the back of his hand on her cheek. It was cold against his fingers.

"How could I miss you so much?" he whispered to himself, then paused expecting a teasing response. His heart broke every time there was silence.

"Even though she's dead, you're still enthralled with her." The queen walked in, but he didn't react to her words. He'd endured all her insults and spite for days; he was numb to it now. "When will you start seeing reason?"

"I'm sane," Alix replied. "You've heard my reasons."

"Yes, I understand why you let her walk free. She saved your life, and you returned the favour but—" She grabbed his arm, so he would look into her fierce eyes that mirrored his own. "You didn't owe her any more than that. You brought her into our home."

Alix chuckled bitterly shrugging his mother's grasp from his arm. "She was so angry. She begged us to take her back."

"Why didn't you?"

Alix lifted Lilly's hand and pressed his lips against it, recalling how warm she once was, the scent of the forest on her skin. The cold reached into his soul and made him shudder.

"I wanted to prove to her that we weren't monsters," he said.

"I promised to keep her safe, and I failed. In every way, I failed. Maybe if I'd left her alone…"

"You should have left her alone. Instead, you've disgraced the crown," the queen said, barely holding back the growl in her voice. "Aretia is heartbroken."

Alix could tell that much from the slap he'd received. "I didn't mean to hurt her."

"But you did."

"The engagement was your idea," he barked. "I never said I wanted to marry anyone."

The queen stepped back. In all his years, Alix rarely spoke back to his mother. He made himself her perfect prince, but now he stared her down like he was daring her to talk back. There was frustration in his brow. The past three days had aged his eyes by countless years.

There was a knock at the door. Jenos and Ryalie walked in. Before they could greet her, the queen rushed out the door in a huff.

"What happened?" Jenos asked. "The last time I saw the queen that upset, you appointed Ryalie as your personal knight."

Ryalie shrugged. "She grew to love me."

"She still can't stand to be in the same room as you for more than five minutes," Jenos countered. "And she's never called you by name."

Ryalie took a moment to consider Jenos's words. "So, she's still growing."

Alix gave a wry smile at their attempt at a bit of humour,

though Jenos's words spoke of a bitter truth.

"It's nothing," Alix said with a tired sigh. "Did something happen? Do you need me?"

"No, we are here for the same reasons as you," Jenos said, placing a supportive hand on his shoulder. "Still no difference?"

Alix shook his head. "I miss her."

"Do you?" Rion appeared at the foot of the bed.

All three stood a little straighter, angling their bodies defensively.

"To what do we owe the pleasure?" Alix asked. He couldn't hide his resentment.

"I came to ask you, Prince Alixios, a question," he started. "Are you willing to gamble everything you have on her?"

"Yes," he said without hesitation

Rion's face stiffened. He frowned as though he'd tasted something foul, but his eyes held a glint of envy. "So be it." He lifted his arms towards her and began to speak, reciting the words the others had used to revive her body.

I was falling, air trapped in my lungs, ice on my fingertips. There was nothing but darkness and a sharp hum in my head. The light was a shock to the system.

I woke up.

My eyes darted around, trying to make sense of the shapes and colours that vibrated too loudly and suffocated my mind. I felt someone grasp my hand and saw sapphire.

"Lilly?"

My name sounded distorted, like I was underwater. I blinked through the confusion, trying to push the buzzing out of my head. I had to focus. I grasped the hand over mine, warm and large. It wrapped tighter, firm yet gentle, as though afraid to break it and afraid to let it go. My vision started to clear, and I began to make out Alix's face, his tired and dark rimmed eyes inches away from tears.

"Alix? Are you okay?" I asked. I pushed myself up and found Jenos and Ryalie standing around the bed, looking at me with wide eyes of relief and amazement. "Are you all alright? You're looking at me like I'm a miracle."

"You're nothing short of a miracle." Rion stepped forward with scrutiny etched in the lines of his face.

Seeing him brought all the memories back like a smack to the face. I ran my hands over my body and finally pulled down my shirt to inspect the skin at my sternum. There was a cluster of tiny scars, like broken glass, that were smooth under my touch.

"What happened to me?" I asked.

"You shattered," he said matter-of-factly.

"I died," I gasped.

"No. Death is far more permanent," Rion said.

"Why?" I asked. I looked him in the eye and refused to look away even when his gaze became ice cold. "I was gone. I could've stayed gone, like you wanted. Why bring me back?"

He shook his head. "Because the worst has already happened."

"What happened?" I asked.

Rion swept the room with his gaze and shook his head again.

"That's none of your concern…for now. You have more pressing matters to address."

I paused. "More pressing than the fact that I half-died?"

"Yes," he said. "I've come to make a deal."

I paused at the look he gave me, the plea in his eyes. There was a longing in the stiffness of his lips and tightness of his jaw. Whatever had happened, whatever he couldn't tell me, must have been worse than any curse.

Epilogue

Eons

He was shorter than Zalia had thought he would be, and sickly thin, like a child left for dead. The moment he was reborn, he'd taken her to some unknown forest and hadn't uttered a word since. It had been days and all he'd done was sleep, curled up in a patch of long grass with only a blanket she'd stolen from a nearby town.

He'd woken up on the third day.

He cleaved his way through the forest. Every living thing in his path crumbled and withered. She followed close behind him, towering over his delicate shoulders.

Once out of the forest, he looked up at the full moon. The light illuminated his skin, like that of a doll's. She'd thought his hair was brown whilst in the shadows, but under the light of the moon, it gave off a bright red shimmer.

The boy stared at the moon like he was trying to calculate its distance or find a way to make it fall into his hands. He stood without movement for a whole minute, then turned.

His bright green eyes shone and held a glint of innocence, yet there was an ancient feel to them, as though they'd experienced eons worth of emotions.

His lips curled up into a smile. "She's awake."

END

Maria B. Moses

Acknowledgements

Writing this book has been a test of patience and tenacity. I got the idea at a young age. It was born from boredom and loneliness, which is fitting. Though the key elements of it remained consistent, it went through a metamorphosis of truly stunning proportions. One could say it is unrecognizable, but I would argue it maintained its soul.

I would like to begin by thanking that one critical review I got on the first draft of this book. It was harsh, but it was the kick I needed to make this story into something as special as I knew it could be. I'd like to think I've done better. So, thank you, whoever you are, for disliking my work but giving me feedback in hopes that I'd do better. The world needs more people like you.

To my editors, Cassandra Chaput and Cyan Patterson. Thank you for putting the time and effort into making my work what it is. You both were amazing to work with. And Coral Coons, thank you so much for the edits you did. They helped me take a more critical eye to the page. I only wish you'd stuck by me until the end.

Naturally, I need to thank all my friends that lit the flame and were my guiding light into realizing what I love and what I was born to do. Precious Ampofo, Alande Zungu, Temitope Omoyefa, Edna Ojo-Aramokudu, and Aliyah Ali. This book would not exist without you. You all gave me the courage to write, and I will keep writing. Thank you.

Finally, to Marjie McNulty, my MVP, who read this book more times than should be allowed and never once complained. I owe you a huge debt. You took time out of your day to help me and cheer me on. I feel like the luckiest person in the world whenever you ask me for that next draft. Thank you for loving my work and giving me hope in everything I do. I am thankful for all that you are, and I hope you'll stay in my life.

THANK YOU FOR READING

See you in the next book

A Path of Thorns

About the Author

Maria Bolanle Moses lives in the heart of Toronto, Canada. Her love for stories and creation started at a young age and has gradually taken over her life. She's obsessed with mythology, anime, and the performing arts. When she's not writing, she can be found singing with her choir, reading, and auditioning for her next big part.

Check out her website: www.mariabmoses.ca for more content, a glimpse into her work and the books awaiting release